To Chris
with love
from
Anita x

The Quest to Xegeron

Anita Gilson

Pen Press

First published in Great Britain by Pen Press

All paper used in the printing of this book has been made from wood grown in managed, sustainable forests.

ISBN: 978-1-78003-733-2

Printed and bound in the UK
Pen Press is an imprint of
Indepenpress Publishing Limited
25 Eastern Place
Brighton
BN2 1GJ

A catalogue record of this book is available from the British Library

Cover design by Jacqueline Abromeit

Dedication

This book started life as a film, and I would like to dedicate it to Gwen Lyndhurst, who helped to draft the film script, to Barrie, our intrepid cameraman, and to Nicky, who had the unenviable task of editing it. Also to our cast of thousands, and especially our seven lead characters, all of whom sacrificed their spare time and got up at six o'clock on some very cold mornings to perform.

This book is also dedicated to all the kind souls who let us use their homes, gardens, places of work and land, as film locations.

I also dedicate this book to my dear mother, Lucie, who was our "angel" and paid for the editing of the film, besides speaking the voice of the dragon mother.

Also, thanks to Sarah and Bruce, who helped with the film, and to Sarah for coming up with the name Zephrena for the Dark Sorceress, and to Annie, who let me develop Droco the Sprig, her *Dungeons and Dragons,* character into the delightful lovable rogue he became. To Simon and Emma, who helped us so much at the beginning, and to Kris who helped with the filming one cold and crucial morning. Thanks also to Vic, who let me use his "profile" and the name of his character Torvic Shinetop. And this book is dedicated to them too.

Many thanks to Dawn and Brian at Saltdean Library for their endless patience, and all the times they flew to my rescue, when the computer seemed to have Zephrena's curse on it.

Finally, this book would never have been written without the kind help of my dear friends Ron and Dot, who let me sit in their house every Wednesday and type the manuscript on their computer. To Ron for his endless patience in sorting out the computer every time it went wrong and to Dot who kept me going on delicious cups of coffee and scrumptious biscuits.

To all of you, *The Quest to Xegeron* is dedicated with love.

Chapter One

The Temple of the Golden Unicorn

The early sun was pale. As yet its white rays gave out only the faintest heat, but its light promised growing strength as the day progressed.

In U-Llashkar at the Temple of the Golden Unicorn, this faint white light was the signal for the ringing of the temple bell, calling the priests and priestesses of Shara Sorian to their daily morning prayers. Soon their voices could be heard, chanting their prayers to the goddess.

The two young acolytes whose task it was to sweep the courtyard this bright morning were already at work, but at the sound of the dawn chant, they set down their brooms and stood with arms upraised joining joyously in the sung prayers.

Usually at this hour, Kestrel Moonblade, the chief warrior priestess, would enter the courtyard with Lord Aragal ni Tourleth, the high priest, and they would perform the Ritual Battle of the Dawn. This morning, however, Lord Aragal entered with Lady Maia Paladine and they took up their cloaks and swords for the battle.

The two young acolytes were accustomed to this, for Lady Kestrel had been away on her quest for many months, but now she had returned in triumph and rested for 13 days and they had fully expected her in the courtyard this morning. They exchanged fleeting glances of surprise as they left the courtyard.

"Perhaps the Lady Kestrel is still weary after her quest," suggested Elastor Zar Aishan in a whisper, as soon as they were alone.

"Maybe so," agreed Llashka Starsong. Then she remembered something. "No, that is not the reason she has not come to perform the Battle of the Dawn. I have heard it spoken that she is retired to record the story of her quest in The Book of Ages."

Elastor's face lit up.

"And think you we shall be allowed to read it?"

"I hope we shall," Llashka replied, "for it must be a wondrous tale."

And the two young acolytes hurried off to join their companions for the dawn meal in the refectory.

***

Kestrel Moonblade sat in the meditation room. The sun poured its pale warmth in at the window of the centaur, Shara Sorian's bridegroom. The stained glass made bright flower patterns on the stone floor. Kestrel sat cross legged on a purple cushion in deep meditation.

She was a woman whose age could not be determined from her outward appearance. Her face was unlined, but held great wisdom. Her body was lean and lithe, like a spring maiden's, but she carried herself with the assurance of maturity. Her hair was corn coloured and hung in ripples to her waist. Her eyes were the grey of a stormy sea but they were tranquil, and, at present, unseeing, focused inwardly.

After a while, her eyes saw the world around her once more and she rose from the cushion and went to the plain window, overlooking the courtyard. The warrior acolytes were training in the use of the sword. As usual, Cleander Larkrise was the swiftest and strongest. Kestrel smiled. She saw herself as a young girl, when she had followed her vision of Shara Sorian and come to the Temple of the Golden Unicorn as an acolyte. For a while she watched the sword training. Then she turned away to the massive book, bound in gold, that lay on the large stone table in the centre of the room. The Book of Ages.

Taking up her reed-quill, Kestrel began to write in the great book. As she wrote, her eyes took on a faraway look, as though she saw things that no longer were. Sometimes a smile stole across her lips. At other times there was a shadow of sadness on her face.

"It is now thirteen days since I returned from Xegeron and six months since I set out on my quest," wrote Kestrel. "Lord Aragal ni Tourleth has decreed that the story of my quest be recorded in The Book of Ages."

Six months and thirteen days, thought Kestrel. It seems much longer than that.

She looked up at the stained glass window, through which the sunlight was now pouring with greater strength. Then she dipped her reed-quill into the silver inkstand and continued to write.

"Lord Aragal ni Tourleth, high priest of the Temple of the Golden Unicorn...his soul was stolen by Zephrena, the dark sorceress of Xegeron, who wished to spread evil through Zar-Yashtoreth and I was used to separate Lord Aragal's soul from his body."

The quill trembled in Kestrel's hand and she stopped, unable to continue writing.

Even now I cannot write these words, she thought, without being overcome by grief and remorse.

Kestrel's resolve failed her. She covered her face with her hands and her tears fell. After a while she grew more composed and began to write again.

"There were seven of us in that band of adventurers on the quest to Xegeron. Myself, Kestrel Moonblade, warrior priestess of Shara Sorian at the Temple of the Golden Unicorn, Droco the Sprig, the thief, Taṇith-Medea, the dragon-maid, Zakarius, the wizard, Lindor Estoriel, the elf minstrel, Giles de Sorell, the Knight of the Falcon, and Torvic Shinetop, the dwarf trollslayer.

As she wrote, Kestrel paused, seeing in her mind the companions of her adventures. Droco, slim and agile, the incorrigible scamp, with a heart of gold. Tanith, with her delightful innocence her eyes full of wonder and suspicion at the world beyond her home, Zakarius, whose bumbling manner and apparent vagueness masked his true power and wisdom. Lindor, beautiful and light of heart, spreading joy and loveliness with her magical music. Giles, fearless and devoted, determined to prove his valour and honour. And Torvic, with his quick temper, his surly scowl, his courage and loyalty and his well-disguised kindness.

Kestrel was surprised to find tears in her eyes. "By the light of dawning, I miss them," she said aloud. "The times they drove me to distraction with their quarrels and their exploits. But all the same, they were good friends. May Shara Sorian be with them all, wherever they may be."

Chapter Two

The Dark Tower

The Island of Xegeron lay in the extreme north of Zar-Yashtoreth. Here was the great sea of Xegos, where lay the island of Xegeron, and it was on this island that the Dark Tower of Zephrena stood.

Zephrena, the Dark Sorceress, had gathered her evil powers secretly. She had grown in strength, until now, her power was the strongest single power in Zar-Yashtoreth. She had subdued all Xegeron and turned it into a land of fear and darkness, and now her powers were seeping further, bit by bit, drawing the rest of Zar-Yashtoreth to her.

She surrounded herself for protection with evil monsters of her own creation and with grey skinned kraul warriors, whose strength and ferocity were a byword. Krauls and Goblins served her, too, and did her bidding.

Zephrena, with her dark magic, had fashioned a huge iron globe. It stood in the darkest room of the Dark Tower. And in this globe, the sorceress had imprisoned the souls of the many who would not follow her evil path and had died at her hands.

By means of her dark magic, Zephrena had also entrapped a scarlet fire dragon of the mountains, named Neis-Durga Talahindra. The fact that she had succeeded in taking captive one of the dragon-folk spoke of the immense strength of her dark powers. The krauls brought the tranced dragon to the Dark Tower. Here, Zephrena had used her magic to extinguish Neis-

Durga's fire and to chain her to the Globe of Souls with a chain of evil sorcery. Now, anyone that tried to approach the globe, hoping to set free the souls within, would be afraid to do so, on seeing the huge dragon.

Then the evil sorceress laid her most powerful spells around the Dark Tower, to deaden the sound of any cry for help that Neis-Durga might send by voice or mind. She also laid magical barriers around the tower, so strong that not even a dragon could break through. For Zephrena knew well the bonds of friendship, love and kinship that united the dragon race; knew that once Neis-Durga's captivity was known, every dragon of Zar-Yashtoreth would storm the tower to rescue one of their own kind.

When Neis-Durga emerged from her trance and found herself captive and her magic drained from her, she did what any dragon would do in such a plight – she fretted and pined and refused to eat. The lovely, shining creature became thin, and her scales became lustreless. Nevertheless, Zephrena thought that her size and very presence would deter anyone who tried to approach the Globe of Souls.

The Talahindra Clan of the Mountains, finding one of their number missing, sent word to all the other dragon clans of Zar-Yashtoreth. The Shirakalinzarin of the Guadja, the Valley of the Sun and Moon Lakes, the Sa'arourat of the Waters, the Vaneschi of the Air, the Ushani of the Caves, the Kaboora of the Winds, the Varatozi, the Crystal Dragons and the Shanadari, the Rainbow Dragons of Bright Magic.

And Neis-Durga herself sent out the mind call of her people, which penetrated all spells and was immediately heard by every dragon. They would respond to it at once. But when they tried to follow this call, they could get no further than the shore of Lake Xegos, and then the call was lost, so great was the power of Zephrena's evil. At length, the dragon-folk believed that Neis-Durga was dead. They returned home and mourned her, and Neis-Durga, feeling all hope of rescue fade, grew more and more sick and weak. Finally, she determined that, even in death, she would defeat Zephrena's purpose. For no dragon surrenders its freedom without a struggle, and every dragon has a small reserve of magic that can be called on when all else is lost.

Zephrena reclined upon a black couch. Beside her stood Thirghiz Gorblitz, her kraul servant, a hideous creature with grey and grimy skin and yellow teeth. Her grey green hair hung in tangles and her clothes were foul and ragged.

She was complaining bitterly about the dragon, Neis-Durga Talahindra. She was afraid her mistress would blame her for this latest, terrible thing that had happened, and was anxious to exonerate herself before she told the sorceress the dreadful news.

"She won't eat and she won't drink, Oh Exalted One," whined the kraul. "Though I've slung in some tasty little morsels, such as I wouldn't refuse myself."

Zephrena thought, privately, that any dragon would be too fastidious to touch the kind of morsels that a kraul would find tasty.

"If you ask me," Thirghiz's voice grew confidential, "she'll let in any enemy who chooses to come."

A shadow crossed Zephrena's face, momentarily, but then lifted as she replied, "No matter. The sight of the monster will be enough to stop anyone approaching too closely. She is a fearsome-looking beast."

There was no putting off the dreadful moment of truth. Thirgiz trembled and whined, "Aye, but that's where the new trouble begins, Oh Exalted One."

Zephrena's eyes were as cold as stone.

"What new trouble?" she asked, her voice sharp as daggers.

"I don't know how to tell you, Mistress." Thirghiz wrung her hands. "I hopes you won't hold it against me. I'm only a servant and I don't know no magic. There wasn't nothing I could do to stop it."

"Stop whining and tell me what has happened," ordered Zephrena. "Speak, before I have you sliced in two and your entrails fed to the nvarwolks."

The kraul slattern trembled in every limb. "I don't rightly know where to begin, Your Magnificence."

"Thirghiz Gorblitz," the sorceress's voice cracked like a whiplash, "either tell me what has happened, or I'll have your worm-gnawed body carved and send your miserable soul to the abyss. That is, if you possess such a thing."

The unfortunate Thirghiz moaned and gathered her courage to tell the dreadful news.

"I crave your forgiveness, Mistress. I will tell you all, but remember, it's not my fault."

"Speak then, troll spawn," snapped Zephrena impatiently.

Trembling and terrified, Thirghiz spoke.

"The dragon, Mistress. She has changed her shape."

"What?" demanded Zephrena in a voice like a desert of ice.

"By the blood of Grak, mistress. I couldn't help it. She just changed afore me eyes."

"Changed into what, you scum of a stagnant pool?"

"Into a woman, Oh Magnificent One," quavered the unhappy Thirghiz.

Zephrena rose to her feet. She had drained all the magic from the dratted creature. How had she managed to shape-shift? Why, oh why had she troubled to capture that wretched dragon? Why hadn't she used one of her own monsters to guard the Globe of Souls? They were just as large and fearsome looking, and their loyalty was unquestioned.

"The curse of Kasperus on the wretched beast!" she cried. "And on you too, Thirghiz Gorblitz. Use a little persuasion to make her change back into a dragon!"

"I've tried, Mistress," whimpered Thirghiz, "but though she has a woman's skin, she seems armoured 'gainst pain, as if all her dratted dragon scales were still on her. Wouldn't it be easier to turn her loose, Mistress, and save ourselves the trouble of keeping her?"

"Imbecile," Zephrena cried scornfully. "Let her go and bring every dragon in Zar-Yashtoreth against me? A thousand times the creature has heard me use my secret spells to open and close the Globe of Souls, and, if I know anything about dragons, she'll know them herself by now. And you say let her go, and return with her people to release my captives and slaughter me! The creature must be killed and the easiest way to do that is to keep her chained to the Globe of Souls and let her starve herself to death. But first, I'll take from her her powers of speech, so that she cannot reveal the secrets of the globe to any who might be foolish enough to travel this way."

"Mistress," cried Thirghiz, sycophantically, "you are clever beyond all nightmares."

Zephrena dismissed her with a wave of her hand and the kraul shuffled into the darkness, relieved to be alive and out of the dreaded presence of the sorceress.

Left alone, the sorceress rose from her couch, and walked to the far end of the room. Here, in its darkest recess, lay the Pool of Azolak. Immeasurably deep were its inky waters, and still as death. Though once, before Zephrena's evil days, the waters had been living and bright.

Zephrena stood by the edge of this pool and called, "*Erez metrigal ursha zigfra.*" At once a mist spread over the dark waters. Zephrena took up her black staff of khazwood and cried, "Come forth Ishta'aren, spirit of the pool!"

The waters shivered, and through the mist rose a blue spirit. Her pale blue hair streamed like water and her slender blue arms stretched out over the pool.

Her face was immeasurably sad, for she too was a captive of Zephrena's, and was compelled to tell her nothing but truth and aid her evil work, whereas once she had been free and had rejoiced in the bright waters.

"What is your command, Great One?" her voice, mournful and hollow, echoed across the darkness. Her eyes, yearning for freedom from the dark slavery to the powers of evil, enforced upon her by Zephrena's magic.

"I have captured many souls," Zephrena replied. "They lie imprisoned in the Globe of Souls, but my great work progresses too slowly. I shall not rest until I have taken the souls of all who follow the Paths of Light. Tell me, Spirit of the Pool of Azolak, how can I darken Zar-Yashtoreth with one blow?"

Through the stillness came the voice of Ishta'aren, her words coming against her will, while her tears fell at the evil forced upon her.

"It cannot be done with one blow, Oh Exalted One, but there is a way to gather the souls of light more swiftly."

"Tell me. I command you!"

"You must capture the soul of the high priest of the Temple of the Golden Unicorn," intoned Ishta'aren. "He is Lord Aragal ni Tourleth. Once he has fallen, all other souls of light will follow swiftly."

"Where can he be found?"

"In the land of U-Llashkar, Exalted One. But you must know one thing, his soul can only be gathered into darkness if he is slain by one of his own disciples. And that will not be easy, for all his disciples love and revere him and all of them walk in the Paths of Light."

It was the first truth Ishta'aren had enjoyed telling Zephrena since she had fallen captive to her, but her joy was short lived.

"The curse of Kasperus be upon them!" Zephrena muttered. "However, nothing is impossible." Then, raising her black staff and turning to her scrying mirror in its great carved frame, she cried, "*Oursh an morg li zhegar*!"

The mirror rippled and grew misty. Zephrena's reflection, and the reflection of the room, vanished.

"Show me," demanded Zephrena, "the Temple of the Golden Unicorn, in the land of U-Llashkar."

Instantly, the mirror obeyed. The sorceress saw the temple, and in its courtyard, Kestrel Moonblade and Lord Aragal performing the Battle of the Dusk.

"Who is that?" Zephrena asked Ishta'aren.

"That is Lord Aragal and his chief disciple the high priestess, Kestrel Moonblade," Ishta'aren responded, reluctantly. "They are performing the ritual combat of the Battle of the Dusk. In the morning they will perform the Ritual Battle of the Dawn."

An evil smile crossed the sorceress's face. "That is perfect for my plan." She raised her staff and cried, "*Morg ez kraish legh*!" and Ishta'aren vanished.

Then, turning to the mirror, she saw Kestrel's sword laid to rest for the night, now the Battle of the Dusk was over. Through the mirror she began to cast a spell on the sword. She saw the sword twitch as if in horror and indignation, and she laughed.

"Tomorrow, Kestrel Moonblade, you will kill your beloved Lord Aragal, and his soul will be mine. Soon all Zar-Yashtoreth will lie beneath my power!"

Chapter Three

The Spell

The dawn bells at the Temple of the Golden Unicorn rang out their song. Light and merry, yet strong enough to waken any sleepers who should now be rising to greet the day. Lady Kestrel Moonblade's eyes opened as she lay in her gold and purple chamber.

Kestrel rose. She washed and then went to the window and began her dawn prayer to Shara Sorian. After this she meditated, seated on a purple cushion on the floor of her chamber.

After her meditation, Kestrel rose, refreshed, and pulled the golden bell pull. Almost immediately, the young acolyte, Cleander Larkrise, answered the summons. She was a slender 12-year-old girl, with long red-gold hair and solemn, fearless brown eyes.

"Happy dawning to you, Cleander," said Kestrel.

"Happy dawning to you, Lady Kestrel Moonblade."

Practised and efficient, the girl laid out Kestrel's ritual black sword, black cloak and dark crown, in which Kestrel would enact the powers of darkness, and be defeated by Lord Aragal, in the guise of the Powers of Light.

Kestrel thanked her and walked down the stairs to the Courtyard of Battle. Cleander followed, carrying the sword, cloak and crown, with care and pride. They emerged into the early light through the archway of darkness.

At the same time, Lord Aragal came through the Archway of Light, his young disciple, Daklesh Aishan, carrying his golden cloak and crown and silver sword.

The bell rang seven times and on the seventh, Cleander and Daklesh stepped forward confidently and placed the cloaks around the priest's and priestess's shoulders, then gave them their crowns and handed them their swords, before retreating to the wall, while the ritual battle began with Lord Aragal's prayer.

"Oh, Shara Sorian, Goddess of Light, from whom all our blessings flow, look upon our morning ritual; with favour and bless this day."

Then Kestrel offered her prayer. "We now destroy evil symbolically. Oh, Shara Sorian, make it so in truth."

And Lord Aragal, arrayed in his clothes of Light, proclaimed, "Now am I Kurian, champion of light!"

While Kestrel, in her clothes of darkness, proclaimed, "Now am I Zariax, champion of darkness."

And, as they turned to each other, they both cried, "Now commences the Battle of the Dawn!"

They raised their swords and swung them slowly over their heads, before clashing them together three times. It was then that Kestrel felt her sword take on a momentum of its own, which she could not control. It trembled and pulsated in her hands. The power was overwhelmingly strong, and the weapon moved so swiftly that, before Kestrel was even conscious of it, she felt it thrust through flesh, and saw a rose of blood stain Lord Aragal's white and gold robes, heard his cry of surprise, and watched in horror, as he fell at her feet. Lord Aragal's white face expressed bewilderment rather than pain or fear.

"What treachery is this?" he murmured.

"Never mine, my Lord," Kestrel was shocked that he might think she had done this terrible deed deliberately, "Surely you do not suppose that I..."

"Suspect you of such a deed?" interrupted Lord Aragal, "Never, Kestrel Moonblade. I recognise another hand in this. This is the work of my enemy, the queen of darkness, Zephrena of Xegeron. She seeks my soul."

Cleander and Daklesh stood, frozen at this horror and then, with a single thought, ran to the Calling Bell, and, at the same moment, reached for its rope and began to tug at it.

Immediately the voice of the bell was answered by a stream of priests and priestesses, novices and acolytes, who rushed into the courtyard and stood aghast at the scene.

At their head was Maia Palladine, the high priestess. All stood and murmured in disbelief at what they saw. Maia knelt beside Lord Aragal and helped Kestrel in her attempts to stop the flow of blood. Lord Aragal lay with eyes closed, pale as wax, but as he spoke he kept his voice steady and measured. "Zephrena has tried, this day, to turn the Battle of the Dawn to her victory. Yet, in the end, the victory will be ours."

"Sage of the Path of Light," wept Kestrel, "how can we win this victory? What cure is there for such a fatal wound?"

Lord Aragal laid his hand upon Kestrel's. His eyes closed, but he fought through the pain of his death wound.

"Seek out Morrigan, the Crone of the Moondark, in the Forest of Sourak. She will advise you."

"I will do so," replied Kestrel.

"May Shara Sorian protect you," said the high priest. "May She protect you all. My soul is carried into darkness. Farewell."

Lord Aragal ni Tourleth lay still, white as pale marble. From the priests and priestesses, novices and acolytes, who stood watching, arose a desolate wailing sound. Many of the young acolytes wept in terror.

"He is gone and I have slain him," lamented Kestrel, shedding tears over his body. The high priestess, Maia Palladine, raised her to her feet.

"Not you, Kestrel Moonblade, but some great power of evil."

Through her tears, Kestrel tried to think what must be done. Mourning eased her soul, but it did not help Lord Aragal. She raised her head and spoke to Maia Palladine.

"I must seek out Morrigan, the Crone of the Moondark. She will tell me how to restore Lord Aragal's soul."

Kestrel's voice held a vestige of hope.

Maia Palladine laid her hand on Kestrel's arm. "Go then, and may Shara Sorian go with you."

Then she embraced Kestrel and said, softly, "Farewell, Kestrel Moonblade. May you return safely, soon and victorious."

Kestrel called Cleander to her and the young acolyte took the black cloak, crown and sword from her mistress, as commanded.

"In the guise of evil did evil guide my sword," said Kestrel. "I now cast off that guise and renew my true soul."

She retired to her chamber to prepare for her journey. Cleander laid out her white tunic and breeches, her sword, her cloak, her pack and her travelling boots, but she did not touch Kestrel's staff that held the most powerful magic and could only be touched by a priestess.

Tearfully the child helped Kestrel to dress and brushed her hair for the last time.

"Lady Kestrel, let me come with you. I can help you. I'm the best swordswoman and archer of my years. Please take me with you."

Kestrel seated herself on the couch and drew the child to her.

"And who will take care of my chamber and make the morning and evening offerings to Shara Sorian? Who will guard my magic books and my ritual sword and garments, should an enemy come?"

"There are many who could do these things, my lady," replied Cleander.

"Are there?" Kestrel looked steadily into the girl's eyes.

"Is there anyone who knows this room and its contents so well as you, who has tended me for so many years? Is there anyone who knows my rituals as you do? Besides, if enemies did indeed come, you are the only one who knows my deepest secrets of combat."

A flush of pride brightened the child's face.

"Then I shall remain here, if you wish it, and perform the rituals and perfect my battle skills. But my heart will wander with you, Lady Kestrel and I shall be desolate until you return."

Kestrel held Cleander to her.

"And my heart will be here with you, Cleander Larkrise. May Shara Sorian give you courage. If I do not return..."

Cleander started and began to protest, but Kestrel interrupted her, "I may not return, little one. I may not be successful, and then the Forces of Light will need every telinn of their strength. If I do not return, Lady Syrinx Firefly will take my place. Serve her as you have served me, my child. Have courage, my little one.

"I promise," Cleander's voice broke on the words, but she uttered them bravely. "But you will return and succeed, my lady. I know you will."

"I hope so," Kestrel gave Cleander a last embrace and returned to the courtyard where all had come to see her off.

Kestrel raised her sword in salute and the priests and priestesses, novices and acolytes, returned her salute.

"Farewell, my friends," Kestrel cried. "May Shara Sorian be with you and protect you."

"So mote it be," came the chorus of voices. Maia Palladine stepped forward and embraced Kestrel.

"And may Shara Sorian go with you. Farewell, Kestrel Moonblade. May you return safely and be victorious."

"Farewell, Maia Palladine. Who knows when we shall meet again?"

With that, Kestrel turned and walked out through the gates of the Temple of the Golden Unicorn. Her last glimpse was of Cleander Larkrise, her sword raised in salute, her face white and stricken, but bravely keeping back her tears.

Chapter Four

Kestrel Moonblade

Kestrel was five when she had the vision of Shara Sorian that was to set her on the path she now followed. She was then called Elinda, and she was the youngest of five children. Her father was a weaver, her mother a potter, and they lived happily in the land of U-Llashkar.

Then her father, Ezanor, became ill with the fever. The sickness set deep and he could not shake it. He grew thin and grey. He lay on his bed, half conscious, drenched in sweat. His wife, Peronel, left her work to tend him. She sat by him all day and all night, wiping his face and weeping. The physician visited and prescribed, but nothing seemed to help him throw off the fever. The physician shook his head and said there was no hope of recovery.

Little Elinda did not understand what had happened. She knew only that her family was no longer merry and blithe, but had become anxious and silent. Neryl, the eldest daughter took care of the other children, so that Peronel could tend their father. Elinda grew pale and fearful. She followed Neryl around, terrified of this darkness that had drained the joy from her family.

One day Neryl sent Elinda to the spring to fetch water. The child took the earthenware jug and went to the spring, solemn but proud to be asked to do something to help. Carefully she dipped the jug into the cool, bubbling water. But as she turned towards her home, she tripped on a tuft of grass, and fell, grazing her knee painfully. The jug broke into a hundred pieces, and the water seeped into the dry ground.

Shock and pain overwhelmed the child. Worst of all was the thought that she had lost the water. She had failed in her task. In utter misery, she lay weeping on the ground.

Suddenly she was aware of a bright light before her. In a trice all her grief vanished. Her heart was full of hope. She sat up. Before her stood a beautiful golden lady in bright robes. Her dusky hair flowed to her knees, and she had the sweetest smile Elinda had ever seen.

She held out her arms and the little girl went to her. Then a wonder occurred. First the shining lady laid a gentle hand upon Elinda's knee, and at once, the pain vanished, and the cut was gone. Next she held her hands over the jug, and that, too, was whole, and full of shining water. Lastly, the beautiful lady handed Elinda a small crystal bottle filled with a bright liquid.

"Give this to your father, child," the shining lady's voice was sweet, "and his sickness will leave him."

"Thank you! Oh, thank you!" cried Elinda, but the beautiful lady had gone. Elinda was alone. She would have thought she had dreamt it, had she not held the pretty bottle in her hand, and the water jug been whole, and her knee healed.

Carefully she carried the jug and the bottle home. She went into her father's room.

"Quick, Father, drink this!" she cried. Ezanor did not even hear her. His eyes were closed. His breathing was laboured. Elinda opened the bottle, and, stretching over the bed, let a few drops of the liquid drop on to his dry lips.

At once Ezanor's eyes opened. The liquid sent a feeling of wellbeing through him. He took the bottle and drained its contents. He smiled and sat up.

"I would love a dish of quirren eggs," he said. His voice was strong. The sweat that had drenched him was gone.

Peronel sent Sebka, her eldest son for the physician. He came, expecting the end had come, and was amazed to see Ezanor out of bed, sitting by the window, enjoying quirren eggs.

The physician examined him, felt his pulse, and pronounced him cured.

"This is a great miracle," he cried. "How did it happen?"

"My little one gave him a bright liquid to drink," replied Peronel.

The physician examined the bottle. The liquid had gone, but its sweet scent remained.

"I have never smelt anything so beautiful," cried the physician. "Where did you find this wonderful thing, my child?"

So Elinda told the story of the shining lady, and how she had healed her knee and mended the jug. All her family stood around Elinda and looked at her in awe. The physician murmured, "The child has been visited by Shara Sorian Herself."

"We must send to the Temple of the Golden Unicorn," said Peronel. "Someone there will explain this miracle."

So Aylesha Iphena came to the house of Ezanor and Peronel, and Elinda told her story again. The high priestess spoke softly,

"The child has been chosen by Shara Sorian. Bring her to the Temple when she is seven years old."

Then life returned to its happy round. Ezanor regained his full health and he and Peronel worked and kept the house, while the children helped and studied and played. But always they looked at Elinda with joy and pride. For she had been chosen by Shara Sorian Herself.

After her seventh birthday, Elinda's parents brought her to the temple. She was taken into the Chamber of Dreams, and Aylesha Iphena gave her whortle roots to eat, which the child relished. Then the high priestess called Lara Meadowsweet, the Mistress of the Girl Novices, and bade her prepare the child. Elinda was bathed and dressed in a robe of shining white, with a green girdle. Lara Meadowsweet took her to a soft green bed, and told her to prepare for sleep and to try to remember her dreams.

Then the Mistress of the Girl Novices kissed her and lit a sweetly scented candle by Elinda's bed.

Lara Meadowsweet and Elinda's family sat by her bed and watched the child drift into sleep. For hours they waited, until the little girl's eyelids flickered into wakefulness. She smiled ecstatically, and sat up. The watchers by her bed had now been joined by Aylesha Iphena and by Kiriel Phoenix, the healer, Mirinzel Ashai, the warrior, Nightingale Silverleaf, the scholar and Elai Farendel, the craftsman. Each one ready to hear where Elinda's dreams had sent her.

"Have you remembered your dreams, little one?" asked Aylesha Iphena, gently. Elinda's face grew thoughtful.

"Oh yes, Your Holiness. I dreamt I was on a mountain beneath a crescent moon. A beautiful kestrel flew overhead and snatched the sliver of moon from the night sky. The bird placed it in my hands, where it became a silver sword, the most beautiful I ever saw."

Then Mirinzel Ashai stepped forward, and Aylesha Iphena said, "She is yours, Mirinzel Ashai, to learn the skill of the warrior priestess, and her name shall be Kestrel Moonblade."

So Kestrel entered the Temple of the Golden Unicorn as a warrior priestess, all those years ago. Now she was one of the high priestesses.

Her mind travelled back over her life at the temple and how she had been chosen for this life by the Goddess Herself. As she made her way towards the Forest of Sourak, she wondered whether her whole life had been planned and shaped for this moment and purpose.

Chapter Five

The Crone of the Moondark

The Forest of Sourak had an aura of peace and light. The trees gave out feelings of friendship – even of love. They seemed to beckon to Kestrel, showing her which way to go, and Kestrel, never doubting them, followed the path through the deep silences, broken only by the myriad voices of the birds. The sunshine slid through the leaves, and fell in little pools upon the pathway, so that Kestrel seemed to step in and out of their golden brilliances. Her travelling boots were dark and bright, dark and bright as she stepped from light to shadow, along the parti – coloured path.

Now Kestrel's ears became accustomed to the silences, as eyes grow used to darkness. She heard other sounds through the birdsong. The dry crack of a twig. Leaves rustling. Some creature scuttering into the undergrowth.

Kestrel held out her staff at arm's length. It glowed faintly, which told her she was heading in the right direction, towards some good and wise magical power.

Kestrel followed the path.

***

Morrigan, the Crone of the Moondark, sat in the centre of the forest, in a small clearing. Before her the light of the fire flickered.

Into this fire, Morrigan stared and saw. Her eyes fixed on the flames, the wise woman began a slow, soft chant.

"She comes this way, the seeker, the pilgrim. She comes this way. The Warrior Maid. Out of the darkness that leads her to Light. Needing my darkness that leads her to Light."

Then she sat, unmoving, still as a stone figure, staring into the fire. Waiting.

***

Kestrel followed the forest track through the silent trees, hearing only the birdsong and the forest sounds, until, suddenly, there was the clearing and the old wise woman before her.

Kestrel's heart lifted. Soon the Crone of the Moondark would give her a potion, or tell her some words of healing, and then she could restore Lord Aragal. All would be well. It had been so much easier than she had thought. She had imagined that the forest would be full of dangers to be overcome. But there had been only birdsong and light.

Kestrel walked into the clearing and stood before the old woman, waiting for her to end her deep meditation. But Morrigan spoke with her eyes still closed,

"Why do you come here, Kestrel Moonblade? Why do you seek the Crone of the Moondark?" Her voice was soft, gentle, crooning.

Kestrel started in surprise. "You know who I am?"

"I know all things past, present, and future," replied the old woman.

Kestrel looked at her. Her skin was dark and wrinkled as a krabnut, but her eyes were as bright as a bushtail's. They watched Kestrel keenly, but with kindness and compassion. One did not mind being watched by her.

Her hair was long, grey and wispy. It hung like mist. Her long-fingered hands danced over the fire. Ancient, clever hands.

She wore a purple robe and a black shawl and an amber filet over her mist-like hair. She could have been any age – seventy, one hundred, one thousand. For she had the wisdom of all ages from the beginnings to the ashes of time. Kestrel could feel this wisdom. Could see it. The crone beckoned to Kestrel and motioned to her to be seated opposite her by the fire. She peered curiously at the high priestess.

"You come to me because Zephrena of Xegeron has slain the high priest, Lord Aragal. What I do not understand is *why* you seek me. I know all things, past, present, and future, but I cannot make the dead live."

A great shock seemed to strike Kestrel's heart. A sense of unreality. A haze danced over the flames of the fire. A nightmare deadness filled her with darkness. That Lord Aragal could not be saved had never occurred to her.

Shaken, she said, "Lord Aragal said you would advise me. I hoped you would have a potion..."

Her voice trailed into emptiness.

"It is not as easy as that," Morrigan's voice was kindly. She laid a brown, wrinkled hand on Kestrel's arm and Kestrel felt the old woman's courage flow into her.

Even so, her voice trembled and her eyes filled with tears as she asked, "Then he cannot be saved?"

Morrigan smiled at her. "That is not what I said. Lord Aragal's life was taken by trickery, before his appointed time, and his soul still lives in Zar-Yashtoreth. The soul stealer, Zephrena, has it in her clutches, imprisoned, with countless others slain by her, in a great iron globe. Release his soul and he will live again. But remember this must be done before the Sands of Doom run out. You have a half-year's run to complete this task.

"How can I release Lord Aragal's soul?" asked Kestrel.

"You must go to Xegeron," the Crone of the Moondark replied. "You must destroy Zephrena and open the iron globe and release the imprisoned souls within."

"How do I reach Xegeron?" asked Kestrel.

The Crone held out a scroll. "This shows you the way. Go first to the Shaman of Silence, who dwells at the edge of this forest. She will give you a silver chalice. When you release the souls from the iron globe, Lord Aragal's soul will fly into this chalice and can be brought back to his body in this Vessel of

Light. But remember, this must be performed before the Sands of Doom run out."

Kestrel faltered. "It seems an impossible task."

The old woman nodded understandingly.

"It will not be easy," she agreed. "There are many dangers on the way, and the road is rough and the path is twisting and thorny, but you will not be alone."

The Crone's body began to sway rhythmically, her eyes half closed, in a trance, as if she saw things that Kestrel could not see. Suddenly she began to chant in a high, sing-song voice.

"You shall have as your companions,
The thief,
The dragon-maid,
The wise fool,
The elfin minstrel,
The sword bearer,
The seeker of honour,
And that is all."

Her voice dropped to a whisper, as she repeated, "That is all."

There was complete silence. Not a leaf, not a grass blade stirred.

These are strange companions indeed, thought Kestrel. But as Shara Sorian desires, so mote it be.

She rose to her feet and handed the old woman a small pouch.

"Thank you for your help, Mother Morrigan. Please take this gold in return."

Morrigan shook her head. "I thank you, my daughter, but gold is of no use to me. Keep it, my dear, you may have need of it."

"How, then, shall I repay you for your kindness, Mother of Wisdom?" asked Kestrel.

"Free Zar-Yashtoreth from evil," the Crone replied. "That is all the payment I seek."

For a moment she sat silently, staring into the fire. Then she seemed to remember something. She reached for the scroll, and took it from Kestrel's hand. Then, with a blackened twig from the fire, she wrote some words upon the parchment.

"One thing more. The dragon-maid will not come willingly. But speak these words and she will go with you."

Then she pointed to the words she had just written, and pronounced. "*Ourov selig nestia, vrag Neis-Durga Talahindra.*"

Kestrel repeated the words. They lay strangely upon the tongue.

"What do these words mean?" asked Kestrel.

"It is the dragon tongue," explained Morrigan. "It means 'Neis-Durga Talahindra is in danger'."

"I thank you," Kestrel replied, and then a thought struck her. "One thing more, Mother of Wisdom. If you can see into the future, can you tell me, will I be successful in my quest?"

Morrigan smiled and Kestrel suddenly felt like a young novice, who knew nothing. Yet, oddly, this did not disturb her.

"That is not how the future is revealed," the wise woman said gently. "She is ever veiled. Success is the quest in your own heart and none can flee the snares that fate has set for them."

"I do not understand," Kestrel faltered.

The old woman shook her head and spoke kindly. "Nor is it fitting that you should. And now farewell, my daughter, and good fortune shine on you. Go first to the Shaman of Silence. Follow this path and it will lead you to her. After that your way lies over the Nagli Mountains."

Then she traced the shape of the crescent moon and the full moon on Kestrel's forehead. "The peace of the Moondark go with you."

"Farewell, Mother, and thank you," said Kestrel, and she began to walk along the pathway.

The thief, the dragon-maid, the wise fool, the elfin minstrel, the sword bearer, the seeker of honour, Kestrel thought. "Six companions, and I, myself, make the seventh. Seven. The number of magic and change. Pray Shara Sorian that the magic and change lead us from darkness to light."

Kestrel turned and looked back along the path. The Crone of the Moondark was still waving to her, smiling gently. She looked a long, long way away.

Chapter Six

The Shaman of Silence

Kestrel stuck to the path, though this was not easy to do. It twisted and looped and disappeared into tangles of briar. It divided and forked and Kestrel stood for long moments, wondering which fork to take. But always she seemed to hear the crone's voice within her, guiding her.

At first Kestrel wondered whether the voice within was really the crone's, or whether she was just hopefully imagining it. But each time the path she took seemed to lead her on to smoother roads and the old woman's presence was so strong, that, after a while, Kestrel simply opened her heart to her guidance, and trusted it without question.

As the grassy road reached the edge of the forest, it became wider and the grass became softer and greener. The forest became more and more silent. Yet Kestrel did not feel alone. A sense of peace permeated the forest and seemed to welcome the warrior priestess.

Presently there came a very faint sound, so faint that Kestrel could not be sure she truly heard it. She stood quite still and listened intently. Now it came again, more clearly, borne upon the air. The sweet, woody notes of an orm-pipe.

The music drifted through the leaves and branches, and Kestrel followed the sound, until she came to a clearing, and stood in a circle of bright, cushiony grass, surrounded by trees and forest flowers.

This circle of grass was so bright and green, so lush and soft, that it seemed designed by nature to be an arena of some kind.

The sound of the orm-pipe, deep and sweet, was much nearer now, but the musician was so well camouflaged that, when Kestrel suddenly saw him, she was startled for a moment.

He wore a loose, grey-brown tunic, tied with a brown cord, and baggy grey brown breeches. His long curly hair was brown and his weather-beaten skin was brown. He seemed part of the tree against which he leant, playing the long slim orm-pipe. He did not appear to notice Kestrel. His eyes, brown as the tree trunk, stared, trance-like, into the distance. He seemed hypnotised by his own music.

Kestrel wanted to ask him if he knew how she could find the Shaman of Silence, but found herself unable to speak. She, too, was half-hypnotised by the sweet sound of the orm-pipe.

But, as if her thoughts had called to the shaman, Kestrel suddenly saw her. She was stretched out on the branch of a lorqu' tree. Like the musician, she seemed, at first, to be part of the tree itself. Now she untwined herself and slid, serpent-like, down the smooth trunk of the Sacred Tree to the grass. She was old beyond years, yet, at the same time, seemed like a lithe girl, a spring maiden. Her hair was silver. Her eyes were green as leaves. Her face was lined, yet young. She wore a robe of green. Her feet were bare and they danced upon the grass, like swift, graceful moths. Spiralling and spiralling they whirled to the sound of the orm-pipe, until, suddenly, the music stopped, without warning, and, at the same time, the shaman stopped too, and looked at Kestrel.

She spoke not a word, but Kestrel knew she must approach. She went towards the shaman, drawn by her, and, instinctively, held up her hand, palm outwards. The shaman did the same, and their palms touched, lightly. As this happened, Kestrel felt a warmth leap through her and she knew that the shaman understood everything about the quest, about Lord Aragal ni Tourleth, about Xegeron, and the evil Zephrena. Even about the strange companions who were to accompany Kestrel on her journey.

At last the shaman nodded. The musician's haunting music floated on the air once more, and the shaman began to dance. She danced Kestrel's journey to Xegeron, over mountains, through forests and across lakes and seas, her feet light as clouds floating on the sky. Finally she stopped and flung her arms upward, as if she embraced the sun. Then she brought her arms down and then held one hand out, as if to receive a gift from the air. The next moment a silver chalice, most beautifully engraved, stood upon her palm.

"Where did it come from?" Kestrel wondered, "By what magic?" But the shaman spoke not a word. She handed the chalice to Kestrel, who, instinctively, knelt to receive it. The shaman smiled at her and then twirled into the air and was gone. The music hung in the air for a few moments and then broke off suddenly. Music and musician were gone too. There was an intense silence in the glade and Kestrel suddenly felt an overwhelming sense of loneliness.

Chapter Seven

Droco the Sprig

When Droco the Sprig, master thief of Kironin, was sentenced to ten years in the Islarian galleys, everyone agreed that it was incredibly bad luck. Thieves who learned their profession from the great Zirax Busko were seldom caught, and Droco could count his captures on the fingers of one hand and have several fingers left over.

Droco was born in the poor quarter of Kironin. His mother, Modron Skyle, was a penniless seamstress, who had been seduced and then deserted by a passing lord. Pregnant, destitute and homeless, she was taken in and cared for by the Trilki beggar, Peckle Gubbit, who tended her and loved her, and soon won her love in return.

Peckle Gubbit was a beggar of some talent, and made a fair living at his trade. He bought food and clothing for Modron and nursed her through her troubled pregnancy, but all she had suffered took its toll. Despite all Peckle's care, she died in childbirth, leaving the little Trilki with a baby boy on his hands.

Peckle Gubbit loved the child as if he were his own son. He named the boy Droco, after Droco Gubbit, his own grandfather, and reared him with tender care, through good times and bad.

The boy grew up to be cheerful, affectionate, generous, kind and merry hearted. He was lively, and quick-witted, and a great favourite with the Trilki people and the begging fraternity. As soon as Droco was old enough to walk and talk, Peckle began to teach him the begging trade and Droco proved no mean hand at it.

Droco enjoyed a happy childhood. Life in the crowded slums of Kironin was far from luxurious, but there was colour, adventure and excitement in plenty, and Droco would not have exchanged it for life in the king's palace itself.

On red letter days, Zirax Busko would turn up in the slums of Kironin, where Peckle and Droco begged. He was the great and famous master thief, who could take jewels before the very eyes of the most watchful of guards and slip a lady's ring from her finger as he kissed her hand. He had a thousand disguises and had travelled all over Zar-Yashtoreth, always evading the clutches of the law, always returning to Kironin, his birthplace and home. Droco and his young companions hero-worshipped Zirax Busko, and so indeed did all the inhabitants of the poor quarter, for the great master thief never failed to share his purloined gold with them. When Zirax turned up, he would treat everyone, at the Red Cat Tavern, and regale them all with tales of his exploits and adventures. To Droco, the life of a thief seemed the height of romance and excitement.

Zirax had a band of young apprentices who were the crème de la crème, and learned their profession for seven years before they were accomplished enough to set out on their own. Droco enjoyed begging, but when her heard Zirax or his apprentices talk of a thief's life, he wished with all his being to become apprenticed to the great Zirax Busko. Sometimes he expressed this longing to his stepfather. Peckle understood and would nod his head wisely.

"Aye, it's an exciting life," he agreed, "but begging's a lot safer. You might be kicked or cursed now and again, but they don't flog you for begging, and they don't hang you for it, or send you to the galleys."

Droco knew this was good sense, but Zirax Busko had set something alight in his heart. His thoughts were drawn continually to the profession of thieving and his opportunity came suddenly, when he least expected it.

It came about when Droco was 11 years old. He and Peckle had had a rare bad day. The passers-by were particularly ungenerous. Perhaps because of the cold, sleety rain, or just due to general bad luck. Either way the takings that day were slim.

Peckle shrugged his shoulders philosophically.

"Ah well. That's how it goes," he remarked, as the sky darkened even more. "Let's pack it in for today, son. We've made enough to buy us a brag pie and a cup of khadish, and that's not bad."

Droco agreed, cheerfully. His stepfather was right. A beggar's life wasn't bad at all. If the weather was uncharitable, you did not have to keep working, like most folk. You could knock off and go into the warm and dry.

"Crooked Crab, Pa?" he enquired, with a grin.

Peckle nodded. "I'll say!"

The Crooked Crab served cheap meals, and, in weather like this, they had a roaring log fire. They set off together, when, suddenly, Droco saw a prosperous-looking gentleman picking his way among the market stalls, and, clearly, seeking shelter.

At the sight of him, Droco felt an irresistible urge to pick the man's pocket. He'd heard Zirax describe how to do it, many times and he had even watched the master thief's apprentices at work, and Droco felt, deep within himself, that he knew how to do it.

Carefully, but without hesitation, Droco cut the man's pouch, successfully. It felt very full, and he was just congratulating himself, when he felt a hand on his shoulder. His heart seemed to stop. He whirled round, expecting to see one of the town guards, and found himself looking up at the laughing face of Zirax Busko himself.

"That was well done, my lad. Like a professional," said the master thief, and Droco's heart brightened with happiness and pride.

"You've a natural talent," Zirax told him, "How'd you like to learn the profession properly?"

Droco's eyes widened. "You mean you'd take me on as an apprentice?"

Zirax laughed. "If your people agree. You're the stepson of Peckle Gubbit, the beggar, aren't you?"

Droco nodded. "He's just there down the street," he pointed to where the little Trilki was coming back to see where in Zar-Yashtoreth his stepson had got to.

"I'll speak to him," said Zirax.

Peckle glowed with pride that his beloved stepson should be chosen by the great Zirax Busko. He knew this was the path Droco wanted to follow. He'd never be truly happy as a beggar. And so Droco had started his apprenticeship.

Now he himself was a master thief, and a highly successful one. And to be caught at Lord Ashak's palace in Islaria through a crowd of drunken revellers setting off the alarm bells, was the worst luck anyone could have.

But if Zabris, God of thieves, had been asleep for a few moments, he woke up soon enough now one of his disciples was sent to the galleys for ten years.

After suffering the tortures of the galleys for a week, Droco's luck returned. He saw a small piece of copper thread lying close to his rowing bench. Where it came from, he couldn't tell. Perhaps it was a gift of compensation from Zabris himself. But it was all Droco needed to pick the lock of his chains, and this he did with such skill, that none of the galley guards noticed. Then, in the darkness of night, Droco eased himself over the side of the ship and struck out for land – any land.

***

Kestrel climbed the Nagli Mountains slowly. The wind wailed like a creature in pain. She could hear the screeches of dawcaws and the huffing barks of ghyrinx. Added to these mournful sounds was the desolation of the barren mountain peaks. Sometimes she leaned on her staff and paused for breath. At other times she clung to boulders and even tufts of grass, as the path grew steeper, and the sun hotter. At last she knew she must rest for a while and sat down under the sparse shade of a stunted thorn bush. She took a drink of cool stream water from her flask.

As she sat, leaning her head against the withered trunk of the bush, she was surprised to hear the sound of shouts and the swish of someone beating aside brambles and bushes.

"Where's the skadding little squin got to?" said someone, speaking in Islarian.

"Vanished! Can't see him anywhere!" said another.

"He'll get 50 lashes for this," came a third.

"A hundred if I have my way. I'm scraped to the bone by these quirking thorns," said the first voice.

Kestrel knew enough Islarian to understand the gist of what was being said. She rose to her feet and looked round. Now she saw three lean, but strong-looking men, beating the bushes and long grass with their scimitars.

Their long, crimped blue-black hair and beards, their long drooping moustaches and their gold earrings and wide copper arm bangles, proclaimed them Islarians.

As Kestrel watched, one of them pointed a long, lean finger towards the top of the mountains.

"There he is. I can see him. We've got him!"

Kestrel looked up to where he pointed, and saw a thin ragged figure, climbing among the rocks, clinging to tufts of grass, thorn bushes and projecting stones. Though half dead with terror and weariness, he was as nimble as a mountain goat, and, for a while, it seemed he would escape his pursuers.

But his exhaustion took its toll, and the Islarians began to close in on the fugitive, who, finally, leant against a rock in an attitude of utter defeat.

Kestrel was horrified. As the Islarians reached out to take him, she held out her staff and cried, "*Aya Asherah*!" Instantly the Islarians stood frozen to the spot in a state of trance.

"In the name of Shara Sorian, I command you to depart," Kestrel continued. The Islarians walked away down the mountain, through bushes and burrs, through thistles, nettles and thorns. Unseeing, unhearing they walked and vanished into the rising mist below.

The fugitive seemed to revive at once, though he was clearly amazed.

"Frazz me! All thanks to you, great Zabris!" he cried. The next moment he had flung himself at Kestrel's feet and was kissing her hands in gratitude.

"A thousand thanks, brave, kind and beautiful lady!"

Kestrel saw that his grey rags were stained with blood, where the lash had cut his back, shoulders and arms.

"Who were those people?" she asked gently. "What did they want of you?"

"Islarian galley guards, my lady," replied the fugitive. "I thought my last moment had come."

"Do they pluck victims for the galleys from their homes these days?" Kestrel was outraged. To her amazement, the fugitive grinned. It was an irresistible grin, and Kestrel could not help liking him.

"It's not that, my lady. I've escaped from their frazzing galleys." There was a note of pride in his voice.

Kestrel flinched inwardly to hear him use the worst kind of thieves' cant, and her feelings must have shown, for he said quickly, "Forgive me, my lady, but there's no other word for them. Ten years, that frazz— I mean that troll, Lord Ashak, sentenced me to. Ten years in the Islarian galleys. Might as well have sent me to the gallows and be done with it. Who could survive ten years as a slave in the Islarian galleys? And all for a few jewels and a little gold that the quirking twag wouldn't have even missed. 'The great are protected by lions', as the old saying goes."

Slowly it began to dawn on Kestrel that the fugitive was not some harmless peasant, dragged from his hearth and home to serve in the Islarian galleys, but had been sent there for the theft of gold and jewels from the Lord of Islaria's palace.

"You are a thief?" she asked, hardly liking to put the question.

The fugitive gave her another irresistible grin and rose to his feet.

"The best in Zar-Yashtoreth, my lady. Droco the Sprig at your service," he said, with a flourish.

Kestrel was dumbfounded. She had expected a vehement denial, or else excuses. She had not expected pride.

"I'm not at all sure I should have rescued you," she said. "You probably deserve the Islarian galleys.

Droco was unabashed.

"Bless you, my lady. No one deserves the Islarian galleys. I'm scarred all over from the lash and I was only there a week. Ten years would kill a griffin, let alone a man."

Despite herself, Kestrel was curious and could not refrain from asking him, "How did you escape? And while you tell me, perhaps I can heal those lash wounds."

Droco's pride in his profession took over once more and as he began to recover from his ordeal, and as Kestrel bathed his wounds with a healing salve that took away the pain, he grew quite skittish.

"Ah, now you're asking, my lady. There isn't a lock on Zar-Yashtoreth that I can't pick – unless it's been magicked, of course. I was apprenticed for seven years to the great Zirax Busko himself. Not that the galley chains weren't a challenge, especially as I had to do the job without letting the guards see me. But I like a challenge. I'd have set my benchmate free too, but he was too scared. Wouldn't hear of it. Said he'd swear he was asleep and saw nothing, but he wouldn't go with me. He was past it anyway, poor old grig. He'd never have made it to land."

Kestrel took in his words, and recognised the generosity of his action. To think of a fellow prisoner at such a time was kind and courageous. He might be a thief, but he was not evil. Then she recalled the name Zirax Busko. She knew that name, for his fame had reached even the Temple of the Golden Unicorn.

"Zirax Busko, the thief?" she asked.

"The master thief," Droco replied. "*The* master thief! A legend in his own time."

"Are thieves apprenticed to their trades like cobblers?" wondered Kestrel.

"Profession, my lady. Not trade," said Droco, with dignity. "Thieving is a profession, you know. Naturally it needs an apprenticeship. It can't be learnt in a day."

Kestrel felt it incumbent on her to show some disapproval, though it was difficult to disapprove of Droco, for his charm was irresistible, and his light-heartedness infectious. However, she tried to speak seriously.

"But, Droco, have you never considered how degrading, how dishonourable it is to be a thief?"

Droco was not one whit offended. He simply said, "Now hold on, my lady..."

The mountain wind blew. It sounded like a voice singing. It brought to Kestrel's mind the voice of Morrigan, the Crone of the Moondark, as plainly as if the old wise woman were there beside her, "You shall have as your companions...the thief."

Kestrel stood as if turned to stone. This, beyond all question of a doubt was the thief. But would he go with her to Xegeron? Kestrel turned to Droco.

"Maybe I spoke in haste," she said. "As it is, I have need of a..." she could not bring herself to utter the word, which she felt was an insult. Instead she said, "Of one of your profession." Droco smiled to himself at her evasion and Kestrel continued, hastily

"I am Kestrel Moonblade, warrior priestess of the Temple of the Golden Unicorn of U-Llashkar, and I am on a quest to Xegeron to destroy the dark sorceress, Zephrena. Will you go with me?"

Droco looked startled.

"To Xegeron?" He considered for a moment. Then he continued, "Well, I reckon, if it hadn't been for you, I'd be getting branded and flogged half to death in the galleys, so I'll go with you, my lady. In which case, I'd better return these. If I'm to work for you, I can't exactly steal from you. It would be against our code, you know."

He handed Kestrel her purse and her ring. It took Kestrel a moment to take in the fact that they were hers. When she realised, all she could do was ask in amazement, "How did you come by these?"

"Took them from your belt and your finger, my lady," Droco replied, casually. "Not that I'd have kept them. Not after what you've done for me. I just wanted to be sure that, after a week in the galleys, I hadn't lost my touch."

Again, Kestrel's disapproval melted under Droco's charm. She shook her head.

"I'll say one thing for you. You're certainly good at your work."

Droco acknowledged the compliment.

"None better," he agreed. "Unless you were to hire the great Zirax Busko himself." Then a thought struck him. "How do we reach Xegeron?"

Kestrel took from her pack the scroll that Morrigan had given her. She unrolled it and laid it on a flat stone, tracing, with her finger, the route to Xegeron so that Droco could see it.

"First we must continue over the Nagli Mountains, and when we have crossed them, we descend to the Valley of the Sun and Moon Lakes."

Droco started. "Take care, Lady Kestrel, that's dragon country."

"I know, Droco," Kestrel replied gently. "If you would rather turn back, I shall understand."

Droco's face grew determined. "What – turn back from an adventure of a lifetime? Never in a thousand years. I'm with you to the end! Besides, I haven't forgotten what you did for me this day."

Kestrel was touched. She would never have guessed that a thief could have so much honour.

"Thank you, Droco," she said. "Then on to the Sun and Moon Lakes. And Droco…"

"My lady?"

"I hope you don't propose to try your skills on a dragon's lair."

Droco was outraged, "Lady Kestrel, I'm a professional thief. I'm not a fool."

Kestrel could not help laughing. "I'm glad to hear it," she said.

As they made their way up the steep mountainside and along the narrow paths, Droco regaled Kestrel with his life story and his exploits, and, though Kestrel tried to be disapproving of the latter, his way of telling them was so amusing and so free from any malice, that she could not help smiling at his tales.

Droco the Sprig made a good travelling companion, and his light-hearted chatter made the journey a lot less lonely, and a lot more hopeful. It shortened the dreary way, for, suddenly, Kestrel realised, they were over the mountain peaks, and making their descent. It was growing dark, however, and they would never reach the Valley of the Sun and Moon Lakes before nightfall. Kestrel knew they must find a place to rest for the night. There was a large sheltering boulder, and some small jarl bushes, which would keep off the wind. It was as good a place as any.

"It's growing dark," Kestrel said. "We must camp here for the night and go on to the Sun and Moon Lakes tomorrow."

She unrolled her blanket, "Take this," she offered. "I shall keep watch first. You must be tired, I'll wake you later."

"You are generous, Lady Kestrel. I thank you," replied Droco.

He wrapped himself in the blanket, and, for a while, lay looking up at the darkening sky. It had been a frazzing amazing day, he thought. Last night he had been a galley slave. This morning he had been a fugitive. Now here he was on an impossible quest (for Kestrel had told him, as they travelled, what she hoped to do) with a mad priestess, who hadn't a hope in Kasperus of succeeding, and who was about to take him into dragon country. Truly, life was a mirrafly. She hovered and darted.

Kestrel's warning against using his skills on a dragon's lair came back to him. He smiled sleepily to himself. Plunder a dragon's lair indeed! You'd have to be frazzing crazy! Not even Zirax... Mind you, he thought, that *would* be a challenge! The challenge of all challenges! If you succeeded, how you would go down in legend! Why, every minstrel would have your name on his lips.

"Droco!" Kestrel's voice broke into his thoughts. "Do not so much as consider it in your dreams."

Droco sat up like a flash of lightening. Surely he had not spoken aloud? Frazzing Kasperus! She'd read his mind!

"No, Lady Kestrel," he sighed, and lay down again.

By Zabris! he thought, "I'm in with a quirking mind reader now!"

He stretched out on the blanket, pulling one end of it round him, and fell asleep. Kestrel sat beside him, and watched the stars come out.

Chapter Eight

Tanith-Medea

After the Purging Wars, the victorious Troll Queen, Mugdrug of Oglaf, slaughtered every elf, trilki, human and dwarf on whom she could lay hands, until even the dwarfs fled her dark lands. Only trolls, goblins and the grey skinned krauls remained. Oglaf was a wasteland, a land almost as dark as Xegeron itself.

But one day, a ray of brightness lit the land of Oglaf. A young elf minstrel walked, singing, through the desolate crags, strumming the qu'enga, heedless of the evil around him. The Purging Wars had ended long before his birth, and he knew nothing of boundaries or prohibitions, and cared less. He lived only for love, and music, and song. So he walked like a sunbeam through the darkness, sending forth his beautiful voice, and the sweet strains of the qu'enga, oblivious that he was watched by grutsk, sitting hunched on mountaintops and by kvark flying high on their leathery wings.

These swooped to Mugdrug's palace and told her that an elf was strolling through her country, as bold as a trog. Mugdrug's face grew thunderous. Her troll courtiers watched her, terrified. The Troll Queen was dangerous in this mood. Her voice sounded like boulders grinding.

"Fetch the squin-dung to me, I'll show him what it is to defy my command. I'll have him torn by nvarwolks!"

The nvarwolks by her throne strained on their chains, sensing something good coming their way, while those in the pit, in the corner of the throne room, paced, restlessly, their hackles rising.

The troll courtiers cackled and rubbed their hands in glee. The grutsk messenger clapped its great wings and flew off, followed by the kuark messenger, calling harshly to the others.

One of them heard and immediately swooped down and grasped the young elf in its huge toothed beak. The elf was terrified. He clung to the qu'enga, as if for protection. The kuark bore him to Mugdrug's palace and dropped him at her feet.

The elf minstrel's heart almost stopped beating, as he found himself surrounded by hideous trolls, by leering goblins and by ferocious kraul guards.

"What," rasped Mugdrug, "are you doing in Oglaf, elf scum? Have I not banished you filthy squin from my land?"

The elf trembled. "If you please, Oh Great One," he hazarded, for she wore a huge iron crown, sat on a throne and talked of her land, "I am a traveller and did not know this was your land, nor that I should not be here."

"A likely tale!" snapped the Troll Queen, "You've never heard of the Purging Wars, I suppose?"

"No indeed," the elf minstrel spoke no more than the truth. "I am a minstrel, Your Greatness. I know nothing of politics and war. I live only for music and song."

The Troll Queen screeched with laughter, and her courtiers cackled sycophantically.

"You twagging bit of filth! You dare to come into my land!" Her green-skinned face loomed over the young minstrel. He cringed at her great mouth with its blackened and broken teeth. At her small grey eyes, full of cruel hatred.

"Now learn your fate, squin-dung. You will be carved by scimitars, and thrown, still living, to be torn to pieces by my nvarwolks. What do you say to that, my fine elfling screecher?"

Terror made the elf minstrel quick-witted. He bowed low before the hideous creature.

"If I have offended your gracious and beauteous Majesty, I am more than willing to die," he said. "Indeed I am honoured to die at your hands. But let me beg one favour from your greatness. Let me sing a song before I am slain – a serenade to your beauty."

Mugdrug was flattered. "Then chirp your last chirp, swamp-fly. When you are finished, the kraul scimitars are ready for you. And let your chirping be short, for the nvarwolks are hungry.

Then the elf minstrel began to strum the qu'enga, and his sweet voice filled the great stone hall beneath the huge hanging stalactites, green with slime.

"The Queen of the Trolls
Is as beautiful as lilies.
Her soft hair ripples like a sunset lake.
Her eyes are like blossoms on the arapan tree,
Her voice is as sweet as the honey bee."

As Mugdrug's rust-coloured hair hung in filthy knots. Her eyes were small and squinting and her voice was like a hurricane, it was only terror that prevented the young minstrel from laughing out loud at this great lie. He continued.

"The Queen of the Trolls is as sweet as a flower,
She makes my heart flutter, like a butterfly.
If her lovely face is the last thing I see,
Then my life is complete, and I'll happily die."

Mugdrug had no ear for music, but she liked the compliments, and the qu'enga's lovely notes had a hypnotic effect, even on the unmusical trolls, krauls, and goblins. Even the nvarwolks in their pit stopped pacing and listened, while those chained by the throne crouched and were still.

And Mugdrug couldn't help thinking how beautiful this young minstrel was, and how delicate, and how much she would like him as a lover. But, of course, no one must guess her thoughts. It would be the greatest dishonour for the Queen of the Trolls to take an elven lover. So she narrowed her tiny eyes and planned. At last, she thought of something.

"Put the little song bird in a cage!" she ordered. "And set him in my chamber. He can chirp for my pleasure. It would be a pity to silence that voice for ever."

So the young elf minstrel was put in a cage and taken to Mugdrug's chamber. When she retired for the night, and was alone, she opened the cage and took him to her bed. Afterwards, overcome with lassitude, she fell asleep, without securing him.

Crushed, bruised and sick with revulsion, the young minstrel took his qu'enga and escaped from her window, vanishing, for ever, into the night. Mugdrug's fury knew no bounds when she discovered he had gone, and everyone trembled at her rage.

Some time later, Mugdrug knew she was with child. She told no one, but took a young troll warrior as her lover. Now everyone would think the child was his.

When the time came for the child to be delivered, Mugdrug retired with Ozilgax, the royal midwife. Ozilgax had served the royal family of Oglaf for many years. She was devoted, trustworthy and discreet. She had seen much, yet even she was not prepared for the baby she delivered.

It was a girl child, tiny and delicate, with a mop of thick black hair, green skin and claws, but with her father's delicate features and the pointed ears of the elven race.

When Mugdrug saw the child, she was horrified.

"Ozilgax, you understand what has happened?"

"Majesty," replied Ozilgax, "I have known many secrets in my time, but spoken of none."

"Indeed, I know I can trust you," Mugdrug told her. "You are sure as rock. This thing cannot live." Mugdrug opened her window and lightly tossed the sleeping infant into the River Kvar, which flowed outside her palace.

"We will wait a few hours. Then you must carry a bundle out to the grave-ground, and have it buried. Then we give out the news that the child is dead and in its grave. Khirazak, my consort, must only know once the burial is complete."

"It shall be done, Your Majesty," said Ozilgax. And so the unfortunate incident was ended.

***

The unhappy baby, the result of so strange a liaison, floated, unconscious, on the River Kvar, not even waking when a swooping grutsk picked her up in its great claws and carried her off over the Nagli Mountains and high over the Valley of the Sun and Moon Lakes.

A passing huntsman on the mountains sent a well-aimed and fortunate arrow and struck the grutsk, who let its prey drop, and hurtled, dead, to the ground.

The child, who seemed to have divine protection, fell into one of the green moon lakes, amongst a clutch of dragon eggs. Morgana-Semiramis Shirakalinzarin and her consort Shitak-Shagreet Talahindra, were crooning to their first little hatchling, whom they had named Hecate-Magreet, and all the dragon clans who had gathered, as they always did, for a hatching, were also crooning, "Welcome, welcome, welcome," to the little newcomer.

Then the next egg hatched, and out came tiny Lilith-Medusa, and at the selfsame moment, the baby, lying in the clutch of eggs, awoke, and began to wail. And the dragons, still chanting their welcome song, gathered round curiously and found the tiny, green-skinned, pointed-eared, long-clawed baby in their midst.

"What is this?" cried Morgana-Semiramis.

"It is a wonder!" replied Shirak-Shagreet.

And Lady Tiamat-Ananta, Morgana's mother and the clan matriarch, marvelled, "This Hatching is blessed. Mother Tiamat has sent you a Gift Child."

Lady Hochma-Sofia, the Dragon of Wisdom, was sent for. She was of the Ushani, the mystic black dragons of the Zarasti Mountains of the South. She gazed into the distance with her second sight. Then she told them of the little one's strange parentage.

"The poor little quodling!" cried Morgana-Semiramis." She has been sent to us for protection, and we will rear her as one of our own. Shall we not, my dear one?"

"Indeed we shall," agreed Shirak-Shagreet. "Poor little quodling, alone and cast out by her cruel mother. What shall we name her, my dearest?"

It was the custom of the dragon people for the mother to choose the first name of their girl children and the father to choose the second name. This was reversed for their boy children.

So Morgana-Semiramis spoke first. "I name the little one Tanith."

"I name her Medea," said Shirak-Shagreet.

Then together they said "She is Tanith-Medea Shirakalinzarin."

And her elder sister, Hecate-Magreet, and her "twin" sister, Lilith-Medusa, who had hatched as Tanith-Medea was discovered, snuggled close to her, as if to keep her warm and safe, while the dragon clans crooned, "Welcome, welcome, welcome…" and the other eggs, though not yet ready to hatch, rocked rhythmically to the crooning chant.

***

To be adopted by the dragons of the Sun and Moon Lakes, was to live an idyllic life of joy and luxury. The Valley of the Sun and Moon Lakes, or the Guadja (as the dragon people called it, in their tongue, and which meant, simply, "Paradise") was one of the most beautiful lands of Zar-Yashtoreth. In its tropical climate grew the most luscious of fruits, the sweet scarlet quetsch-fruit being the general favourite. Tskai flies built their nests, and then abandoned them, leaving their old homes dripping with thick, oozing honey. Huge brilliant flowers grew everywhere. Bright birds darted among the graceful trees, flashing their brilliant plumage, and warbling their exquisite songs. Beautiful insects, like jewels, flew or crept among the grasses and flowers and over the warm, magnificent lakes that gave the land its name.

Waterfalls and pure springs were everywhere, so food and water were plentiful, and the dragon clans that lived there lacked nothing. They lived lives of pure enjoyment. In the morning they rose and bathed in the lakes, the older ones washing the little ones. Then they breakfasted. Then followed their devotions, giving praise to Mother Tiamat, who had brought them safely through the night to this day. Though, indeed, dragon devotions were more a continual conversation with their beloved Mother Tiamat, who was interested in everything her little quodlings did.

They spent their days reading and telling stories, and lazing in the sun. The little ones went to Aunt Xanthe-Bathsheba, and Aunt Drusilla-Cassandra, who taught them dragon lore and dragon games. Most popular was the memory game "Dragon Tree", which taught them the difference between physical treasure, like gold, or rubies, emeralds, diamonds, silver, or garnets, and spiritual treasure, like happiness or kindness, peace or contentment. Any gathering of dragons, of any age, would often, spontaneously, form a circle for a game of "Round and Round the Dragon Tree".

The older dragons went to Grandmama Tiamat-Ananta, Tanith's grandmother, the clan matriarch of the Shirakalinzarin clan, who taught them dragon magic, and to Lady Hochma-Sofia Ushani, and Great Grandfather Tanin Cyprianus Ushani, who taught them dragon wisdom, and philosophy, and the meanings of dreams, and how to speak the tree speech and the common tongue, though the basic common tongue was really imbibed from birth.

Uncles Phineas Coprinius Shirakalinzarin and Apolonius Mercury Shirakalinzarin, renowned fighters and vanquishers of armoured murderers, taught them how to defend themselves, should they ever need to.

Aunt Cordelia-Aurelia and Uncle Orion-Orlando Sa'arourat, and Aunt Berendrith Inzilbian Talahindra taught them etiquette and Uncle Glautur Meriog Talahindra, the famous raconteur, taught dragon legend and taught the little ones how to read.

There was much the young dragons needed to learn, but there was no hurry, so most of the day was spent at leisure, basking and sleeping and playing, reading and bathing, creating and telling stories, making beautiful artefacts, and marvelling at the beauty of their treasure. Treasure, to the dragon-folk, was valued, simply for its beauty. They cared nothing for wealth. Freedom and joy were prized far more.

Or they would frolic with their friends and families. Whole flocks of dragons would go off cloud diving, the little ones, who could not fly, riding on the backs of their elders. Or they would explore the small jewel-like islands off the coast of the Guadja. At night they gathered in their caves and slept, curled up together, after a joyous thanks to Mother Tiamat for their happy day, until the sun caressed them awake, and the whole happy round began again.

Bathing, playing, learning, feasting when they were hungry on the luscious food around them, drinking from the sparkling springs and streams when they were thirsty, sleeping in perfect safety, when they were tired, life for the dragon people was a round of joy.

The only dark cloud in their lives was the fear of the dreaded Armoured Ones, who sometimes caused tragedy with their murderous assaults; but they never came near the Guadja, and if they did, Uncle Phineas Coprinius and Uncle Apolonius Mercury would be ready for them. Tanith's own father, Shirak-Shagreet, was a redoubtable fighter too, though he preferred lazing in the flowers, or cloud diving.

So Tanith's life passed in happiness. When she was old enough to realise that she did not look quite the same as her brothers and sisters, Morgana-Semiramis told her of her origins, and added, "But you are of the dragon people, despite your outward shape." And since the dragon-folk accepted her completely and never gave her outward shape a thought, Tanith, too, forgot about it, and enjoyed her trouble-free life to the full, accepting, completely, that she was one of the dragon people.

Chapter Nine

The Dragon-Maid

That memorable day, which was to change the life of Tanith-Medea Shirakalinzarin so greatly, began quietly and ordinarily enough. Tanith awoke in the happy security of the family cave, with her sisters' arms around her and her arms around them. Her parents' sheltering wings spread overhead. The sun shone as usual. She could hear the peaceful sound of the great Sun Lake beside their cave, gently lapping against the shore. She could smell the sweet scent of the quetsch-fruit groves and the abgennas and kala flowers and the khola grass.

Her younger brothers, Caramoon Liskander and Merlin Melchior, lay curled up with them, while the youngest of the family, Thespis Hyperion, Circe Delilah, Mordecai Caladrian, and the latest, newly hatched baby, Accacia-Laburnum, were snuggled between Morgana-Semiramis's encircling paws.

Tanith stretched, luxuriously in the glorious, humid heat. A great love of her family surged through her and she cuddled down with Hecate Magreet and her twin, Lilith Medusa, and listened to the kritch-kratchs' songs, and the birds' warbling hymn to Mother Tiamat.

Soon they, too, would greet each other and offer up their devotions to Mother Tiamat. Then they would bathe and meet and greet the others of their clan, and all the other clans, and then they would begin their morning feast in the sunshine.

Just now, however, Tanith-Medea was the only one awake. She lay, drowsily, happy as the morning unfolded outside their cave, and Mother Tiamat opened her golden eye, while all her little ones curled up and went to sleep.

After a while, the sunlight called to her and she began to think that an early bathe would be very pleasant. The dragon people often did this, for the Guadja was a place of complete safety. No harm could come to anyone here.

So Tanith, moving quietly, so as not to disturb her sleeping family, disentangled herself and slipped into the glorious morning. She poured forth her joy to Mother Tiamat, including Her in her plans and chatting to her, as all the dragon-folk did. She stretched her slender arms with their long-clawed hands to the sky and cried, "Good morning, dearest Mother. My thanks to you for this radiant day and for my sweet sleep last night. I am going to bathe now, and perhaps find fruit, and then I will return to my dear ones in our beautiful cave."

So saying, she stepped into the warm, clear emerald lake, and swam for a while, before emerging and making for a quetsch tree. The sun dried her skin. She plucked one of the scarlet fruits and bit into its luscious sweetness.

"Dear Mother Tiamat, thank you for our beautiful lakes and thank you for these delicious quetsch fruits," she said inwardly, as she held the fruit and ate daintily and delicately, as her mama had said she should.

"Don't eat like a troll," Mama would say, if any of them gobbled too greedily. Tanith never took offence at these words, nor did anyone feel embarrassed by them. For all of them had completely forgotten Tanith's troll blood, including Tanith herself. She was a dragon, as far as they were all concerned.

***

Droco had been keeping watch now for several hours. Kestrel had woken him, gently, and now she slept, and it was his turn to make sure no danger threatened. It was not the first time he had ever kept watch. He'd kept vigil for days on houses he planned to rob, but that was different. Then there had been the excitement of the job to be done. This, however, was tedious. He could see nothing, because of the darkness, and the heat was suffocating, and the silence was unnerving.

To Droco, bred in a noisy, bustling town, these still mountain foothills were disturbing. Every rustle made him start, and he became very conscious of the fact that below them lay dragon country. So he alternated between terror and boredom, until the darkness lifted and he saw the Valley of the Sun and Moon Lakes spread beneath him.

He gasped in wonder, and all his weariness evaporated, for he had never seen anything so beautiful in his life. The great lakes were of the brightest blues and greens. Even at this early hour steam rose from them in the heat. These lakes were surrounded by huge trumpet-like flowers of vivid scarlet, magenta, peacock blue, flame and dazzling white. Tiny delicate blossoms intermingled with these large flowers, their colours iridescent and jewel-like. Their fragrance wafted on the air and reached even the foothills where Droco and Kestrel were encamped.

A glistening waterfall, rainbow hued, rushed down the mountainside. The mountains were bright with soft grass and flower carpets. They also held huge caves. Dragon caves thought Droco, nervously. However, nothing stirred in the valley.

Presently, to Droco's intense surprise, an elf-woman emerged from one of the lakeside caves. She looked like an elf, as far as Droco could see, but her skin was green. She was quite naked.

She entered one of the lakes and swam for a while. Then she sat under one of the gently falling waterfalls and groomed herself, washing her long, thick black hair. She reminded Droco of the way an animal might groom itself. She spent a long time doing this. Then she stood up and the shining water dropped off her like khargstones. She shook herself, again, as an animal might, and then waded back to the shore, through the shallow water. She plucked one of the large red fruits growing on the lower branches of a tree. She washed it carefully in the lake, and then began to eat it, holding it delicately in her fingers.

Droco was fascinated and horrified. How could this elf-maid act so nonchalantly in dragon country? He watched, mesmerised.

"Well, frazz me!" he murmured. "If that don't beat everything! Now I've seen it all!"

Kestrel's sleep was always very light. At the sound of Droco's voice, she was awake, instantly. She sat up and laid her hand on her sword hilt.

"What is it, Droco?" she whispered. Droco pointed down to the valley.

"Look at that, my lady. Did you ever see anything like it? An elf with green skin, and what's more, she's just walked out of that cave as if she owned it. And I'll wager it's a dragon's cave too."

Kestrel knew his guess was right and she was horrified. It was clear that the elf-woman knew nothing of the danger she was in. If the dragons found her trespassing in their domain they would destroy her instantly.

"I must warn her of the danger of entering a dragon's lair, uninvited," she told Droco. "Stay here. I'm going down"

Droco went ashen at the very idea. "But then *you* are entering uninvited…" he began.

Kestrel simply smiled serenely. "Shara Sorian will protect me. I shall come to no harm."

So saying, she left Droco, who stood, shaking his head and muttering "Frazzing Kasperus!" and she began to descend to the Valley of the Sun and Moon Lakes.

The heat grew more and more intense and oppressive as Kestrel moved nearer to the valley. She felt the sweat run down her back and her legs. Now she could smell the overpoweringly sweet scent of the flowers. She saw tskai flies and ryzka moths shining like jewels. She heard strange liquid notes of birdsong that she had never heard before. She could feel the spray of the rainbow-hued waterfall cascading into the bright lakes, but all the time she kept her eyes on the elf-woman. But *was* she an elf? Now that Kestrel saw her closer, there was something not quite elfin about her. It puzzled Kestrel. She had the slim build, graceful movements and pointed ears of an elf. Ears that were mostly hidden in her thick, long black hair that fell almost to her knees.

But then there was something else, Kestrel could not quite define it, that was not quite elven. What really startled Kestrel was the animal quality in her movements. The way she sat, the way she climbed over rocks and fallen tree trunks, was graceful, but not quite human, and not quite elven. Certainly the way she ate reminded Kestrel of some dainty, fastidious animal. She was startled to see that the elf-woman had long claws on her fingers, though not on her toes.

Kestrel approached cautiously, not wishing to startle the strange creature, but the green-skinned elf-woman noticed her. She rose in alarm, dropping the fruit, and gave a hiss, like a serpent's hiss. It was an alarming sound coming from such an elfin-looking creature.

"I don't wish to alarm you," Kestrel said gently, "but you are in danger here. This is the land of the dragon-folk."

The green elf held her arms out stiffly, as if they were wings. She shivered her arms and her whole body, and hissed again. Then she spoke. She used the common tongue in a slightly stilted way as if she were unaccustomed to using it frequently.

"What have you come for, evil one? I know you. You are one of the armoured ones. The death bringers. But you shall not harm me this time. Miscreant! Armoured fiend! *Avaunt* before I call my family!"

This was such a quaint way of speaking, that Kestrel found it difficult to restrain a smile, but she managed to remain quite solemn and simply said, "I only came to warn you. You and your family are in great danger here." For she thought that, perhaps, the green-skinned elf-woman's family had innocently taken shelter in one of the large caves, not dreaming that they were dragon caves.

The elf-woman did not seem alarmed by Kestrel's warning, but turned on Kestrel.

"The danger comes from such as you! We know your kind. The armoured ones, the death bringers, slaughtering and laying waste, plundering our treasure. Murderer! Drinker of innocent blood! Go or I shall bring the strength of all our peoples upon you!"

Kestrel was utterly bewildered by this speech. Whatever could the elf-woman mean by it? One thing was clear, however. She was suspicious and fearful of Kestrel, for some reason. So she spoke carefully and kindly.

"I mean you no harm. I must speak with you." Kestrel took a cautious step towards the elf-woman.

The elf-woman retreated at once.

"Oh, you're clever!" she said. "You would lure me within reach of your sword. But you are not clever enough to trick me!"

Then she cried in a strange tongue that Kestrel had never heard in her life,

"*Mama masqu'ata olerin vrazh laqu'en zildren*!"

These words were followed at once by the sound of rushing feet and the beating of wings, and an enormous green dragon appeared from one of the lakeside caves, followed by a slightly smaller, but still huge, red dragon and many young ones, ranging from half-grown to the tiniest, that tumbled out over their little feet.

From other caves came other dragon families, and yet more swooped down from the mountains, and emerged from the lakes.

Kestrel stood motionless, frozen with fear. "Shara Sorian protect me," she murmured.

The green elf ran to the first dragon and put her arms around its neck and the huge creature kissed her and folded its wings protectively around her.

"*Ourlen qui seldan rhoureveleg zhanbour*," said the elf. The green dragon raised her head and addressed Kestrel in the common tongue. She, too, spoke in the quaint, archaic way that the elf-woman did.

"Armoured murderer! What do you seek? What harm has my daughter done to you?"

Kestrel's composure was so shaken that she cried,

"This elf-maid is your daughter?"

"Do not call me elf," replied the elf-woman. "I am of the dragon people, despite my outward shape."

The other dragons murmured in assent and the red dragon took a step towards Kestrel, wings raised defensively. Kestrel spoke hastily,

"Forgive me. I am from the Temple of the Golden Unicorn. We have always been dragon friends. I would never, willingly, cause distress to the dragon people."

At this, a shining emerald green dragon of great beauty took charge of the situation. She had just arrived at the scene, and by her air of command, and the way the others stood back for her, it was clear that she was the clan matriarch. She was flanked by two enormous and ferocious-looking dragons.

The clan matriarch now spoke.

"I believe this is no armoured one, though she bears a sword. She speaks the truth. She has the look of a warrior priestess, and is, indeed, no enemy to our people. Those from the Temple of the Golden Unicorn mean us no harm."

Then she addressed Kestrel. "What do you seek here in the Guadja?"

Kestrel was about to explain how she had believed the green elf to be, inadvertently, trespassing, and had come to warn her. The elf-woman now stood with her arms round two of the young dragons, while their wings protected her.

And as Kestrel stood amongst the overpowering scent of the flowers, and the rush of waterfalls, and the drone of jewelled insects, she seemed to hear the voice of Morrigan, the Crone of the Moondark, chanting:

"You shall have as your companions,
The thief,
The dragon-maid."

For a moment, Kestrel turned her head. The voice was so clear, she half expected to see the old wise woman beside her, but, of course, there was no one there at all.

The dragon-maid, thought Kestrel. This is she if anyone is.

Aloud she said, "I believe that this maiden is the one I am seeking as a companion on my quest to Xegeron to destroy the evil sorceress, Zephrena."

The green elf drew herself up to her full height, which was not very tall, and replied with dignity, "Quests are for armoured ones. They are always on quests and they always end in the slaughter of our people. I have nothing to do with quests."

"Spoken as a true dragon, Grand-daughter," said the clan matriarch. "You are answered, Warrior Maid. And now, depart in peace."

The dragons turned and began to make their way towards their homes.

Kestrel was horrified. The wise woman had said that the dragon-maid would be one of her companions on the quest. Yet she was refusing to come.

And then, as clearly as if the old wise woman were beside her, Kestrel heard Morrigan's voice: "One thing more. The dragon-maid will not come willingly, but speak these words, and she will go with you..."

Kestrel drew out the scroll on which the Crone of the Moondark had written the words in the dragon tongue, and spoke them slowly.

"*Ourov...seleg nestia...vrag Neis-Durga Talahindra.*"

The effect of these words was amazing. The dragons turned as a single creature and retraced their steps, immediately.

The clan matriarch cried, rapidly and in tones of great concern, "*Qu'eren zele shourag estalion, koura pral dris vrag enzilbion Neis-Durga?*"

"I do not understand," said Kestrel." I do not speak the dragon tongue."

"But just now you spoke in our language," the matriarch replied, "and told us that Neis-Durga is in danger."

"Those words were taught to me by the Crone of the Moondark," Kestrel explained. "She said I must repeat them to you. Otherwise I am ignorant of your language."

"Neis-Durga is of our people. She is of the Talahindra clan, the Fire Dragons," said the matriarch. "But I do not understand how we did not know of her danger. For all dragons can call for help, whenever they need it, and wherever they are, and our people will hear it and respond. We have long sought Neis-Durga, and called to her. But when we heard nothing, and even Hochma Sofia, the Dragon of Wisdom, could find no trace of her, we mourned her as dead.

"She is not dead," said Kestrel, "But she is in great danger. Maybe Zephrena, the dark sorceress, has surrounded her tower with spells so strong that no cry for help can penetrate it."

"They must indeed be powerful," murmured the elf-maid's mother, "if not even Lady Hochma Sofia could tell where she was, for she knows all things."

"If Neis-Durga is in danger," said the clan matriarch, "every dragon of Zar-Yashtoreth will fly to her rescue."

For a moment Kestrel was tempted. With these beautiful creatures to help her, how swiftly Zephrena could be destroyed! Then she recalled that the wise woman had said only "the dragon-maid", not "the dragon people". There must be some reason for that. Besides, if Zephrena had surrounded the Dark Tower with spells to stifle Neis-Durga's cries for help, might she not also have surrounded it with magic to protect her from the dragon-folk?

"I thank you for your kind offer of help," she said, "but Shara Sorian has decreed that I can only take a few on this journey. If all your people come, the quest may be endangered. It must be this maid alone," and she indicated the green elf.

The elf-woman looked horrified and drew back against her mother, who put sheltering wings around her.

"You mean I would have to leave my people and go with you alone? This is a terrible thing you ask of me."

"Tanith-Medea is too young to leave us," put in the mother dragon.

At first Kestrel could not understand this, for Tanith-Medea, as the elf-woman seemed to be called, appeared as old as Kestrel herself. Then she recalled that a dragon was not considered adult until the age of 1,500 years. Tanith would, of course, by dragon count, be a mere child. Still the Crone of the Moondark had said that the dragon-maid would accompany Kestrel.

"Tanith-Medea is needed to set Neis-Durga free," said Kestrel, though she could not explain why she had said this. It almost seemed as if someone else had spoken the words for her.

There was a long pause. Tanith's father, as the red dragon appeared to be, closed in protectively, wings raised to shelter his daughter. And so did her two eldest siblings. Her mother enfolded her still closer beneath her wings and Tanith put an arm round her mother's neck. The clan matriarch drew closer to Tanith and all the dragons seemed to draw in towards Tanith in protection.

Then the clan matriarch spoke again. "We must speak together about this," she said, and, turning to the dragons she spoke in the dragon tongue.

"*L'askar'il meren drazh eglin.*"

"Wait here," she said to Kestrel. With that the dragons made their way through the sweetly scented, brightly coloured bushes and vanished from sight.

Kestrel stood, waiting patiently. She was startled to see Droco suddenly appear before her. Looking cautiously around, he spoke in a whisper, "Lady Kestrel, thank Zabris you're safe. You were gone so long, I thought the dragons had got you."

Kestrel was touched. "It was brave of you to come and seek me."

Droco shrugged. "Well, what's life if it hasn't a few risks and a bit of adventure? I was getting bored up there. Where's the green-skinned elf-woman?"

"Do not call her an elf, Droco," replied Kestrel. "She says she is of the dragon people."

"Poor creature," Droco sympathised. "Is she a little touched in the head?"

"I do not think so," said Kestrel. "It is very strange and I cannot understand it."

For a long time Kestrel and Droco sat and talked. Kestrel told him what has passed between her and the dragons, and why she was waiting. They admired the beautiful valley with its warmth and brilliance of colour, and the music of its sounds. An hour must have gone by. Then there were rustlings and movements in the bushes.

"The dragons are returning," Kestrel warned. "Perhaps you'd better leave now, Droco."

"Are you sure you'll be all right?" asked Droco, already retreating as he spoke.

"Quite sure, I thank you," Kestrel assured him. Droco had already vanished.

The dragons re-emerged. Tanith-Medea looked stricken, but resolute. She was no longer naked, but was dressed in a tunic of green dragon scales and hose of green. She wore shoes and gloves also of dragon scales, and her long claws protruded through the gloves.

Kestrel wondered from where these strange garments came. Perhaps magic had produced them.

"If I am needed to set Neis-Durga free, then I shall go with you." Tanith's voice was tearful and shaky but determined.

"I thank you," replied Kestrel, "with all my heart."

"I must first say farewell to my loved ones," said Tanith.

And then came the Great Leave Taking. One by one, each dragon embraced Tanith and she returned their embrace. They came from everywhere. Out of the forests and caves they came. Down from the mountains they flew. Up from the lakes and streams and rivers they rose.

The air was filled with dragon voices, all speaking in the dragon tongue. And though Kestrel did not speak their language, yet she understood what they were saying. Advice, admonitions, encouragement, reminding, warnings and well-wishing, and great love lay in those voices, as Tanith-Medea took leave of her family and loved ones. Finally she gave a last wave.

"I am ready," she said to Kestrel. Her voice was still shaky but Kestrel smiled encouragement and Tanith followed her out of the Valley of the Sun and Moon Lakes.

Still that was not the end. When they reached the foothills of the Nagli Mountains, the entire dragon population of the Valley of the Sun and Moon Lakes came swooping and swarming into the air. The little ones, who could not yet fly, riding upon the adults' backs.

Round and round they wheeled and dipped, calling their farewell messages and Tanith stood below, waving and throwing kisses to them and calling back in the dragon tongue.

It was a terrifying and a splendid sight. The air sang with loving voices and the beating of magnificent wings.

And then, quite suddenly, they circled, dipped and were gone. Kestrel and Tanith stood alone. Droco, deciding it was safe, crawled from his hiding place beneath a barrathorn hedge.

Tanith stopped, rigid and tense. Her heavy lidded eyes widened in terror.

"Who is this?" she asked Kestrel.

Droco replied with a flourish, "Droco the Sprig, at your service. And who, may I ask, are you?"

Tanith hesitated. Her eyes became full of suspicion. Kestrel reassured her,

"It is quite safe. Droco is our companion on the journey."

Tanith appeared to trust Kestrel, for she answered, "I am Tanith-Medea Shirakalinzarin, daughter of Morgana-Semiramis Shirakalinzarin and her consort Shirak-Shagreet Talahindra."

Droco looked startled. "Frazz me!" he muttered, but immediately recovered himself and said aloud, "Delighted to make your acquaintance."

"The first thing we must do," said Kestrel, "is to go to the nearest town and acquire provisions for our journey."

It was Tanith's turn to look startled.

"What are pro...pro...whatever you said?"

Droco turned his eyes heavenward. "Provisions," he explained patiently. "Food, water and packs to put them in." He could not hide his amusement at Tanith's ignorance, but she did not notice. She was too busy being surprised at what he said.

"But there is food in the forest and on the mountains. Food is all around us, and so is water, in the streams, rivers and lakes. And what is...packs?"

She spoke the last word hesitantly, as if it were quite foreign to her, which indeed it was.

Kestrel smiled, but she spoke gravely.

"There may be places where food and water are scarce. I shall explain as we go."

So with the thief and the dragon-maid, Kestrel set off for the nearest market town, which lay a long way off.

Chapter Ten

The Town of Uz

Uz was a small market town in Uhatt-an. It throbbed with activity. Ox carts lumbered past, their wheels rattling and grating on the cobbles. Dwarfs, elves, nereids, humans, trilki, goblins, gnomes, and minataurs thronged the place, buying and selling, haggling, arguing, standing and staring.

Tradesfolk shouted their wares. Children and hounds darted through the crowds, shouting and barking. Acrobats tumbled. A juggler was juggling with hoops of fire. At one end of the marketplace a company of strolling players was performing the comical tale of *Grinn, the Troll, and his Magical Fiddle* to a delighted audience. Musicians played. There were sideshows, contests of strength, contests of skill, contests of wisdom. A conjuror performed feats of magic. A healer demonstrated her powers. A dentist offered to pull teeth painlessly, for only five copper draskas. There were cobblers, and tinkers, and knife grinders, stilt walkers and wire walkers and snake charmers. There were silk merchants and jewel merchants and wine merchants. Whores and pickpockets plied their trades, despite the presence of the Watch. Beggars tried to coax coins from passers-by. Tipplers reeled unsteadily through the crowds and fortune-tellers told of the past and the future.

Tanith took one look at all this bustle and noise, and, with a screech of terror, fled back through the gates.

"Frazzing Kasperus!" cried Droco. "What's wrong with her?"

"She has never seen a town before. She has never even left the Valley of the Sun and Moon Lakes," Kestrel reminded him.

"She has never been away from her home?" Droco was incredulous and Kestrel began to explain.

"Do you know how old a dragon has to be before it is considered fully grown?"

"I've no idea," Droco replied. "Can't say I've had many dealings with dragons, my lady."

"One thousand and five hundred years," Kestrel continued.

Droco whistled. "Frazz me!" He saw the look on Kestrel's face. "I mean, my goodness!"

"So you see," Kestrel continued, "in Tanith's world she is still regarded as a child, to be petted and protected. I'm surprised she was permitted to come with us at all. I'm afraid she will find things very difficult."

"Don't worry, Lady Kestrel," said Droco, "I'll help you to look after her." A thought struck him. "In the dragon world, she'll never live long enough to grow up, will she?"

"She may do," replied Kestrel. "She is part elf, and they are a long-lived race. And she is partly something else, though I can't think what, but, possibly, she has the blood of another long-lived race in her veins. She may live to dragon adulthood, without even changing in appearance very much. But for now she is a child to her family, and thinks and acts as one."

They found Tanith. Wide-eyed and trembling, clinging to the gatepost of the town gates, while people squeezed past her, making some very uncomplimentary remarks. Tanith did not seem to hear. She was terrified.

"What is this dreadful place?" she whispered. "Have we reached the Abyss of Kasperus?"

"No, no, Tanith," said Kestrel, gently. "It's only a small market town. Come, don't be afraid."

Tanith remained frozen. She neither moved nor spoke. A shudder ran through her.

Droco patted her arm. "We won't let anything hurt you," he said.

Tanith never moved.

So they might have remained for ever, had not, at that moment, an elfin musician walked through the gates, playing the raiatan. Tanith stared, hypnotised by the haunting elvish music, and, drawn by it, crept, cautiously forward, following it.

At the gates, she paused, but the music still drew her on, and Kestrel and Droco encouraged her, until they all passed into the town.

The elfin musician had vanished into the crowd. Tanith, confronted with the noise and rush of the town, gave a cry of terror, and prepared to take flight again.

"Hey, it's all right." Droco told her gently. "It's only a town. Nothing to be afraid of."

Tanith, sensitive to his tone, grew a little calmer, though she still trembled.

"This is a terrible place," she murmured, "no wonder my people never come here."

Kestrel refrained from saying how fortunate this was. She imagined the chaos and terror that would ensue if a dragon came flying over this little town.

At that moment, the troupe of strolling players began their second performance of the tale of *Grinn, the Troll, and his Magical Fiddle*. They had set up their stage quite close to the town gates. Their music and bright colours attracted Tanith, and, of course no dragon can resist a good story. So Tanith forgot her fear and drew closer to the watching crowd and finally settled down and followed the tale, fascinated.

Kestrel and Droco sat beside her. Kestrel had not wanted this diversion, for she wished to continue their journey as soon as she had purchased the things they needed. She was constantly aware of the Sands of Doom running relentlessly. But she was relieved to find something that distracted Tanith enough to lessen her terror of the town. It was a lively and comical play, and the performers were skilled, so she began to be drawn into the tale as much as Tanith and Droco so that when the play ended, she felt the strange sensation of returning to reality from a world of fantasy. She rose to her feet and so did Tanith, whose eyes, too, held the bewilderment of one transported from one world to another.

Kestrel made ready to continue with the business in hand, namely buying equipment for the journey, when she became aware that Droco was no longer there. He had watched the play. She had seen him. Now he was gone. She scanned the crowd, but he was nowhere to be seen. Her heart sank in disappointment. She had not expected him to desert them like this.

Tanith had also noticed Droco's absence. "Where is Droco, Lady Kestrel?" she enquired.

Kestrel shook her head, "I do not know," she answered. "He seems to have vanished."

"Is he a magician?" asked Tanith.

Kestrel smiled, in spite of herself. "No, Tanith. I don't think so."

Well, if Droco had deceived them, so much the worse, thought Kestrel. The wise woman had said he would be her companion, but she had not said he would be there for the whole journey. Perhaps he was only supposed to go a little of the way with her. The quest would continue, nonetheless, but she missed his light-hearted company.

"Come, Tanith, follow me," she said, with determination, and she led Tanith towards the market stalls.

All at once, an ox-cart lumbered past, stirring up dust-whirls and scattering the crowd. Tanith stiffened with terror and shrank back, distressed. She flexed her claws and gave a menacing hiss. Startled, the oxen shied, lowing and huffing. Tanith nervously lashed out with her long claws, raking the flesh of one of them.

The huge animal bellowed and bolted, dragging with it its yoke companion, and the cart. The drover cursed and tried to hold back the great creatures, but to no avail. The oxen plunged into a fruit stall, upsetting the contents and sending them sliding and rolling over the ground.

"Hoy!" shouted the stallholder, a sturdy looking dwarf with a large black beard. "What are you playing at, you clumsy great cokskull?"

The drover was a large, leathery skinned man. "Who are you calling cokskull?" he roared. "I'll put my fist through your puny jawbone, dwarfling!"

"Oh, you will, will you?" mocked the dwarf. I'd like to see you try that caper, troll dung!"

So saying, the dwarf took a swing at the drover and the drover retaliated, while the onlookers cheered and jeered, took sides, and joined in. Before long a first-class fight was in full flood.

The oxen, disturbed by the noise, backed the cart into another stall, selling copper bowls. These came bumping and tumbling from their boards and rolled in the street, tripping several passers-by. The passers-by got up cursing and the trilki stallholder screamed abuse at dwarf, drover, oxen and cart, and hurled her wares at them all.

This was too much for Tanith. Never, in all her life, had she witnessed such noise and violence. With a blood-curdling screech of terror, she fled from the scene of confusion, with Kestrel in pursuit, vainly trying to calm her.

Madam Tabour, the fortune-teller, sat in her gold and scarlet booth, reading the palm of a bearded Islarian merchant. Her long, slender finger, with its violet-painted nail, traced the lines of his brown, well-manicured palm.

"Prepare for a great surprise," she told him. "It is coming very soon."

No sooner had she spoken these words, than Tanith appeared in her booth, seeking shelter in the nearest thing to a cave she could see. Her eyes were wild with terror. Her long black hair was bushed out to three times its normal size.

Madam Tabour sprang up with a shriek, which was echoed by the merchant, and then by Tanith herself. Tanith suddenly felt trapped in the small dark booth, where she had hoped to find peace and protection. Panicking, she could not find her way out and flung herself at the booth's woven walls, like a trapped bird. Kestrel followed her vainly trying to calm her, and at the same time apologising to Madam Tabour.

Tanith, finding no way out of the booth, grew desperate, and began to claw at one of the walls with her talons, ripping it to shreds. The wall collapsed, trapping Tanith beneath its folds. Tanith shrieked more than ever as she struggled to free herself, while Kestrel attempted to extricate her from the tangle.

Meanwhile, Madam Tabour, believing she had, inadvertently, conjured up some demon from the abyss, held her arms aloft, waved her hands, and chanted, "Sprit of the darkness, be gone! *Avaunt!*" while the merchant grew pale, and shrank into the furthest corner of what remained of the booth, where he stood, frozen with terror."

Tanith continued to tear at the booth, in her efforts to escape from this place of horror. She had ripped herself free of the tangle of material that had buried her, and now tried to carve a way out for herself with her claws. Her screeches grew more and more anguished, until the entire booth collapsed in tatters around them all, and Tanith, free at last, fled across the market square, scattering startled folk to left and right. Kestrel gave Madam Tabour a hurried apology, crossed her palm with a whole bag of silver, and set off after Tanith.

She found her at last, crouching in the ornamental fountain. She was using its curtain of water as protection and speaking softly in the dragon tongue. She was, in fact, invoking the aid of Mother Tiamat. A large and curious crowd was beginning to gather round the fountain, gazing at her in amazement.

Kestrel ignored the crowd. She sat on the rim of the fountain's basin.

"Come, Tanith. You can't stay there. I promise you'll be quite safe from now on."

"I want Mama!" said Tanith, wide-eyed with terror.

Kestrel began to worry in earnest about Tanith-Medea. Having her on this quest would be like having a young child with her. Tanith might be an adult in Kestrel's eyes, but to a dragon family she would be a mere child, and she was used to the loving protection of those around her. However, the Crone of the Moondark had said that the dragon-maid was to accompany her to Xegeron.

Kestrel sighed. Perhaps, like Droco, she was destined to be Kestrel's companion only for part of the way.

"I'll look after you," she told Tanith, and waded into the fountain's bright water.

The crowd shrugged and tapped their foreheads sympathetically.

Kestrel reached Tanith and sat down beside her in the water. She put her arm round her. "Come out now, Tanith-Medea. Just think how proud of you Mama, and all your family, will be when you return."

Then she dropped her voice, for Zephrena might have spies anywhere, "And you want to set Neis-Durga free, don't you?"

"Yes," agreed Tanith. "You are quite right, Lady Kestrel. I must have courage."

Then she spoke to the fountain, in the dragon tongue, clearly thanking the water for its protection and then she crawled cautiously out, and, clinging to Kestrel's arm for safety, went with her back into the marketplace.

As they approached Madam Tabour's wrecked booth, Kestrel noticed that the fortune-teller had gathered quite a crowd around her, and, with the merchant confirming her story, was regaling all and sundry with the tale of how she had, not long ago, been visited by a malignant green spirit, which had uttered fearful screams, and torn her booth to shreds, and how it had taken all her magical powers to banish it. For proof, she pointed at the shreds of her booth.

"I think we had better go the other way," Kestrel said, and turned to avoid the fortune-teller, and the crowd. And, as she turned, Droco was, magically, at her side once more.

For the first moment, Kestrel did not recognise him, and Tanith did not recognise him at all, so great was his transformation.

He had clearly visited the bath house and been bathed, shaved, perfumed and curled. His galley slave's rags were gone. His hair hung sleek and shiny. He was dressed in a wide-sleeved shirt of shimmering gold schai, tied with tasselled lacings, and he wore breeches of emerald sheen. Round his waist was a wide scarlet sash. His calf-high boots were of the softest grey bannin. He wore a gold ring in his left ear. His fingers were adorned with large rings of gold, silver and toquaq, and he had a gold chain round his neck.

He had acquired a pack, which looked suspiciously full. He grinned at Kestrel and Tanith, and winked.

"Sorry I left you. One or two little things I had to do. You didn't think I'd gone for good, did you?"

Kestrel was so relieved at his return, that she could not sound reproachful, even when she asked, "Where did you get all those things?"

"Oh, here and there," replied Droco, in a manner most suspiciously innocent. "You know how you pick things up in these market towns, my lady."

Kestrel knew, only too well, how Droco had probably picked things up and expected the town guard to descend upon them at any moment. She entreated Shara Sorian to deliver them from Uz as soon as possible. She could see the stall that sold items needed by pilgrims, and other travellers. There were packs and wineskins, flasks and horns, pouches and shoes and cloaks. There were charms for luck, and charms for protection, and charms for fair weather. There were also light weapons, such as bows and arrows, slings and catapults.

Tanith showed no interest in such drab and prosaic objects. Her heart was fired by the next stall. The jewel merchant's stall. The bright and glittering gems in their vibrancy and brilliance went straight to her heart. She drew close to them, transfigured with delight. As if in a trance, she took now this gem, and now that, into her hands, stroking and kissing them and crooning to them in the dragon tongue.

"Hoy! What are you up to?" growled the dwarf jewel merchant. "Are you buying, or what?"

Tanith, hastily, remembered her manners. For one of the first things a dragon learns is that a treasure hoard is sacred to the owner. She put down the huge diamond that she held and said, politely, "Forgive me. Your treasure is so beautiful, I forgot what I was doing."

She then added, with carefully learnt courtesy, "May the glory of your valour be renowned," as her mama had taught all her children to say to a dwarf, should they ever meet one.

"Humph!" snorted the dwarf, somewhat mollified, but keeping his eyes firmly fixed on Tanith.

"Come, Tanith," coaxed Kestrel, "we don't need jewels, but we *do* need packs and flasks."

She drew Tanith away to the neighbouring stall with the dull things that held no magic for her.

"It seems that I do not need to purchase a pack for you, Droco," said Kestrel. "You appear to have one, and, no doubt it is full."

"Pretty well, my lady," Droco agreed, cheerfully.

Kestrel sighed. Droco was incorrigible, but it was impossible to be angry with him. She returned to the business of equipping Tanith for the journey ahead. Suddenly Tanith gave a cry of joy and wonder and approached the travellers' stall, startling the little trilki stallholder nearly out of his wits.

"Look! Look!" she cried ecstatically. "Oh, see! How beautiful!" and she pointed to a pack from Ileskion, made in the vibrant and brilliant colours of the Ilesque fashion. "How brightly it shines! Like the eyes of Mother Tiamat's little ones at night!"

The pack was, indeed, lovely. It was bright gold, and had hundreds of tiny mirrors stitched into it with threads of vermilion, rose, emerald, turquoise, sapphire and purple. These miniature mirrors glittered in the reflected sunshine.

Tanith drew forwards towards this treasure. Her eyes clouded with an ecstasy of love. She trembled at the beauty of it, though this time, she remembered her etiquette, and refrained from touching the treasure.

"Would you like to have that pack, Tanith?" asked Kestrel, feeling that here was one way of keeping Tanith happy and distracting her from any fear or homesickness she might feel.

Tanith's dark, heavy lidded eyes grew wide and lustrous. "Oh yes, Lady Kestrel, but it is part of the little man's treasure. He won't part with it, I'm sure." Then a thought struck her. "Perhaps, if I told him a magic spell in return…"

"I think he'd prefer to have 12 copper draskas," Kestrel smiled, and handed him the coins.

"I could have got it for you for nothing," offered Droco.

Tanith was shocked. "Oh *no*, Droco. A gift demands a gift."

Droco turned his eyes heavenwards, in mock exasperation.

"I wish you'd remember that, Droco," Kestrel said. "A gift demands a gift."

She found a flask for Tanith made of amber, encased in scarlet quan and patterned with gold, emerald and blue. Tanith's eyes filled with tears at its beauty. She held out her hands to the flask as if to the warmth of a fire, and when Kestrel gave it to her, she put her trembling arms round Kestrel and kissed her lightly on the cheek. Utterly at peace, she settled down on the ground, cradling her treasures, brooding over their colours and brightness. Finally, Kestrel purchased a blanket of Vaschien design, with gold moons, suns and stars on an indigo background, and Tanith's happiness was complete.

"But I have nothing to give you in return," she cried suddenly in distress. Then, brightening, she cried, "I shall tell you a Magic Spell and a Prayer to Mother Tiamat for protection."

"Thank you, Tanith," said Kestrel, "that will be a beautiful gift."

Tanith drew Kestrel aside.

"Excuse me please, Droco," she said politely. "But this is Lady Kestrel's special gift and must be secret. I hope you don't mind"

"Not at all," replied Droco, strolling away nonchalantly. "I quite understand."

He watched Tanith solemnly imparting her gift to Kestrel, in silent amusement. To him, Tanith was as good as a permanent entertainment troupe. Though he felt a gentleness, a protectiveness towards her too. She seemed so innocent, so vulnerable and naïve.

Kestrel procured food and led the way to the pump, so they could fill their flasks. At first Tanith viewed the pump with some suspicion.

"Is it a trap?" she asked.

Droco laughed, and worked the pump, and Tanith was delighted when she saw the flow of water.

"It's a tiny waterfall!" she cried, and held out her hands to it. When Droco stopped pumping and the flow ceased, Tanith gave a gasp pf concern.

"It has died!" she cried in dismay.

Droco seemed to have grasped, with remarkable speed, the way Tanith's mind worked.

"No, no. It's only sleeping," he said. "I'll wake it up if you like."

Obligingly he pumped the handle, and the stream of water gushed over Tanith's hands.

"Oh, how *cold* it is!" Tanith cried, withdrawing her hands. "Oh look, the little waterfall sleeps again! Are you sick, my quodling?"

Droco pumped the water again, and Tanith watched, entranced.

"The waterfall will give you water to take with you on your journey," said Kestrel. "See, you must hold out your flask, like this."

Kestrel filled her flask and Droco followed. Finally, Tanith held her own flask under the water, exclaiming again at its coldness.

Kestrel was anxious to leave Uz now and to be off on the road to Xegeron.

"The waterfall is tired now and wants to sleep, once more," she told Tanith. "Come, let us leave it."

Tanith nodded. "I thank you for your water," she said solemnly, "and I wish you golden dreams." She blew the pump a kiss and followed Kestrel.

"Frazzing Kasperus!" murmured Droco, once more turning his eyes heavenwards. He relieved a passing merchant of his purse and followed Kestrel and Tanith out of Uz.

Chapter Eleven

Father Zakarius

Zackery Tzen was the middle child of three. His father. Septimus, was a shepherd, who guarded Lord Mirmin's flocks in the land of Talen-Zhin. He was a mild and gentle man. His wife, Leonora, was a laughing, jolly woman, to whom everything was a joke.

Their eldest daughter, Zaria, was a scholar, a philosopher. Their youngest son, Sharan, was a tailor, who worked in the town, with his mother's brother, Federin.

Zackery, on the other hand, was like his father. He was gentle and dreamy and a born shepherd. But he shared his sister's love of books.

From the age of seven, he had gone with his father into the mountains, guarding the sheep. At first Septimus worried when he saw his son deep in a book, and, apparently not watching the animals. But the boy seemed to possess a sixth sense for when a sheep or lamb was in danger and needed his help.

Then one day, disaster struck. Lord Mirmin's favourite ewe, Flossilda, went missing. Septimus and Zackery searched and called, but there was no sign of her. Septimus was distraught. He had never lost a sheep in all his years as a shepherd.

"T'will be the end of us!" he moaned. "Lord Mirmin will dismiss me, or even have me thrown into his dungeons. What will become of us?"

"Don't fret," Leonora tried to calm him, "Flossilda'll turn up. Even if not, you've never lost a sheep yet. Lord Mirmin will forgive you."

"Never!" cried Septimus. "She's his most precious ewe. It's the end of us all."

Zackery put his hand on his father's shoulder.

"Don't cry, Father, I'll find Flossilda."

He was amazed to hear these words issue from is lips, for had he not searched with his father in vain? And were not the Talen-Zhin mountains vast and cavernous? Yet deep within him he knew he could find the missing sheep.

That night Zackery sat in his room and prayed to the Cloud Father for help. Long he sat in meditation. Then he rose, opened the door quietly, lit his lantern and slipped out of the house.

All was dark and quiet. His parents had long since gone to bed. Without a moment's hesitation, Zackery took his way over the mountains. It was as though someone were leading him by the hand, and he knew just where to go. Over rocks and boulders he scrambled, until he reached a cave, and there, bleating piteously, was Flossilda.

She followed Zackery home, and again, he knew the way, as if someone were leading him. Once home, he called his parents joyfully.

"I've found Flossilda. She's here with me!"

Such joy! Such celebration! Such horror and concern when Zackery told his parents how he had wandered the strange and perilous paths, with only the light of his lantern to guide him.

"You could have been killed," his mother cried, clasping him to her.

"You should not have risked all this for me, my dearest son." Septimus said, his tears falling, as he, too, clasped his son to him.

But Zackery only laughed. "I was in no danger, for the Cloud Father led me by the hand and lit my way, and showed me where Flossilda had strayed. I had a greater light than that of my lantern, for the Cloud Father made it as light as day for me."

His parents stared at him in awe. They told the priest the strange story.

"The boy has the gift," said the priest. "You should take him to the temple."

So the child was taken to the Temple of the Crystal Brotherhood, and the chief priest gazed at him in wonder.

"This child has an aura of pure light," murmured the grand wizard. "He should be trained in the arts of high magic."

So little Zackery came to the Crystal Temple and learnt the high arts. Now, an old man, Father Zakarius was a high wizard. His memory was no longer what it had been, but he was still a force to be reckoned with and a magician of great power.

On a bright day in spring, in the beautiful Temple of the Wizards of High Magic and Followers of Light, Aeurian, the grand wizard called a meeting of all the high wizards.

"My brothers in Light, I have been consulting the Cloud Father on how to defeat the evil that is creeping over Zar-Yashtoreth and darkening its peace and beauty. And, in His goodness, the Cloud Father has advised me. He says that one of our number must travel to the Temple of the Sacred Cats of Kushli and seek the guidance of its high priestess, Lady Vashti-Bastet."

A murmur of agreement arose amongst the grey robed wizards.

"I have meditated long and prayed long to find which one of you should make this journey, or whether I myself should go. In my meditation, the Cloud Father has spoken to me, telling me that one of you already has the marks of wandering upon the soles of his sandals, namely, a small reian leaf. If you will kindly look and let me see the soles of your shoes, we will know who that is. Firstly, my own."

He removed his sandals and held them aloft, but they bore no leaves.

Then one by one, the wizards showed their sandals, but none bore a reian leaf, and each was disappointed, for all wished to be the one to go to Kushli.

At last Zakarius stepped forward, and, on his left sandal, was a small reian leaf. He smiled gently. The grand wizard clasped his hand in congratulation.

"Father Zakarius, my heart rejoices for you," he said. The other wizards also congratulated him, for each knew that he was, indeed, the right one for such a journey.

"I am unworthy to be so honoured," Father Zakarius replied, "but my heart rejoices to be chosen for such a noble task."

He turned to the others and raised his hands aloft.

"Remember me in your prayers and in your meditations. Keep me ever in your thoughts. If you do so, no danger can harm me, and I cannot fail to return from Kushli with the knowledge we need"

***

Zephrena sat in the scrying chamber of the Dark Tower. With narrowed eyes she watched Kestrel, Droco and Tanith enter the Forest of Svorg-Skenda and settle down for the night. Her scrying glass brought them before her eyes as clearly as if she were in the forest herself.

Beside her stood the captain of her krauls, Bragazh Gourbag, his face contorted in a sneer as Zephrena told him what she saw, for he had no powers of scrying himself.

"Not much to fear then from Kestrel Moonblade, Oh Great One," he said, complacently. "If she has no help, save a thief from the gutters of Kironin and a petted dragon brat, as yet unskilled in magic."

"Do not underestimate our enemies," Zephrena snapped. "The dragon brat has imbibed dragon wisdom from her birth and though she has, as yet, little magical skill, what magic she knows can be deadly. As for the thief, he is a *master* thief. No uncharmed lock can hold him. And Kestrel Moonblade herself is a high priestess with great skill in magic and with weapons. However, as you say, they are no danger to me yet. I must be vigilant, but they are not worth squandering my powers on. Not yet."

Once more Zephrena gazed into the black-framed mirror. This time she saw a tall grey building made of polished stone, set high in the mountains.

Its roof reared into delicate stone pinnacles, thin and fragile as needles. Zephrena knew the place to be the Temple of the Crystal

Brotherhood, Wizards of High Magic and Followers of the Paths of Light. Her lips curled in revulsion.

She watched Aeurian come forward and address the grey clad brethren. Watched Father Zakarius produce the reian leaf. Watched him pack his few belongings and say farewell to the grand wizard and to his Brothers in Light, and set off from the temple, trudging down the mountain path. She laughed a laugh of chilling evil.

"Foolish, doddering old man," she murmured. "Now you have stepped outside your sanctuary, I'll take your memory. You will have no idea where you are going. You'll never reach the Temple at Kushli."

But Father Zakarius went serenely on his way, completely unaware that he had forgotten his destination.

***

In the Forest of Svorg-Skenda, Kestrel, Tanith and Droco rested. Kestrel made up a fire and now they were sitting beside its golden warmth. Around them the shadows lengthened, deep and indigo. Tanith began to feel desperately unhappy. At this time, in the Guadja, they would be snuggling together in their cave. Here she felt alone and vulnerable. The trees around them, ancient and gnarled, linked their branches in a twisted dance. Tanith spoke a little of the tree language, but just now she felt like speaking to no one.

She thought of her brothers and sisters, snuggled for the night, under Mama's and Papa's great protective wings, and a terrible homesickness assailed her. She felt tears make their way up from deep inside her. But before the tears could fall, there was a rustling in the bushes and a twig snapped. Cries and flutters of night birds came from the bushes and then the skittering of some startled animal. Kestrel drew her sword. Tanith's body tensed all over and she gave a snake-like hiss, while Droco retreated up the nearest tree, catapult at the ready.

An elderly wizard emerged from the bushes. His long, grey, dishevelled hair was tinged with green, a sign of his age, but his beard and whiskers, by contrast, were startlingly white and very curly.

He wore a grey robe over a long white robe and a battered hat of gold and scarlet. In one hand he carried a long staff and in the other, a pack made from an ancient blanket, rolled round and tied with thick black cord. On his feet was a pair of very old, battered sandals.

He sounded somewhat vague and bewildered and yet possessed an air of wisdom. He had the most benevolent face any of the three travellers had ever seen. Instinctively they all relaxed their vigilance for all felt there was not a trelin of evil or malice in the old man.

He came forward, quite unaware of the three travellers, searching his pockets and pouches as he came and murmuring vaguely to himself,

"Now where can it be? I'm sure I had it with me just now."

He began looking in his pack. Then spilt the entire meagre contents on the ground, searched through them and then put them back in the pack. They appeared to be an assortment of dried herbs, tied in bundles, and candles and old parchments.

"Bless my beard and whiskers!" he murmured. "It's vanished without trace!"

A terrible suspicion arose in Kestrel's mind,

"Droco..." she began.

Droco's eyes were wide with amused innocence.

"My lady! I've never set eyes on him till this moment!"

But he looked with interest at the old man's many pouches and pockets.

Immediately Kestrel was overcome with remorse. "Shara Sorian forgive me. That is quite true. My apologies, Droco." For, of course, Droco had not been out of her sight since they had entered the Forest of Svorg-Skenda. Not even he could have taken anything from the old man.

Kestrel was afraid she had offended Droco, but he appeared to find her suspicions extremely funny. So she forgot her embarrassment and walked towards the old man.

"What are you searching for, Father?" she asked gently.

The old man started. "Bless me! Where did you spring from?"

Kestrel smiled, reassuringly. "Perhaps we can help you, Father. What are you looking for?"

The old man removed his hat and scratched his head meditatively. "Ah, yes," he murmured. "I was looking for something. Blessed if I can remember what it was."

"We've got a right crabbick here!" Droco said softly to Tanith, "The old grizer is a complete fool."

Tanith shook her head and replied solemnly, "No, he has magic about him. I can sense it."

Then, turning to the old man, she asked, "Are you a wizard, ancient wise one?"

"Why, yes," replied the old man, gently. "That is what I am!"

Suddenly a flash of light seemed to spurt from his fingers, startling them all – most of all the wizard himself.

"Good gracious! How did that happen?" he cried. He tried to do it again, but without success.

"Oh well. Never mind," he sighed, and sat down on the moss-covered trunk of a fallen tree.

"I seem to be a bit lost," he continued. "I was on my way to...to... Bless me if I haven't forgotten where I was going. Now that's awkward, isn't it! How will I get there if I can't remember what my destination is?"

He was interrupted by an agonised squeal from Droco, who had dropped to his knees and was nursing his injured hand.

"By Zabris!" complained Droco "What do you keep in your pockets, baby dragons?

Tanith looked concerned. Baby dragons needed to be with their mamas, to be loved, cosseted cared for and protected. Not put into pockets and accompanying wizards on long journeys far from their homes. She tried to peer into the wizard's pockets to see if any little dragon needed her help, but there seemed to be nothing there. The old man's next words to Droco reassured her.

"Ah!" he cried. "You seem to have found my fire spell. Thank you. How clever of you. I've been searching for that for days."

Kestrel smiled, realising that Droco's accident had been the result of his trying to pick the wizard's pocket. He might be the best thief in Zar-Yashtoreth, but he was not proof against magic.

"That'll teach you to keep your fingers off other people's things," she told him, laughing.

"You might have a little sympathy, my lady," Droco protested. "I'm in agony."

The wizard appeared quite unaware of Droco's intentions.

"I can soon put that right," he said, cheerfully. "Give me your hand. It's the least I can do after you've so kindly found my fire spell. One good turn deserves another. Now let me see..."

He made a pass in the air with his hand and intoned solemnly the words, "*Azag nin memzet, Bournag zol shadrik*!"

Droco let out a cry of terror as his fingers stiffened like icicles.

"My fingers, they're frazzing frozen! For the love of Zabris. These are the tools of my profession, you know!"

He held out his hands. The wizard was all concern.

"So sorry. Wrong spell," he said meekly. "Silly of me. Let me try again."

And raising one hand, he cried, "*Aboura, salina voorzh, zan ha-potra*!"

Droco uttered a scream of anguish. His fingers had turned to stone.

Tanith, who had been watching all this with awe, now spoke.

"I know a spell like that," she remarked with great interest."

"I'm delighted to hear it!" replied Droco dryly, and, turning to the wizard, he added, "I believe you're doing this on purpose."

The old wizard's face was anxious and gentle, but a twinkle in his eyes suggested that there might be some truth in Droco's words. He shook his head.

"Oh dear, oh dear," he sighed. "If only I could remember the correct words. If only I weren't such a complete fool."

He emphasised the last two words very slightly, and looked straight at Droco as he said them.

"All right," Droco conceded, "I must admit, you're no fool, and I'm sorry about you're fire spell, but I should think you've had you're revenge several times over."

The wizard's lips twitched slightly. Then he said "Wait...I have it!"

"Are you sure?" Droco asked "My fingers won't drop off, will they? Or turn into a griffon's claw? Frazzing Kasperus, I was better off in the galleys. There I only had to worry about starvation, thirst and the lash."

The wizard smiled benignly. "Have no fear, my son. I remember the words of the spell."

He closed his eyes and chanted, *"Zhan-ai lar torquil. Zhan-ai praz gh'ayl."*

Tentatively, Droco looked at his hand. It had returned to normal. Relieved, he wriggled his fingers and then clenched and flexed them once or twice.

"Have your fingers healed?" asked the wizard.

"Yes," replied Droco, "Thanks, old man."

"That is good," the wizard said gently. "But take care how you handle spells in future, should you – er, find any more."

Truly, thought Kestrel, this old man is no fool, but has great wisdom, for all his bumbling manner.

And once again, the words of Morrigan, the Crone of the Moondark, came to her, as clearly as if the old wise woman were before her at that moment. That strange singing chant from the silent Forest of Sourak.

"You shall have as your companions
The thief
The dragon-maid
The wise fool."

The wise fool, of course, thought Kestrel. It is exactly as the wise woman told me.

Aloud she said to the old man, "Father, we are travellers on our way to Xegeron, to destroy the power pf Zephrena, the soul stealer. I have need of your help. Will you go with us?"

"I would gladly accompany you," the wizard replied, "but I have to go to...to...now where was it I was going?" Zephrena's spell took hold of his mind. "Blessed if I can remember. Well, I dare say it wasn't important, and, anyway, if I can't remember, then I can't go there. So I may as well go with you to…where was it?"

Kestrel suppressed a smile, and said, patiently, "To Xegeron."

"Ah yes, to Xegeron," the old wizard nodded as if to make it quite clear in his own mind. "To Xegeron."

"Let me introduce you to our band of travellers," said Kestrel. "I am Kestrel Moonblade, warrior priestess of the Temple of the Golden Unicorn." She indicated Droco. "This finder-of-spells is Droco the Sprig, and this is Tanith-Medea, whose clan name I cannot even begin to pronounce…"

"Shirakalinzarin," put in Tanith, obligingly.

"Daughter of the dragons of the Sun and Moon Lakes." Kestrel concluded.

"Delighted to make your acquaintance," said the wizard. "I am Father Zakarius of the Crystal Brotherhood."

"We welcome you," said Kestrel.

The sun had now sunk below the hills and it was growing darker by the minute.

"I think we should sleep now, for we have far to travel, suggested Kestrel. "I will take the first watch. Father Zakarius, will you take the second. Droco, the third and Tanith, the last.

"What is watch?" asked Tanith, who seemed to be growing more and more uneasy and restless as the darkness increased.

Kestrel explained that someone always had to keep guard at night in case of danger. She drew her time glass from her pack and showed Tanith how the sand ran through, and how to watch two glasses by the light of the watch lantern and the fire.

Tanith was fascinated by the sands running through the glass. She turned it this way and that, and, for a while, appeared to forget her uneasiness.

All was peaceful beneath the moon. Kestrel began her devotions to Shara Sorian. Tanith whispered a prayer to Mother Tiamat to keep her safe, and to take care of her beloved family at home. Zakarius murmured his prayers to the Cloud Father, while Droco uttered a swift word of thanks to Zabris for his deliverance from the galleys and for success in the marketplace.

Then Kestrel took her blanket from her pack and spread it on the ground ready for sleep when her watch ended. Zakarius unrolled his old and worn blanket that also formed his pack, wrapped himself up like a huge cocoon and fell asleep at once.

Droco climbed into the broad, flat branches of a cimiba tree, flung his blanket over himself and was soon fast asleep too.

Tanith had watched the others take their blankets from their packs, and now attempted to do the same. Unaccustomed to such things, she struggled to pull it from her pack. Her long claws became entangled in the blanket. She hissed in annoyance. Kestrel came to her rescue.

"Let me do that for you," she offered, and spread the blanket on the ground. Tanith thanked her politely, then combed her hair half-heartedly with her claws, and fidgeted with the blanket. She looked utterly forlorn.

"Do you miss your home, Tanith?" Kestrel asked.

"Yes, Lady Kestrel," replied Tanith. Tears hung in her voice. "It feels so strange to be here, away from my people."

"I'll sing you to sleep," said Kestrel. She smoothed the blanket and Tanith curled up in it. Then Kestrel covered her up and spread the lowest branches of the cimiba tree over her. Tanith lay with her arms embracing her pack, her whole body tense and trembling a little. Kestrel stroked her long thick hair, and began to sing softly. It was the song that Lara Meadowsweet, Mistress of the Girl Novices had sung to Kestrel and the other novices, long ago, when Kestrel was a small girl and had just entered the temple, and when they had felt the pangs of homesickness.

"Shara Sorian brings the sun
Shara Sorian brings the silver moon,
Through the night, she sheds her light
And she will bring the daylight soon.
Shara Sorian is the glorious sun,
Shara Sorian is the glorious moon,
Through the night she guards our dreams
And she will bring the daylight soon."

Tanith listened to the sweet voice, relaxed a little, wondered who Shara Sorian was and fell into an uneasy sleep.

Kestrel sat by the fire, concerned. Would they have to take care of Tanith like this all the time?

Chapter Twelve

Night in the Forest

It was Droco's watch and he was not finding it easy. He had been woken from the most delightful dream by Father Zakarius, and was, even now, only half awake.

What the frazz was there to watch for here? He thought. It was as peaceful as a nest of shurries. He looked at Kestrel, lying gracefully under the blanket, one hand resting on the hilt of her sword. Her arm across her staff, in readiness, even in sleep.

Then he watched the old wizard, Zakarius, whose long beard moved gently with his measured breathing. And then he was startled by the most pitiful, desolate sobbing he had ever heard. By the light of the watch lantern he saw the slight form of Tanith curled against a tree, tears running down her face.

Droco was amazed. What in Zar-Yashtoreth could have caused her such distress? Immediately he was filled with compassion for the strange, green-skinned elfin dragon-maid. She seemed so lost, so defenceless away from her home. He remembered what Kestrel had told him about dragons not being mature until they are 1,500 years old, and that Tanith was like a child away from home for the first time. Of course she'd be feeling homesick and missing her family.

He knew, vaguely, how she must be feeling. The first night in the galleys had been the worst and he'd nursemaided his old benchmate through nights when he'd been despondent.

"What's wrong?" he asked gently, squatting down beside her. "Are you homesick?"

Tanith tried to explain how she was feeling, but could not, at first, put it into words. When the dragon-folk slept, the little ones nestled close under the sheltering wings of their parents. These people slept far from each other. It was this void round Tanith that was so terrible to her. It was cold, too, compared with the tropical warmth of her home. Tanith had tried to pull her blanket round her, but she had found it an insurmountable obstacle. It twisted like a live thing, and tangled and caught on her claws. In the end, she had crumpled it up with her pack, and slept with her arms round the jumbled heap, using it as a pillow.

She had tried to press her body against a tree, but that was no substitute for her mother's reassuring body.

Horrid sounds came from the trees and bushes. At home, the sounds were gentle and friendly. The contented cluckings of zhieka, the liquid croonings of Ilhira birds, or the "pik-pik" of a wakeful mur-mur, and the kritch-kratches chirping. Here the sounds were hostile and frightening, The fear of the unknown.

All this Tanith wanted to tell Droco, but her words spilt over into tears. "I want to go home!" was all she could say.

Droco was sympathetic. "Hey! It's not as bad as that. You'll go home soon."

Tanith regarded him, half trusting, half suspicious. He was kind, but he was not of her people. She wanted dragon company.

She shivered in the night air that seemed, to her, so cold.

"Here," said Droco, gently, "let me spread your blanket for you."

Instinctively, Tanith laid her hand on the crumpled blanket.

"It's all right," said Droco, keeping his eyes warily on the long claws. "I'm only going to straighten it for you, so you can wrap it round yourself for warmth.

Tanith surveyed him, suspiciously. He was a thief, and thieves stole treasure. But something told her that his heart was good. He would not steal from her. She withdrew her hand, cautiously. Equally cautiously, Droco spread the blanket.

Tanith shivered again. "Why don't you come closer to the fire?" Droco offered. He moved the blanket nearer to the flames.

Tanith drew closer to the warmth. Now, however, there were no trees to nestle against. Tanith began to whimper piteously, like a terrified animal.

Droco couldn't bear to hear that desolate sound. It tore pity from his heart. He stretched out his hand and gently stroked Tanith's long thick black hair.

"It's all right," he said, soothingly. "It'll be all right."

At last Tanith tried to explain to him about the great void, the dark emptiness that was so troubling.

"At home we sleep entwined," she told him, shakily. "The night is warm and alive with friendly sounds. Here it is cold, and cruel, and we are each alone."

"No we're not," Droco reassured her. "We're all together."

Tanith shivered. Tears streaked her face. Droco wiped the tears with her hair and wrapped the blanket round her.

"Try to sleep, Tanith, or you'll be too tired for your watch."

Suddenly something occurred to Tanith. She examined her long thick black hair, ran her hands over it, and then said, "Please, who will smooth my hair for me?"

She spoke with complete innocence and simplicity, inefficiently trying to comb her hair with her claws.

"Don't you know how to comb your hair, little Tanith?" he asked kindly.

"Yes," Tanith replied, "but my sisters always do it for me."

The tears came again. She did not know how to explain the wonderful ritual of combing her hair each evening. She would lean against her elder sister. Hecate Magreet and her twin sister, Lilith Medusa, and they would gently rake their claws through Tanith's thick mane of black hair, never pulling it, gently scratching her scalp and teasing out tangles, while Tanith's dark, heavy lidded eyes closed with pleasure. The happiness of the evening, surrounded by her family, with one or two of the little ones in her lap and in her arms, while the jewelled mur-mur birds darted overhead, uttering their warbling notes, and the shushi birds waded past on their four stilt-like legs, and the kritch-kratches chirped in the reeds. The peace, the security. Tanith felt very far from all this and she wept unrestrainedly.

"I'll comb your hair for you," Droco offered. Tanith grew a little less tearful.

"Thank you, Droco, but you have no claws."

It so happened that amongst his other purloined purchases, Droco had a jewelled comb. Now he drew it from his pack.

"I have a false claw," he said.

Tanith's tear-stained face grew transfigured, as she looked at the treasure.

"Oh, how bright!" she cried. "How beautiful." She put out a long-clawed finger and stroked the comb reverently. Then she leaned against Droco as if he had been one of her own family and let him comb her hair. Once, the comb's teeth caught on a tangle and Tanith whimpered.

"Sorry," said Droco. "I'll be very careful," and he solicitously teased out all the tangles until Tanith's thick hair hung like a sheet of black silk.

Tanith's tense little body relaxed at last. "Thank you, Droco," she murmured, but suddenly she became aware once more that she was with strangers and she began to cry again.

Droco put his arm round her."Don't take on so," he said. "You'll go home soon. Just think how proud of you your family'll be when you tell them your adventures."

Unknowingly, Droco had said the best thing he could have said, for storytelling was one of the chief delights of the dragon people. The idea of sitting, safely returned, amongst her family and friends, recounting her adventures, made her brighten up a little. She dried her eyes and then looked up to the sky, seeking courage from Mother Tiamat. And it was then that she saw how far away the Great Mother seemed. She was puzzled. At home Mother Tiamat's silver eye looked so close you thought you could touch Her. She would ask Droco about it. He was wise and knew things. And as naturally as she would have asked her elder sister, Hecate Magreet, she turned to Droco and enquired, "Why is Mother Tiamat so far away?"

Droco looked startled. What on Zar-Yashtoreth was she talking about?

"Ah," he replied, noncommittally, "there you have me."

"At home," Tanith continued, as if he had not spoken, "she is so close, you feel you could touch her, especially at night, when she opens her silver eye, and all her little ones come out to play. She is a little further away by day, when she opens her golden eye and brings the light, and her little ones go to sleep, but she is still closer than she is in this strange land."

Then Droco knew of what she spoke, and, at once, his quick mind thought of a reply.

"I reckon she's climbed a little further up the sky, so that she can watch over you here, and still see your family at home."

Tanith brightened. "Of course! How wise you are."

Droco shrugged, "I try my best," he said.

Tanith relaxed a bit, but Droco could see she was still restless. To take her mind off her homesickness, he said, "Tell me about your family. If you talk about them, they'll seem close to you."

So Tanith told him about her elder sister, Hecate Magreet, so gentle and kind and loving, like a second mama to them all. About her twin sister, Lilith Medusa, so full of fun and joy, who would be pining for her now at home. About her younger brothers Caramoon Liskander and Thespis Hyperion, and her little sister Circe Delilah, who were little imps of mischief and had the spirit of Lord Krilgos Telmar, the trickster in them, but were all so lovable. Of her quiet timid younger brother, Merlin Melchior, whose chief delight was reading great tomes of dragon lore, and creating beautiful images. Of her tiny adopted brother, Mordecai Kaladrian, the only survivor of the horrific massacre on the Isle of Iliac. Of her newly hatched baby sister, Accacia Laburnum.

She told him of her wise, beloved loving mama, Morgana-Semiramis and her sweet, brave adoring papa, Shirak-Shagreet Talahindra. Of her gracious grandmama, Lady Tiamat Anahita and her wise grandfather, Lord Tanin Cyprianus, and her cousin Fleurdelis Mandragora. Tanith would have continued with a list of her other cousins, her uncles and aunts, had not sleep, at last, overtaken her, and she lay, curled up in a ball, her slight green form nestled against Droco and her head in his lap.

Gently, Droco put out his hand and stroked her hair. Then he shook his head, resignedly.

"No one said anything about playing frazzing nursemaid to a dragon child," he said, softly, to the silver eye of Mother Tiamat.

Tanith slept peacefully at last. The hourglass turned twice, but Droco hadn't the heart to waken her, so he continued to keep watch in her place.

Chapter Thirteen

Lindor Estoriel

Lindor Estoriel, the elfin-maid of Tilioth, was born in that fairest of all fair cities of the elven lands. Her father, Selandar, was a minstrel, who wandered from place to place, singing and playing the qu'enga, and charming all who heard him. Her mother, Lyria, was a dancer and those who saw her called her "the winged foot". Lindor inherited both her father's and her mother's talents. Her voice was sweet and she plucked the qu'enga's strings with silken fingers. She could dance with butterfly feet too, and while yet she was only small, would trip lightly over the grass, singing and playing.

She was the youngest of four children, Serinda, her sister was the eldest. Then came her twin brothers, Persis and Philemon. The family travelled throughout the elven kingdom, and even beyond it. Every village, town, hamlet and city welcomed them. They played in marketplaces and great halls. They had even played at the Royal Palace before the King and Queen, of which they were vastly proud.

Serinda danced and played the qu'enga and sang. Persis and Philemon sang and tumbled and danced and played the reed pipes, but Lindor could play, sing, dance and extemporise with the greatest skill, by the time she was ten years of age.

It was a merry life, travelling Zar-Yashtoreth. Never staying long in one place, but always returning to beautiful Tilioth after several years. There was always a welcome for the family of minstrels, who brought such light and gaiety into everyone's lives.

But what Lindor loved best in her life, was the storytelling. Every night, no matter where they were, under the stars if it was warm, in a barn if it was not, Selandar laid aside his qu'enga and told them all stories. He must surely have been the greatest teller of tales on Zar-Yashtoreth.

He told them stories of heroism and adventure. Stories of far-off times. Stories of love and romance. Stories that made them all laugh and stories that wrung tears from their eyes and hearts. Stories of daring escapes and stories of thrilling rescues.

Many of these tales involved Selandar himself. In some, he outwitted trolls, monsters and giants. In some, kings and queens had honoured him. No one really believed these tales to be true, but everyone pretended to. And however many times they were told, they were always enthralling.

Lindor listened to these tales with all her being. She loved the descriptions of glaciers and volcanoes, of mountains so tall that only kwarks could inhabit them. Of deep caverns with stalagmites and stalactites. Of pink and gold sunsets. She vowed in her heart that, as soon as she was old enough, she would see these wonders for herself. For, though she knew that many of her father's adventures had grown in the telling, she felt sure that his descriptions of the faraway places of Zar-Yashtoreth were true indeed, and she burned with wanderlust when heard them. Travelling to strange towns and villages, even to strange countries outside the elven lands, was well enough, but Lindor longed for those great rivers and vast caves and huge mountains.

Meanwhile the slender, golden elf-maiden travelled with her family. Persis and Philemon married twin sisters, who added to the troupe.

Then came the darkening of Tilioth as Zephrena's evil began to cast its foul mantle. It grew slowly at first, setting elf against elf, causing greed, cruelty, violence and dishonesty. The elven race, once so noble, good and true, began to grow corrupt and dissolute. The joy and light, that pervaded the elven lands, faded. Elves no longer recognised their obligations to one another, or to elven society. Indeed, they no longer recognised that their society even existed. So selfishness and cynicism set in, and, as this grew, their love of beauty diminished. Elves no longer loved the music and song of minstrels, and the things in which they had once delighted were heard less and less in those once-beauteous lands.

Selandar and his family struggled to make a living. There were still some elves that loved and followed the old ways, though they were few and far between. It grew harder to survive.

At last Lindor decided that this was the time to leave the troupe and set out on her own.

"I shall be one less to provide for," she said, "and I have always longed to travel to far-off lands. I shall go and make my own way, and return when times are better. But I will always hold you in my heart, my dear ones."

The others were horrified and begged her to stay, but her father understood her longing for travel and adventure.

"One cannot clip the wings of a bird," he said. "A bird must be free to fly, or she cannot sing. So go, my daughter, and our blessings go with you. Spread song and laughter and joy throughout Zar-Yashtoreth. Never has she been more in need of them. I shall miss you, my daughter."

All the family understood the wisdom of these words. They kissed and said their tearful farewells. At last, Lindor took up her qu'enga, smiled bravely and set out on her journey.

***

The day dawned warm and cloudless in the Forest of Svorg-Skenda. Kestrel awoke to find Zakarius toasting mushrooms by the fire. Droco, tired by his double watch, had fallen asleep the moment the old wizard had risen for the day. Tanith was awake and bathing cautiously in a stream, which seemed to her cold and hostile compared with the steaming waters of her home. When she was cleansed, she greeted Mother Tiamat, thanking Her for her safety through the night and invoking blessings on Droco, who had been her protector and a true dragon friend.

Kestrel began her own devotions to Shara Sorian. When these were over, and Droco had still not woken, she approached him, concerned that, perhaps, he was sick.

Droco opened his eyes, stretched and yawned, "Frazzing Kasperus, is it morning already?"

"Did your watch tire you?" asked Kestrel, anxiously.

"Not my watch alone. I took Tanith's as well," Droco replied. "She was homesick and worn out with crying. I didn't like to wake her."

Tanith overheard this. "You took my watch for me? Thank you, Droco. That was kind. Then I will take yours tonight."

"There's no need," said Droco, lightly, "I was happy to do it. Mind you, I wouldn't like it to become a habit!"

"No," Tanith insisted. "Amongst my people, we say, 'A gift demands a gift'. That means also a kindness demands a kindness. I shall not forget your kindness to me last night. No dragon ever forgets a kindness or a wrong. You watched for me when I was overcome with grief. Tonight you will be weary, so I will watch for you."

"Well, if you insist," said Droco.

"Who's for toasted mushrooms?" asked Zakarius, as they gathered round the fire.

"For these, your blessings, Lady Shara Sorian, we give you thanks," said Kestrel.

"*Uru lai zarque faramoula, Tz'aru Tiamat,*" murmured Tanith, while Zakarius, sat for a while in silent meditation.

Droco, who had stretched forth his hand to take a mushroom, resignedly withdrew it and cast his eyes upwards in good-natured exasperation at the delay. He waited till it seemed to be the right moment to try again.

"Who is Shara Sorian, Lady Kestrel?" asked Tanith.

"She is the Goddess of the Sun and the Moon. The Creatrix of Zar-Yashtoreth and our guardian," explained Kestrel.

Tanith looked thoughtful for a moment and then light dawned on her face.

"Ah, I understand. It is your name for Mother Tiamat."

"Well, in a way," said Kestrel. "Although we see Her in a different form."

For had not Shara Sorian lived in many bodies and as many creatures, so as to understand the minds and souls of Her creations? Until, as a golden unicorn, she had leapt back into Aeulandis, Her home. And if it was in the form of a dragon that Tanith could understand the love of Shara Sorian, then so mote it be.

Tanith thought it sad that Lady Kestrel could not see the Great Mother in Her true shape. The dragon-folk's prayers took the form of a perpetual dialogue with Her, including Her in all they did, so, while she ate, Tanith, silently, asked Mother Tiamat to grant Lady Kestrel the sight of Her as a glorious dragon, since Lady Kestrel was a true dragon friend.

They finished their mushrooms. Kestrel found them zailie eggs, which Droco poached over the fire, and Tanith found wild honeycomb, her green skin, apparently, was impervious to stings.

Droco finished the meal off by producing a skin of skai wine, sweet, purple, sparkling and refreshing. Tanith nearly choked on it, never having tasted wine in her life before. Kestrel refrained from asking how Droco had acquired it, knowing that some wine seller of Uz was a skin short.

"Ah," said Zakarius, combing his long beard with his fingers, "That was a truly satisfying meal. Thanks be to the Cloud Father."

To Droco's amusement, the devotions started again, each of them thanking their deity for the meal.

If we have this skadding pother every time we eat or drink, he thought, we shall never get to Xegeron. Thank goodness Zabris, God of Thieves, didn't demand all that. A quick plea, or rapid thanks for help, often on the run, was enough for Zabris. He understood the pace of life.

"I think," said Kestrel, "we should be on our way now. The Sands of Doom never cease to run."

They rose to their feet, knowing the wisdom of these words, but Tanith's legs seemed to give way beneath her. She slid to the ground, where she sat laughing, helplessly.

"Whatever is the matter?" asked Kestrel. Tanith shook her head. She did not know why this wonderful feeling of happiness had suddenly bubbled up within her. Everything was incredibly funny. She laughed and laughed until she collapsed in a helpless heap on the ground.

"Oh dear, oh dear," murmured Zakarius.

"It's the wine," said Droco. "It's gone to her head. Tanith, are you tipsy?"

The word "tipsy", amused Tanith and she repeated it with fresh mirth.

"Tipsy! Tipsy!" she chuckled. "Tipsy, tipsy, tipsy, tipsy."

"Well, we can't go on with her in this state," said Droco. "She can't even stand, let alone walk. Who'd imagine a drop of skai wine could have that effect?"

"She isn't used to it," Kestrel suddenly realised. "She won't have drunk wine before." As she spoke, she searched through her pouch and at last brought out a small vial filled with amber liquid.

"Drink this, Tanith," she said.

Tanith took the vial and looked at it. "It's pretty," she said and began to laugh helplessly once more.

"Try it," Kestrel urged. "It's delicious."

She took a sip of it herself, to encourage Tanith, then handed it back to her.

Still laughing, Tanith put the vial to her lips and drank it.

"It tastes of honey," she said, and drained the small glass vial.

The effect was immediate. Tanith's laughter subsided. A look of puzzlement spread across her face and she got to her feet, as if nothing had happened.

"Frazzing Kasperus!" said Droco, impressed.

"Wonderful! Quite wonderful!" cried Zakarius with greater decorum. "An instant cure for intoxication!"

"You could make your fortune if you flogged that in Kironin, my lady," said Droco.

"I'm sure I could," Kestrel said, laughing. "But that is not for what it is intended. Now, Tanith, have you recovered?"

"Was I sick?" asked Tanith.

"Tipsy as a whinfly," Droco told her.

Tanith looked blank and Kestrel said, "Don't worry about it. The skai wine was a bit strong for you and made you giddy."

"The water of laughter," said Tanith, but she could not remember any more. Just that something she has drunk had made her feel deliciously happy.

"All's well now," said Kestrel, and they resumed their journey.

The forest was a place of great beauty, and Kestrel and Zakarius felt peaceful as they travelled through the ancient trees, though they never ceased to be watchful. Tanith found the place fascinating, now that it was daylight, and held up everyone's progress by stopping to gaze, pick up strange stones, smell flowers or to use her smattering of knowledge of the tree speech to converse with the trees.

Droco, however, who came from a noisy, lively, bustling town, found the forest dull and tedious in the extreme.

At last they reached a clearing, lit by the sunshine, the trees rustling softly in a light breeze. Delicate yala blossom and sweetly scented madral dotted the grassy mounds, and in the centre was a forest pool of shimmering clearness.

By this pool sat a young elf minstrel, playing the qu'enga. Her voice was sweet as she sang to her own accompaniment. Birds drew close to her in the boughs of the trees. Rabbits and deer and other wild creatures peered out at her, as she played and sang.

"*Qu'enda sai touran,*
Qu'enda sai touran,
Shala mourla, Estari la lai.
Estari amal'n. Estari amala'n,
Qu'enda sai touran. Qu'enda sarai."

The Elvish words carried on the air, as the minstrel played and sang, lost in her music, and quite unaware of her audience. All of them were transfixed by the beauty of the sound of the qu'enga and the minstrel's sweet voice.

At last the song came to an end.

"Good day to you, stranger," called Kestrel.

The minstrel looked up and rose to her feet with a smile. She was dressed in a green Elvish tunic and green hose. She wore a gauzy cloak of shimmering rainbow hues. In her hair she wore an ivy wreath.

"Good day, travellers," she replied, as she advanced to meet them. Tanith, who had been greatly moved by the music, tentatively touched the qu'enga's carved wooden frame.

"What are you singing?" she asked. "And what is this wonderful singing wood?"

The minstrel looked at Tanith, recognising her elfin form, but puzzled by her green skin.

"Do you not recognise the qu'enga, nor speak the Elvish tongue? Where have you been travelling, my friend? You must have long been absent from your native land."

This in turn puzzled Tanith. "I speak only the language of my own people," she replied, "and, of course the common tongue. Also a little of the tree speech."

"But surely your people…?" Began the minstrel.

"I am of the dragon people, despite my outward shape," said Tanith, as her mama had taught her.

The elfin minstrel decided to say no more, though she could not understand this, and Kestrel introduced them all.

"This is Tanith-Medea, and this is Father Zakarius of the Crystal Brotherhood. This is Droco the Sprig, master thief of Kironin." (The minstrel at once laid her hand on the purse she wore at her waist, and Droco laughed.) "And I am Kestrel Moonblade, warrior priestess of the Temple of the Golden Unicorn in U-Llashkar."

The minstrel bowed slightly to each, then introduced herself.

"I am Lindor Estoriel from the fair city of Tilioth."

"Tell us of your song," said Zakarius.

"I was singing of my homeland," replied the minstrel.

And she began to sing again, but this time in the common tongue, her sweet voice silvery beneath the trees of Svorg-Skenda.

"The trees are like emeralds, shining with sunlight,
The waters sing with joy as they flow o'er the earth,
In the forests of my homeland
The forests of my own land,
But I am far, far from the land of my birth.

"It sounds bettering Elvish," she concluded.

There was a burst of applause from the delighted travellers and Zakarius said, "You certainly sing well."

Lindor at once took up a flamboyant pose.

"If you have enjoyed my song, perhaps your generosity could persuade you to throw a coin or two to the singer."

"Gladly," Kestrel agreed.

"My thanks to you from Lindor Estoriel, minstrel extraordinaire. I will, at your command, extemporise, immortalise and surprise. I can make ballads of your greatest deeds and turn your smaller acts into great ones. I make 'is' out of 'might have been'. I can capture your exploits as you perform them. Recapture them in retrospect and inspire them before you begin them, with my songs of great adventure.

"I can sing magic spells to assist you in danger and draw evil magic away, as poison is drawn from a wound. I have songs to make you laugh, and songs to make you weep, songs to make you wake, and songs to make you sleep. And for this monumental task, a coin or two is all I ask."

Droco had heard this kind of ballyhoo many times from itinerant performers in Kironin, but never done so well or with so much charm. He laughed and applauded and threw Lindor three coins.

Kestrel and Zakarius did the same. Tanith had no coins. Coins were things to gaze at for their bright beauty, to run your fingers through to feel their smoothness and to hear their musical clinking sound, or see them glitter in the light that filtered into your home through cracks and fissures. To carry them in a pouch seemed pointless and foolish. But seeing they were giving gifts to the beautiful minstrel, she immediately picked a blossom and gave it to Lindor.

"Tanith has no coins," explained Kestrel. "The dragon people look on money differently from the way we do. So let me give you an extra coin on her behalf."

"I thank you, generous lady," replied Lindor. "I thank you all. This will buy me food, wine and a bed for the night on my wanderings."

"And where are you travelling, with your songs for all occasions?" Zakarius asked.

Lindor shrugged, "I travel wherever the sun and moon call me," and then she began to put her words into song.

"I travel the road, as it calls, as it beckons,
I travel the road with dust on my feet.
Where does it call me? I do not know.
Where does it lead to? I do not care.
I just follow, follow, follow.
For all roads are mine and I am free,
And the road to everywhere belongs to me.
Along paths I roam
Far, far from my home,
But all paths are home to me."

The listeners broke into spontaneous applause and through the applause Kestrel once again heard the voice of Morrigan's eerie chant. Heard it as if the old woman were beside her in the forest.

"You shall have as your companions
The thief
The dragon-maid
The wise fool
The elfin minstrel."

This, then, is surely the elfin minstrel, Kestrel thought. Aloud she asked, "Lindor Estoriel, we travel to Xegeron to destroy the dark sorceress. Will you come with us? No doubt our adventures will make wonderful ballads in days to come."

"I would be honoured to come with you," Lindor replied. "Zephrena's evil is beginning to spread its shadow over all Zar-Yashtoreth."

"So, then," thought Kestrel. "Our party is nearly assembled. We need only the sword bearer and the honour seeker. How wise is Morrigan."

Chapter Fourteen

Krauls

The Dark Tower flickered with torchlight. The walls leapt in a fiendish dance of death. The shadows reached out with long, bony fingers. The sorceress, Zephrena, looked into her scrying glass and watched the progress of the five travellers. Five creatures of light, she thought with contempt. All the same, she was uneasy. Kestrel Moonblade's powers were too strong for her liking, though she could match them with ease. Father Zakarius worried her too. She had taken his memory and prevented his journey to the Temple of the Sacred Cats of Kushli, but, just the same, he had managed to find his way to another path to her defeat and she knew that the high priestess at Kushli would have sent him to Kestrel anyway. The powers of light were strong indeed. Now the elfin minstrel had joined the party with her music and song, both great dangers to her dark magic. That wretched little gutter shrike thief had no magic, but possessed great skill in his fingers, which was not to be forgotten; and the dragon's brat had the power to summon every dragon in Zar-Yashtoreth to her aid, if need be, though they could not approach the Dark Tower. Besides, Tanith possessed more magic than she was even aware of.

"They are not yet strong enough to harm me," she murmured, "but they must be destroyed before they grow any stronger. A small party of my krauls should do it, I think."

The sorceress pointed a long finger at the bell pull set in the wall. It rang at her command. The kraul captain, Bragazh Gourbag, appeared in answer to the summons.

"You sent for me, Great One?" he asked.

"Take a party of your company and go to the Forest of Svorg-Skenda," commanded Zephrena. "I will send you there by magic, for it is too far for any other means of travel. We must not underestimate our enemies. I want them all slain. But I have special plans for Kestrel Moonblade. Let her be taken and brought to me alive."

The kraul captain's face broke into a leer of pleasure. "I shall do as you command, Oh Great One."

Zephrena dismissed him with a wave of her hand, and turned once more to her scrying glass.

The five travellers were walking through the forest, unaware of any trouble to come. Lindor was playing her qu'enga and the others were singing an elven song she had taught them.

Zephrena's lips curled in a sneer. "Farewell, my brave adventurers," she said.

***

At midday the five travellers stopped to rest, eat and drink. Suddenly, Kestrel felt a chill shiver through her. She looked at the others. They had, clearly, felt it too. Father Zakarius had a troubled look in his eyes. Tanith was tense in every limb, and gave a hiss, like a startled snake. Lindor had stopped playing and Droco had frozen into alertness.

"There is a presence," whispered Tanith. "I can sense it."

"So can I," Kestrel agreed. Then they all heard the coarse cries of the krauls, in their harsh language, carried on the air.

"Krauls!" Lindor's voice trembled.

"Sent by Zephrena," added Zakarius.

By now the krauls were in view, heading straight towards them. Kestrel drew her sword and placed herself before the party.

With alarm they saw there were about 50 krauls. They were utterly outnumbered.

The kraul captain saw them and shouted a command, and the whole troop charged towards them. Tanith retreated into the undergrowth, hissing and screeching with terror.

An evil-looking kraul drew his scimitar and attacked Kestrel, who held him off, valiantly with her sword, hoping to conserve her magic powers for later on, if she needed them. The steel of their weapons clashed and glinted in the sunlight. The kraul seemed to be made of iron. No matter how Kestrel slashed at him with her sword, he remained invincible. He was cunning too, but finally Kestrel ran him through and he fell dead at her feet, his blood staining the ground.

Immediately another kraul made for her, but no sooner had his attack begun, when Tanith came from the bushes, held up a clawed hand, and cried "*Zan esk maranaza*!"

The kraul froze into stone and when Kestrel turned to thank her, she saw several hideous kraul statues standing round the undergrowth. Tanith had had her own battles, just as Kestrel had.

The krauls were not easy to defeat. Now a band of them surrounded Lindor. But Lindor simply smiled serenely and began to strum her qu'enga.

At once the krauls' faces became blank. All the evil died out of them. In a trance, they began to revolve slowly to the music, gradually getting faster and faster, until they could hardly be seen. Round and round whirled the krauls, swifter and swifter, until they seemed to blend with the air and vanished, without trace.

Zakarius stood contemplating the scene of battle, stroking his beard, thoughtfully, and shaking his head, as three savage-looking krauls advanced towards him.

"Dear me!" he murmured. "What unpleasant-looking characters. I wonder if I can turn them into creatures of light. Now, how does it go, that spell that turns evil into good? Ah! I think I remember. He raised his hands and cried, "*Quilith Sh'an*!"

The krauls vanished. Zakarius blinked in surprise. He was struck suddenly by the sight of two large beetles crawling on a nearby bush.

"Dear me! That seems to be the spell that turns people into beetles. Oh well, never mind. I'm sure they'll be much more useful as beetles than as krauls, and certainly much prettier."

Droco, who had taken refuge up a tree, was using his catapult to good effect, when, from his vantage point, he saw Kestrel in combat with a fearsome-looking kraul. He aimed his catapult and was about to fire, when he saw, on the ground, a knife that sparkled in the sunshine. He fired his catapult and distracted the kraul long enough to allow him to leap from the tree, retrieve the knife, and retreat up the tree once more. Swiftly, he examined his loot.

It was a small knife with no sheath and a long slim elegant blade.

"Nicely made," said Droco to himself. "This would fetch a good price from any fence in Kironin."

As he looked at the weapon, he noticed some letters on the hilt. They spelt words written in the common tongue.

"I serve whomever owns me," Droco read. "What does that mean, for the love of Zabris?"

The knife began to twist in his hand and to take on a life of its own. Then it flew through the air, like a bird on the wing, straight into the kraul attacking Kestrel.

"Hey! It's killed a kraul all by itself," Droco cried. The next moment, the knife returned to his hand.

Droco's face broke into a grin of delight. "Here's a turn up for the sunshine! So that's what it means, 'I serve whomever owns me'. Here it goes again!"

Once more the knife tore itself from Droco's grasp, flew into the heart of a kraul and returned to Droco's hand.

"My luck's in. Zabris be praised!" cried Droco. Zirax always told us that once in every thief's career comes a haul blessed by the gods. I think mine's just arrived. He gave a thumbs up sign to the clouds. "I thank you, Zabris!" Then he kissed the knife. "Welcome and bless you, little one. With your help, I'll become a hero!"

The knife twisted free once again, and flew, unaided, to its target.

"And another hit!" chuckled Droco, "But I think I'll keep you as my own little secret. No need for anyone else to know."

The little knife continued. It was swift, fierce and endless. The five travellers used skill, strength and magic, and many krauls were slain, wounded, turned to stone or transformed, but they seemed indestructible.

All the travellers had wounds and were bleeding profusely. They were getting exhausted, too. Their strength and magic were beginning to wane.

Then, suddenly and amazingly, an unforeseen wonder occurred. From nowhere, there appeared a fearsome-looking dwarf trollslayer and a knight. With loud war cries and weapons raised, they rushed headlong to the travellers' assistance.

The knight's sword spun, shining, in the sunlight, as it cut and slashed, parting the krauls like grass. And the dwarf's huge double axe hacked left and right with such force that kraul heads and limbs flew and the air was thick with blood.

In a short time, the ground was drenched in kraul gore and covered with kraul corpses. Those still alive fled in terror.

The battle was won!

Chapter Fifteen

Torvic Shinetop

Torvic Shinetop, the dwarf, was born in Karak van Dorm, and lived there all his life. His name then was Torvic Runegild, and he was the eldest son of Gruss Runegild, the runemaster and Brendhild Dorenhold, the healer. In his youth, he studied the runes, as his father had done, and he seemed set to follow in his father's footsteps, and, maybe even surpass him in excellence. His two younger brothers, Kalig and Raven, hero-worshipped Torvic and studied the runes too, aspiring to be like him.

There was one strange thing about Torvic, and that was his height. He was unusually tall for a dwarf, which singled him out from his companions. However, he thought little about such things. He was a fine-looking fellow and a good runesmith. Those who knew him honoured and respected him and that was all Torvic cared about.

His life was placid and methodical. His days flowed with the rhythm of a swinging axe. Like most dwarfs, joy was not an emotion he often experienced, but he was content and at peace with himself.

Then came the goblin attack. The dwarfs fought as only dwarfs can, but the goblins had strength too and great numbers, and dark magic as well. By the time the dwarfs had routed the invaders, many dwarfs had been slain.

Amongst the dying was Brendhild. It was dreadful to see her strong, kind, brown face with the sickly yellow-green pallor of death, and her eyes, usually so full of life and determination, grow listless and vague.

She was carried to her house and there she called Torvic to her bedside. He came and sat beside her. In a display of affection, unusual for dwarfs, Brendhild took her son's hands in her wasted ones.

"My son," she said, her voice faint and tense, "I cannot depart to the halls of my ancestors without shedding a little of the secret that has weighed down my heart all my life. It may sadden your days but you have the right to know. Say nothing of this to Gruss Runegild. He is a good soul and I would not have his life blighted with this knowledge.

Torvic's eyebrows knotted. What on Zar-Yashtoreth could be troubling her so? She went on, her fingers tightening their grip.

"My son, I hope you will not hate me when I have told you this thing that has hung on my life like a great stone. I hope you will not reproach me. Remember that I was very young and had not yet acquired the wisdom that comes with years."

"I shall never hate or reproach you," muttered Torvic, embarrassed by the emotional tone of this talk. He had never heard his mother talk so much in all her life. It was not the dwarfs' way. "Tell me what troubles you so." He wanted this conversation over.

Brendhild sighed. "When I was very young, before I knew your father, I was gathering orestone herbs in the Khazveld Caverns, when I came upon a manling mountaineer, who had fallen and injured his leg. I tended him and healed him. Brendhild paused, and then continued. "The healing took some moons and in that time, we came to care for one another, Arvid Kresten and I. We became one.

Torvic felt as if someone had struck him a heavy blow to the stomach. As if his whole being had been ravaged by an earthquake. His mother, whom, all his life, he had revered and honoured, lay on her deathbed, telling him that she had defiled the dwarf code of honour, by taking a manling as a paramour. But worse even than this was to follow.

"My son," Brendhild went on, "I can see you are outraged by my action and yet I have told you only the beginning. I found myself with child."

Torvic felt his whole body go rigid with shock. "You had a child by this manling?"

Brendhild nodded. "Yes, Torvic. And shortly after that Arvid Kreston fell sick again. This time all my skill could not save him. He was already weakened by his fall. He died. I was heartbroken. I buried him and returned to Karak van Dorm. Your father asked me to wed him. He was a good soul and very handsome. I consented. We were very content. The child was born; a fine son. Your father believed it was his, and I have never told him otherwise. You have guessed now, have you not, that you are not the son of Gruss Runegild? That is why you have always been taller than is usual for our race."

Torvic gave a howl of despair and buried his head in his hands. He wanted to slice his flesh and let the skreely manling blood out of his veins. He felt sick, soiled, dishonoured.

He was brought back to himself by the calming touch of his mother's hand on his arm.

"Try to forgive me, my son. I loved your father and he loved me. He was a good and honourable man. There is no disgrace in having his blood run through your veins."

But to Torvic it was both a disgrace and a violation. He loathed himself for the manling blood that was in him. He wanted that blood spilt.

When Brendhild died, Torvic told his father that he wished to work in Ulv, which was famous for its runesmiths. He could not bring himself to tell Gruss Runegild his mother's terrible secret. Besides he was sworn to secrecy and would not violate his oath. But he could not remain in Karak van Dorm. He went to Ulv, indeed, but not to work with the runes. He shaved his head, studied the arts of warfare and became a trollslayer, to try to recover the family honour, lost by his mother.

Soon he was renowned for his fearlessness and ferocity. Where there was danger, there was Torvic. They called him Torvic

Shinetop now, because of his shaven head, covered in war paint, and with only a crest of wild black hair at its centre.

In every battle, in every fray, in any dangerous exploit, Torvic Shinetop was at its centre, seeking an honourable death, goaded always by the memory of his manling blood, that taunted him. He kept this a fiercely guarded secret.

He made no friends, though all regarded him highly. He spoke to few and when he spoke, he spoke as briefly as possible. His thoughts were as dark as a cave at midnight. His only true companions were courage, his great sword, Talven, the swift death, and his double axe, Valdur, the blood spiller.

Dour and surly, Torvic Shinetop travelled Zar-Yashtoreth, seeking honour. He had no inkling of the way in which he was about to find it.

Chapter Sixteen

Giles de Sorell

When Giles de Sorell was five years old, he saw a sight that was to mould his whole life. His father, Gabriel, was a well-to-do merchant of Eloskan. His mother, Aishalind, one of the first ladies of that land. Giles, their only child, lived a life of ease and happiness, loved and indulged in all things.

Their large, low, white house, with its turreted roofs, was surrounded by a huge, well-kept garden. Its green lawns sloped, willow-clad, down to the river. Here, safe behind the wrought iron swirls of the gates, little Giles would stand, watching the river, the water birds and the beautiful water lilies.

On one wonderful day, however, Giles saw something else, something that drove the river and all its loveliness out of his mind, completely.

As he peered through the iron intricacies of the gate, a company of glorious knights rode past on white steeds, their armour silvered by the sun. Bright plumes fluttered on their helmets. Their horses' manes waved in the breeze, kissing their white necks. On the knights' shields were depicted golden falcons.

Giles was stunned by the beauty of the scene. His eyes grew heavy with tears. He had never before known tears for anything but pain or sadness, and he could not understand them now.

He turned to his nursemaid, his little face glowing with delight, and asked her about the wonderful apparitions. The nurse, a sweet, pretty young woman named Linet, took his hand and smiled.

"They be knights, Master Giles," she told him. "Knights of the Falcon. They live up yonder on the hill in a great stone castle. You can't see it from here, for the trees, but there it stands, nonetheless."

Giles sighed with a feeling both of content and of restlessness.

"What do they do, the Knights of the Falcon?"

"Noble and brave deeds," Linet replied. "Most of all they protect us from the dragon people."

Giles's eyes widened. "Dragons?"

"Oh, fearful things they be, rampaging and breathing fire," Linet told him. "But don't you be afeared, Master Giles, for no dragon will ever come near Eloskan, while a single Knight of the Falcon lives."

"I'm not afraid of dragons – or anything," responded Giles vehemently.

For he had, at that moment, resolved never to be afraid again. He had made up his mind that, come what may, he would, one day, be a Knight of the Falcon too, and slay the biggest and most ferocious dragons of Zar-Yashtoreth.

From that day on, Giles dedicated himself to achieving his ambition. He persuaded the gardener to make him a little sword out of wood, and the cook to give him an old saucepan, which had lost its handle, as a helmet, and a pan lid as a shield.

Every day, when he had finished lessons with his tutor, he vanquished imaginary dragons, or went on imaginary quests through the gardens. He read every tale of chivalry on which he could lay his hands and begged his tutor, a mild, learned, dedicated man, named Don Pellinet, to tell him more. Then he relived them in the shrubbery, the herb garden and the rose garden. His heart was enthralled.

At first his parents smiled indulgently, but, as the years went on and they saw his desire to become a Knight of the Falcon increase rather than wane, they took him seriously. At last they sent him to the Castle of the Falcon, where, after Jules de Mausiac, the Golden Falcon, as the knights termed their leader, talked with him, and after this, accepted him as a squire. Giles thanked Argavan, the God of Chivalry, and Ursos, the God of Battle, in tears of happiness. This time he understood those tears.

He killed his first dragon on the Isle of Iliac and slaughtered her young ones too, won his spurs, was dubbed a Knight of the Falcon, and waited for his first quest to be granted.

The granting of a novice knight's first quest was a grave and moving ceremony. Jules de Mauriac and his lady, Linden, presided. Every Knight of the Falcon was present, with his lady, if he had one. Giles's parents watched, proudly, from the public gallery. The young squires and pages gazed, wide-eyed, at Giles, who had so recently been one of their number, but was now exalted beyond their ranks. The torches danced and blazed against the castle walls.

Giles stood in his white tunic, with its golden falcon emblazoned on it. His heart quickened and his cheeks were flushed.

Then Lady Linden, who granted all quests, smiled at him and spoke.

"Giles de Sorell, the time has come for your first quest, and tonight I tell you what that quest will be. It may seem strange to you, for I do not say, 'rescue this captive', 'destroy that dragon' or 'storm such a castle'. Your task is less easy than these things, for it is less tangible."

Giles's heart beat fast with pride and anticipation.

"Giles de Sorell," continued the Lady Linden, "A great darkness is spreading through Zar-Yashtoreth. We feel its shadow here in Eskolan, yet we cannot tell what it is. Your quest – a most difficult one for one so young – is to seek this evil and to destroy it."

Giles felt a quiver of excitement run through him, as this most difficult of quests was given to him. He knelt to kiss the Lady Linden's hand and replied in the time honoured manner.

"My gracious lady, I thank you for this quest, which I accept with all my heart. I hereby pledge unto you, and unto all who are here this day, that I will fulfil it, or die with honour attempting it."

"That is well spoken," said Lord Jules de Mauriac. "Take, then, this surtout that proclaims you a true Knight of the Falcon."

And Lady Linden placed, over his head, the blue surtout with its golden falcon.

Then all cheered and applauded and raised their swords, and Giles de Sorell turned from the Castle of the Falcon and set out to destroy the evil that darkened Zar-Yashtoreth. Whatever and wherever it might be.

As all Knights of the Falcon who went out on their first quest, he travelled on foot, and without full armour. Full armour and a horse were granted as a reward for a successful first quest. He held his head high and his heart was full of joy, pride and hope, as he set out on his adventure.

Chapter Seventeen

The Sword Bearer and the Seeker of Honour

On a bright, sunshiny morning, Giles de Sorell, on his first quest, left the Inn of the Golden Tamarisk and took up his journey once more. He had had many adventures in his first month of travelling. He had rescued a beautiful young girl from a cruel abductor and restored her to her joyful parents. He had vanquished several krauls and killed a vicious grutsk. He had had a somewhat humiliating encounter with a dragon, who had sent him sprawling with one blow of his claw, called him a foolish young whippersnapper and flown off, leaving him covered with mud and grass. Giles pushed the memory away, flushing scarlet; but as yet he had not found the nameless evil he must destroy.

However, it was good to be travelling through this lush and sweetly scented countryside, on such a bright warm day. Giles was aware that he cut a handsome and gallant figure, tall, slim and golden-haired. He had had many admiring glances from the ladies he had met on his travels. This was far from undesirable to him. He hummed a ballad as he walked.

The sun grew hotter and at last Giles decided to rest. He lay down under a malma tree, hanging his cloak on its lowest branch.

It was wonderful resting in the shade, with the song of the Ilira birds, sweet and liquid above him, and the scent of the malma blossom making him drowsy. Giles was almost asleep, when a huge, double axe whistled over his head and thudded to the ground beside him.

In a flash, Giles was on his feet, sword drawn.

The axe-wielder was a dwarf, unusually tall for his race, but, unmistakably, a dwarf, with a long, tangled, black, bushy beard and a shaven head, apart from a strip of black hair, that bristled down the centre. On the shaven part of his head were intricate tattoos, which marked him as a trollslayer. He was scowling with his thick black brows and swinging his double axe at nothing in particular, as he walked. Giles stared at him haughtily.

"What in the name of Kasperus d'you think you're at, disturbing my rest in that way?"

The dwarf bristled.

"What d'you mean by sprawling there like that, you useless squadge?"

Giles drew himself up to his full height, "How dare you speak insolently to a Knight of the Falcon, you insignificant little mushrump."

The dwarf swung his double axe. "No one says that to Torvic Shinetop and lives."

Giles held his ground. "You terrify me, mushrump," he sneered. "No doubt you pass for a giant amongst your fellow dwarfs, but to me, you're just a little squin to be squashed."

Reminded, so rudely, of his height and his manling blood, his secret dishonour, Torvic let out a roar of rage and rushed upon Giles, his double axe raised. The suddenness of the attack put the knight at a disadvantage. He fought valiantly, but tripped over a tree root. Torvic would have decapitated him, had he not leapt swiftly to his feet.

"Very impressive," he said, sarcastically, "but I defy you to defeat me with a sword in true combat."

Despite himself, Torvic was impressed by Giles's courage and ability, but he did not show it.

"I've slain better than you with my sword," he growled as he drew his sword from his belt.

This time they were more evenly matched and the fight lasted longer. However, before victory could be achieved by either Giles or Torvic, they were interrupted by the harsh screeches of krauls.

Both stopped in their tracks.

"That's a kraul war cry or I'm a wizard," muttered Torvic.

"They've surrounded someone, by the sound of it," said Giles. "If there is anyone in danger from the forces of evil, I must go to their aid. It is the pledge of all Knights of the Falcon and my especial quest."

"You're not the only one," scoffed Torvic. "I'll take on any kraul in Zar-Yashtoreth and finish you off afterwards."

"That I'd like to see," retorted Giles, with scorn, but laying aside their quarrel for the greater enemy, the knight and the dwarf hurried towards the sounds of the battle.

Thus it was that Kestrel Moonblade and the other travellers found this wonderful and unexpected aid, just when they most needed it. At the arrival of Torvic and Giles, clearly skilled warriors, and fresh and untired, the remaining krauls fled.

"Praise be to Shara Sorian for sending us help at our darkest hour," cried Kestrel. "We are victorious! My thanks to you all, my friends, for your help, and to you gallant strangers, who came to our aid like blessings from the goddess. I thank you from the bottom of my heart. You won the day for us, for we were all beginning to grow weary and could not have held out much longer. You shall be our guests tonight."

Giles kissed Kestrel's hand, gallantly. "It will be a great honour and a great pleasure, my lady."

Torvic snorted. "Thanks, but I'll be on my way."

"I would not hear of it," replied Kestrel. "You have the true valour of all your noble and ancient race. We would be honoured to share your company."

Torvic, flattered despite himself, mumbled his thanks and assented. They found a sheltered nook near the forest outskirts and here they made their camp. Kestrel spoke some words over the bodies of the fallen krauls, treating them with kindness and gentleness, though they were savage enemies. She then raised her staff, and the fallen bodies melted into earth.

"I know nothing of their customs," she said. "I do not know what happens when they die."

"You've given them a better send off than they deserve," said Torvic, shortly, but Kestrel shook her head.

"Even enemies should meet kindness in death," she insisted, and Torvic hadn't the heart to tell her how krauls devoured their fallen enemies.

Zakarius had found bushes of gola pods and was now roasting them over the fire. It was a slow process and Droco grew impatient.

"Aren't those gola pods ready yet?" he asked. "I'm starving to death."

"Patience, my son," came Zakarius's measured tones. "Let me see – ah yes – they are plump and crisp and golden. Just let them cool."

The dwarf turned, as Droco spoke, and scrutinised him more carefully.

"I know that voice. What are you doing here, thief? Treasure hunting again?"

Droco, in turn peered at the dwarf. "Frazzing Kasperus! I thought I recognised that ugly mug. By Zabris's nimble fingers, what are you doing here?"

Torvic growled, "Haven't they hanged you yet, thief?"

Droco laughed. "They have to catch me first."

Kestrel was amazed. "Where have you met before?" she enquired.

"Don't ask, my lady," replied Droco. "It'll only start him off again."

Torvic glared at him. "Just don't attempt to set foot in Karak van Dorm again," he warned.

Droco shrugged. "Just an unfortunate misunderstanding, that's all."

"Just a plain thief, you wretched little gutter shrike," Torvic returned.

Droco grinned. "What a fuss over a few little gems, that I genuinely thought were a gift from Lord Arvak Helgrist."

Torvic snorted with disgust.

"I see you haven't changed," went on Droco. "Still the same quirking miserable little squin."

Torvic swung his huge double axe, as if it were a straw. "I'll put my axe through you, thief!"

Tanith screeched and hissed, half in terror and half in protectiveness towards Droco. But Droco needed no protection. He sprang nimbly out of the way, laughing.

Kestrel came between them. "Peace be between you," she cried. "Have we driven off the krauls to quarrel between ourselves?"

Torvic withdrew his axe. "You are right, Lady Kestrel," he acknowledged. "But no dwarf can forgive the loss of the Lady of the Mountain."

At these words, Tanith's eyes grew wide and she quivered with emotion, for the Lady of the Mountain was a fabulous and magical emerald that ran through the very fabric of dragon lore and legend. Though every dragon believed, implicitly, in its existence, to hear it mentioned as a living stone, was a thrill almost too great to be born.

"The Lady of the Mountain! I have heard of that."

"Have you!" Torvic snapped. "Well, he stole it."

Tanith ignored this accusation, overcome by the fact that this fabulous emerald, the size of a grutsk egg, might be close enough to gaze upon. She crawled up the boulder to where Droco sat. "May I see it, please?" she asked, with complete simplicity.

Droco laughed again. "I haven't got it," he told her. "Nor can that skadding little misery prove I ever had it."

"The gola pods are cool now," came Zakarius's mild voice. "Please take some."

The quarrel petered out as everyone took a handful of gola pods and settled down to eat them. The old wizard had toasted them to a perfect and delicious crispness. For a while there was a complete and contented silence. At last it was broken by the voice of the knight.

"These gola pods are truly delicious. I haven't eaten gola pods since I killed my first dragons." He paused a moment to let his words make the desired impression and then elaborated with enthusiasm.

"A pair of fearsome beasts they were, living on the Isle of Iliac. I cut them down and all their brood of young ones."

There was an embarrassed silence from Kestrel, Droco, Zakarius and Lindor. They all glanced, uneasily, at Tanith, who had frozen into stillness. At last she spoke.

"You vile, unspeakable murderer. So you are Giles de Sorell, the slaughterer of Iliac. Lady Hochma Sofia spoke of you. She said the time for our vengeance was not yet ripe, but rest assured, we will avenge your blood lust. You have not escaped. Death to all armoured scum!"

Giles turned to look at her, in surprise. It was the first time he had really noticed her. Up to now, she had kept close to Kestrel, suspicious of the strangers. Now he saw her clearly, and something about her made him shiver.

"That wasn't the most tactful remark to make," Droco informed Giles.

Tanith's face seemed to crumple into lines of hatred. Her green skin darkened.

"May you and your vile people perish in misery, "Tanith continued. "All you armoured ones think of is blood. Always your evil swords must drink blood. The blood of our innocent race."

Kestrel, disturbed by this outburst, turned to Giles and said quietly, "My friend, I would thank you not to speak of dragon slaying."

Giles looked amazed, both at Tanith's anger and at Kestrel's request.

"Forgive me, my lady," he said. "But they are an evil race. As a Knight of the Falcon, I am pledged to rid Zar-Yashtoreth of their dark presence."

Tanith rose, trembling with emotion.

"Evil you call us! By what right do you call us evil? We, who seek only to live in peace?"

Giles was puzzled by the use of the pronouns "us" and "we", but realising that she was, in some way, allied to the dragon people, he replied.

"Live in peace? Is that why you come marauding and stealing treasure that would enrich our land and make us happy? And killing all who stand in your way?"

"Then if we came, it was only to reclaim our treasure, plundered by your kind," Tanith returned savagely. "And if we killed it was only in defence, when you raised your swords against us to keep us from reclaiming the treasure that is rightfully ours."

"Gold and treasure stolen by you in the beginning," returned Giles with equal venom. "Gold and treasure that would give everyone a life of ease and plenty and that you know no better than to heap in piles and sleep on!"

"Why you scum of a Kasperus pool!" cried Tanith, almost in tears. "Our love of gold is no mere greed as yours is. We love our treasure for its very spirit and the flame of its being. You use it only to make yourselves great before your companions!"

The travellers watched this interchange with amazement and concern. Those that knew Tanith had seen her only as naïve and childlike. Sometimes timid and awed with wonder at the sights beyond her home. Kestrel, however, remembered Tanith's first words to her in the Sun and Moon Lakes. Had not Tanith called her an armoured murderer and shown fear and hatred when they first met?

She now attempted to calm the quarrel between the knight and Tanith.

"We are all weary," she said, "and that makes us quick tempered. But we owe a debt of gratitude to these strangers, whose courage has given us victory over the krauls this day. Will you not tell us who you are and where you come from?"

Giles gazed at Kestrel with adoration. For him she was a goddess. He would lay his soul at her feet, offer her unqualified devotion. He was hers to command. She was his Lady. When she asked the newcomers to introduce themselves, he rose instantly.

"I am Giles de Sorell, Knight of the Falcon. It is my mission to wield my sword in defence of all those in trouble and to rid Zar-Yashtoreth of evil."

"To cause it, rather," Tanith murmured.

Kestrel turned hurriedly to Torvic. "And you, my friend?"

Torvic rose, bowed stiffly, and shouldered his axe.

"Torvic Shinetop, my lady. Trollslayer from Karak van Dorm."

And Tanith said, politely, "May the glory of your valour be renowned," as her mama had told them all to do, should they ever meet a dwarf.

"A trollslayer and a knight, who travel the world seeking honour and adventure!" cried Lindor in delight. "I have often longed to travel with such as you and set our adventures into song."

"I should be honoured, indeed," said Giles, thrilled at the idea of being celebrated in ballads. He could almost hear the words, "Giles de Sorell, the brave", "Giles de Sorell the noble", "Giles de Sorell the destroyer of evil".

Torvic, however, simply grunted ungraciously, "I prefer to travel without a lot of Elvish racket."

"Well, thank you for your fair words, kind sir," replied Lindor, annoyed.

Droco chuckled. "You could travel to the ends of Zar-Yashtoreth before you got a courteous word out of him."

Kestrel wasn't listening. For, once more, the wailing song of the Crone of the Moondark came to her, clear and sweet.

"You shall have as your companions,
The thief,
The dragon-maid,
The wise fool
The elfin minstrel,
The sword bearer,
The seeker of honour,
And that is all...
That is all."

The sword bearer and the seeker of honour, thought Kestrel. These are they, surely.

She turned to the two newcomers. "Giles de Sorell and Torvic Shinetop, we are travelling to Xegeron to destroy the sorceress, Zephrena, and release the souls in her clutches. Will you go with us and complete the party?"

Giles bowed and kissed Kestrel's hand. "I should be honoured, my lady, for this is surely the quest on which I was sent."

"I, too, will be honoured to come with you, my lady," said Torvic.

"Well, there's a turn up for the sunshine," cried Droco. "Fair words from Torvic Shinetop. You must be the only person on Zar-Yashtoreth to get them from him, Lady Kestrel."

Torvic turned on him. "Why you little..."

But as he turned, his hood slipped from his head, and Kestrel saw blood streaming from his eye. Only a dwarf could have born such a wound, for so long, without a murmur. Kestrel was touched by his courage.

"Let me heal your eye," she said, taking from her pack a small box of sweetly scented purple ointment.

Torvic shrugged. "It's nothing." But allowed her to smear the ointment on his eye.

"You have shown great courage," she told him. "Shara Sorian will honour you, as she will honour all of you for your courage in driving away the krauls this day." Then, from a nearby likanda bush, she plucked the purple flowers, and tossed them in the dwarf's direction.

"In the name of Shara Sorian, may you be healed."

Instantly the blood flow ceased.

"Thank you, my lady," said Torvic gruffly, but, clearly, impressed. But the damage to the trollslayer's eye was deep, and Kestrel knew that the sight would never return to it.

"I can still kill krauls, even if I have only one eye," he said, unconcerned.

"Take this for protection," Kestrel handed him an eye patch, from her pack. For a moment, Torvic looked as though he might refuse, then changed his mind and put it on, nodding his thanks.

From then on, the trollslayer wore Kestrel's gift with pride and reverence. They were feelings he rarely experienced, but Kestrel had, unconsciously, generated them in his heart.

"You are both welcome," Kestrel told Giles and Torvic. "And now our party is complete."

At this, Lindor struck up the qu'enga and sang.

"We are assembled, the party of travellers,
Travelling to Xegeron, bringing light to night,
May all the powers of goodness attend us,
Victory be ours in our glorious fight."

Torvic scowled at her. "Plague on it, elf, are we to have that infernal din through our entire journey?"

Lindor, offended, replied stiffly, "Most folk like it, but it is well known that dwarfs have no music in their souls."

Her hurt look changed to one of mischief, as she, deliberately, strummed a few more chords on the qu'enga.

Torvic growled, like a disgusted dog and walked away, grumbling into his beard.

"Dear, dear," said Zakarius, gently. "What a bad-tempered creature! And we were such a happy little party."

"Bad tempered is putting it mildly," returned Giles. "Before we arrived here, he insulted me and threatened me with his axe. That made me laugh and I told him he didn't frighten me, even if he was a giant amongst dwarfs. Well, you should have seen him, he flew at me like a thousand furies!"

"If you mentioned his height, you're lucky to be alive," Droco told him. "I've known him kill people for that."

"Why should he kill people for mentioning his height?" Zakarius enquired, somewhat nervously.

Droco turned to where Torvic had departed. He could be seen, at the top of a little knoll, some distance away, seated on a stone, hunched up and the picture of discontent.

"Can he hear us from there?" he asked.

"I think he's too busy sulking," Lindor replied.

"If he hears me tell you his secret, I'm lost. If he even knew that I know, I'd be lost; but the fact is, he is half-dwarf, half-human. What they call a man-dwarf. That's why he's taller than dwarfs usually are."

"How do you know this?" asked Kestrel. "It could all just be idle gossip."

Droco grinned, cheekily. "Oh no. I heard this from a most reliable source. His mother took a human lover. Now that is the most terrible disgrace in the dwarf code. They have some very strange ideas, do dwarfs. So his mother kept quiet about it, but it must have troubled her, for she confessed it to old Shinetop on her deathbed."

"It must have been dreadful for him to hear such news," Kestrel sympathised. "No wonder he's inclined to be surly."

"It shook him rigid," Droco replied, without too much sympathy. "That's why he became a trollslayer, to reclaim the family's honour. But for the love of Zabris, don't let him know I told you."

"I am sure none of us would dream of mentioning such a painful subject to him," Kestrel told him.

She looked up at the darkening sky. "I think we should prepare for rest, now." She consulted her scroll. "Tomorrow we travel to the Port of Kyrd, and from there to Xegeron."

Then, turning to the knight, she added, "Welcome to our band of travellers, Giles de Sorell." And then, glancing at Torvic, who had not moved and was still seated on his stone looking as if he, too, were part of that stone, she continued, with a smile, "Perhaps I should try to persuade Torvic to return to us."

"Well, I don't know that I wouldn't be just as happy without that miserable old twag with us," said Droco.

Tanith was shocked, "But Droco, you must always be polite to dwarfs."

Droco laughed, "Who told you that?"

"Mama," said Tanith.

"I hate to contradict Mama," said Droco, "but dwarfs are made to be rude to."

Seeing Tanith look horrified, he continued, "Besides, he's only half a dwarf. But not a word about that, remember?"

"Of course not," Tanith replied. "It is a deep and precious secret."

She spread her blanket. She was getting quite good at this now and this gave her a great sense of pleasure and delight. "Look!" she exclaimed, pointing to the blanket lying, almost flat on the ground.

"You are becoming an expert blanket spreader!" cried Lindor as she pulled out the corners for her.

Giles watched, tense and hostile. The creature had them all bewitched, acting so harmless and naïve. How fortunate that he was here, with his understanding of what dragons and their kind were really like.

By this time, Kestrel had reached Torvic, who turned at the sound of her footsteps.

"Has that minstrel stopped her Elvish racket, plague take her?"

Kestrel sat beside him. "There's no cause to curse Lindor's music. It has saved us many times in the battle today, though without your skill and courage, we should have been lost indeed."

Torvic's expression became slightly less surly, which showed Kestrel that he was not immune from a little subtle flattery.

"It was nothing," he said, shortly. Then, after a pause, he went on, "Lady Kestrel, for your sake, I would endure more than that bunch of trolls that travel with you."

Kestrel laughed. "You will find that they are not quite such trolls as you think. A fair night to you, Torvic Shinetop, and, again, thank you for giving us victory today, and for joining our little band. With you by our side we have nothing to fear. You have, indeed, the courage of all your noble race."

Under his prodigious whiskers, Torvic almost smiled, but hastily changed it to a grunt. "And a fair night to you, too, Lady Kestrel," and he began to make his way back to the campfire.

As he reached it, and heard Lindor, still strumming the qu'enga, his sullenness returned.

"Another gola pod?" enquired Zakarius, politely. "There are a few left."

"Gargarus take your gola pods," snapped Torvic.

Zakarius was not in the least perturbed. "Oh, very well. If nobody wants any more, I'll eat them myself." He took a bite out of the juicy, savoury vegetable. "Mmm! Quite delicious," he murmured appreciatively. "If there's one thing I do well, it's toasting gola pods, if I do say it myself."

Kestrel stood watching the dwarf make his way back to the camp and prepared to follow, when she became aware of Tanith's shadowy form coming towards her.

"Lady Kestrel," she faltered, "is that armoured scum truly to travel with us?"

"Why yes," Kestrel affirmed, "it is so destined."

Tanith clasped her arm. "Do not take him on this journey," she said, intensely. "He is evil, as are all his kind. I cannot travel with a murderer of my people."

Kestrel's heart sank. To have gathered all the companions foretold by the Crone of the Moondark had cheered her immensely. She felt as though the journey to Xegeron had now started in earnest And to have Tanith say she could not go, unless Giles were dismissed, seemed to Kestrel as if a great obstacle had been placed in her path. But Shara Sorian spoke in Kestrel's heart, so she knew how to reply to Tanith.

"But if we are to set Neis-Durga free, you must go with us, Tanith. You have nothing to fear from Giles de Sorell. Much of his talk is simply youthful swagger, but he means no harm by it. He is of the forces of light, and remember the courage with which he fought against the krauls.

Tanith's expression closed.

"I know the armoured ones, Lady Kestrel. I know all about their deeds and their savagery. And he is the slaughterer of Iliac, one of the worst of his kind. For Neis-Durga's sake I shall go to Xegeron, but I know he is evil and has the blood lust of all the armoured ones."

Kestrel put her arm round Tanith, reassuringly. Slowly she guided her back to the place where they were encamped for the night. Giles volunteered to take the first watch, and everyone settled down to sleep.

Kestrel waited till everyone was asleep and then approached Giles.

"Giles, I would ask you once again not to mention dragon slaying in Tanith's hearing. You upset her."

Giles inclined his head, slightly, in acknowledgement.

"Forgive me, Lady Kestrel, but she upsets me. She makes my flesh crawl and she is, clearly, in league with the dragon people."

"She has been reared by dragons and thinks of herself as one. And they, too, regard her as one of their own," Kestrel explained.

"I see," Giles's face bore an expression of disgust. "That explains the revulsion I feel against her. Now I come to think of it, she reminds me of a dragon. She sits like one. She guards her pack as a dragon guards treasure. I cannot feel at ease in her presence."

"Nevertheless," said Kestrel, "she is necessary to our quest and I would regard it as an act of friendship if you no longer spoke of your dragon slaying exploits before her."

"If you wish it, Lady Kestrel," Giles acquiesced. "But it will bring danger, having her in our company. I know dragons. They are evil."

"It is clear," Kestrel replied, "that you know nothing of the dragon people."

"Not so, Lady Kestrel. I know much of them and I know they are not to be trusted. The Tanith creature may be some kind of monster, with dragon blood in her veins. Why is her skin green? And why does she have long claws?

"I do not know," said Kestrel. "She has elven blood, but is not pure elf. She never speaks of her lineage. Perhaps she does not know it. She simply says she is of the dragon people, despite her outward shape."

"I wish she were not of our company," Giles replied. "It is well that I am with you to be vigilant. Your heart is too good, my lady, and too trusting."

"You will grow accustomed to her," said Kestrel, with a smile. "She has harmed none of us. I am glad you have joined our band of travellers, Giles. Your courage has saved us today. I thank you for it. A quiet watch to you."

"I too am glad to have joined you," said Giles. He kissed Kestrel's hand, reverently. "It is an honour to serve you."

Chapter Eighteen

Zephrena's Message

Zephrena, the dark sorceress of Xegeron, sat before her scrying glass and watched the party of travellers. Now they were complete and they would journey to her land and seek to destroy her and reclaim Lord Aragal's soul.

Zephrena rose, a tall slender figure, clad in her black robes, her black cloak falling from her shoulders and her cold crimson lips in a deadly smile.

"Let them try to come here. They will find me more than ready. A little division amongst them; a few quarrels; a little suspicion. That should break their strength. Now let them feel my power. I think I'll begin with the dragon-maid and the Knight of the Falcon. That ancient feud is already simmering. Let it now come to my aid."

She picked up a black wand, carved and twisted with curious designs, and, holding it high, she cried "*Oorsh' an' Morg li Zhegar*!"

The scrying glass sent forth a mist, which cleared, revealing Tanith curled up asleep on her pack. Zephrena drew close to the mirror and began to whisper.

"Tanith-Medea Shirakalinzarin, you are in great danger."

Tanith stirred, nervously in her sleep. The poisonous voice continued its lying whisper.

"At present your companions are kind, but will they remain so, should they discover your true lineage? That you have troll blood in your veins? What will happen then? As yet they do not know. But you have, in your midst, a Knight of the Falcon. A sworn dragon slayer. The slaughterer of Iliac. He will not show you kindness. He will kill you at the first opportunity. Destroy him before he destroys you."

Tanith woke in terror, from, what seemed to her, a false turning in sleep's labyrinth.

"Mother Tiamat, protect me!" she murmured.

The night was still. Everyone was asleep. Only the silhouette of Zakarius, who was now keeping watch, stood out black, against the firelight.

I must ask Mother Tiamat for help, thought Tanith, and began to make her way to a small clearing, nearby, where there was a pool.

"What is it, my daughter?" asked Zakarius.

"It is the full moon, Father Zakarius, and I go to worship the Great Mother," she replied and continued her journey to the pool.

In the Dark Tower, Zephrena looked through her scrying glass at the recumbent figure of Giles de Sorell. Once again she sent forth her poisonous messages.

"Giles de Sorell, beware the dragon-maid," it said. "No dragon ever forgets a kindness or a wrong. You and your people have killed many of the dragon race and you are the known slaughterer of Iliac. She will seek vengeance the very moment she can. She has gone, this moment, to the forest pool to worship Tiamat, the dragon goddess, and ask Her to give her strength to spill your blood. Why not kill her, before she kills you?"

Giles woke with a start and reached for his sword. He rose and looked around him. Tanith was not amongst the sleeping travellers. Her blanket lay in disarray. His dream had spoken truly and he must follow it and kill the dragon creature, before she killed him.

Zephrena watched through her scrying glass, as Giles rose and took up his sword. She smiled to herself.

"Now," she said, "A little distraction for that foolish old wizard," she stretched out her hand. Zakarius heard the sound of footsteps in the bushes.

"Who's there?" he asked, puzzled, and rose to investigate. At once the footsteps ceased. "Strange," muttered Zakarius, "I must be imagining things." Thus it was that he failed to see Giles as he made his way to the pool.

Zephrena laughed to herself. "And now, let the first bloodshed amongst you begin."

Tanith reached the pool and stretched her hands up to the full moon. Mother Tiamat's silver eye gazed benignly down at her. Tanith raised her arms over her head, in a curious wing-like gesture, which was the nearest she could get to what her dragon family did. She had the uneasy feeling that something was wrong and darted quick, suspicious glances into the darkness.

"Dearest Mother Tiamat, I am in danger. Please give me your protection. Defend me, Mother Tiamat, for I am alone and far from my dear ones."

She looked into the pool and saw the moon's reflection, and beside it, something that made her heart turn to stone, as if it were the victim of the one magic spell she knew. In the water she saw Giles de Sorell, his sword drawn.

Tanith turned. Giles's face was a mask of hatred.

"Dragon spawn, I have come to fulfil my vow as a Knight of the Falcon. You have beguiled the others in our company, but I know the truth about the dragon race."

Tanith was numb with terror. She would have used her stone spell, but her fear prevented her from gathering her energy. But, despite her fear of this armoured one, she managed to reply.

"I am ready for you, murderer!"

Giles struck first. Tanith hissed like a serpent. She knew little about combat, but her uncles, Phineas Coprinius Shirakalinzarin and Apolonius Mercury Shirakalinzarin, were renowned fighters and destroyers of armoured murderers. And these two great green dragons had instructed them all in the rudiments of defence and attack, should the occasion arise. Little Caramoon Liskander was the best at it in Tanith's family and Aunt Belladonna Cressida's young ones, Vashti Cleopatra and Cagliostro Cyprian, promised well too.

"If only they were here now to help me," thought Tanith. For a moment the idea went through Tanith's mind to give the dragon call for help, which would bring every dragon in the vicinity to her aid. But this call was only used in the most dire emergencies. Tanith decided to use it only if this armoured creature became too strong for her,

Giles struck again, wounding the side of her face. Tanith screeched and flew at him, tearing his face with her long claws. Then she tried to coil herself round him, as she had seen her uncles do, when they demonstrated methods of attack, using rocks or tree stumps. Giles felt sick with revulsion at her touch and shuddered to see a human-like creature behaving like a serpent.

He slashed with his sword and saw blood on it. Tanith gave an unearthly, animal-like screech and slithered to the ground, hissing. Then she slid up from behind him, sinking her claws deeply into his neck and face. The hair rose on Giles's arms and the nape of his neck, as he shook her off.

Trembling with terror, Tanith lashed out wildly at him. Giles stepped aside, wounding her arm with his sword, and using his shield to fend her off. Then he moved in for the kill.

***

At the camp, Zakarius wondered why Tanith was so long returning. Then he noticed that Giles was missing and his heart misgave him. He woke the others.

"Can't a body get any sleep here, in the name of the abyss?" grumbled Torvic.

Kestrel said nothing, for she, too, knew what had happened. The noise of the fight came clearly now, on the breeze. She led the way towards the clearing. Here a terrible sight met their eyes.

Tanith had rallied and was now coiled round Giles, once more. Her long claws were, again, embedded in his neck and face, while Giles slashed at her with his sword and tried to throw her off. Blood poured from both of them.

For a moment they all stood, frozen. Then Kestrel stepped forward.

"In the name of Shara Sorian, cease this bloodshed!"

A light flashed from her staff. Tanith dropped from Giles and Giles stepped back. Tanith was trembling, hysterical with fear and anger, while Giles stood like a statue, his face contorted with hatred and revulsion.

"Murderer!" Tanith said, her voice low with intense venom and hatred. "Evil slaughterer who sheds innocent blood." The tears poured down her face and she clung to Kestrel for protection.

"Spirit of Gargarus!" Giles returned with equal malice. "There will come a time when we shall not be interrupted."

"I shall be prepared for you, armoured scum!" Tanith replied.

"Stop!" cried Kestrel. "Can you not see? This is the evil of Zephrena. Whatever enmity lies between your peoples, you must forget it, or the dark sorceress will be victorious."

Giles cleaned his sword as best he could, and sheathed it reluctantly. Tanith was shivering, uncontrollably, but when Lindor strummed the qu'enga, she grew a little calmer.

"Come," said Kestrel, raising Tanith to her feet. "Let us return to our fire."

Giles gave Tanith a murderous look, which Tanith returned. Slowly, coaxingly, Kestrel led the way back to the fire and once again everyone prepared for sleep, though all were shaken by the incident. Kestrel kept watch while she bathed and healed Tanith's and Giles's wounds as best she could. Then she woke Droco, whose turn it was next.

As usual, Droco grumbled good-naturedly. "Another frazzing watch! All right. I'm ready. I'm ready." He yawned and shook himself awake.

"All is peaceful, now," Kestrel assured him. Droco nodded, and, when Kestrel was sure he was fully awake, she lay down, and fell asleep at once, exhausted by the night's events.

Droco stood looking at his fellow travellers. Kestrel lay sleeping peacefully, but her hands, even in sleep, were upon her staff and her sword. Her expression, in repose, was, as in waking, one of serenity and utter goodness.

The old wizard twitched and muttered into his beard as he slept. Droco smiled. Silly old poddle. Though not as silly as he made out. Droco couldn't help liking him.

Lindor lay curled round her qu'enga, her light hair spread around her. She was beautiful. She smiled at some sweet dream. Light seemed to surround her in some strange way. Not physical light, but something magical. Droco shrugged. It was too deep for him.

He moved on to Giles. De Sorrel slept quietly, his fair curls in disarray. Clearly Lady Kestrel had healed his wounds as much as she could, but his face still bore the marks of Tanith's claws.

"Serves you right, you twag!" thought Droco, carefully and expertly removing a little of the knight's gold. Giles's sleep was untroubled. He lay dreaming of slaying dragons and being honoured by Lady Kestrel, when she discovered he was right about them and that they were, indeed, vile and evil.

Torvic Shinetop snored loudly. His great black beard was tangled with leaves and twigs. He grasped his double axe in one hand and still wore his great sword at his side. Even in sleep he was a fearsome sight. Droco could not resist the challenge. He slipped a few silver draskas from the dwarf's pouch. He was pleased to see that his touch was so light, that the dwarf did not so much as stir.

Droco continued his survey of the camp and then he saw Tanith.

She was awake and clinging to the base of a tree, as if desperate for warmth and succour.

"What's the matter?" Droco asked her. "Can't you sleep?"

Tanith never moved. "If I sleep, that armoured murderer may attack again," she whispered.

"No," Droco assured her. "He won't attack again."

"How do you know that?" asked Tanith.

"Because," said Droco, "I heard Lady Kestrel ask him not to and Lady Kestrel can be very persuasive. Besides, our friend Giles worships the ground she walks on."

Tanith shivered suddenly and Droco felt sorry for her. Remembering the tropical climate of her home, the outside world must seem bitter to her, he thought.

"Are you cold?" he asked. "Here, take my blanket." He put it round her, over her own.

"Thank you, Droco, but you will need it."

"I'm not cold." Droco lied, for the night was chilly. He wrapped the blanket round Tanith a bit more. Then he saw that the wound on her face was bleeding again.

"Hey! You're bleeding" he cried. He woke Kestrel, gently, and showed her Tanith's wound. She cleaned the blood off, carefully, and tended it with balms and salves from her pouch.

"There, that will soon heal properly," she stroked Tanith's hair. "All is well now."

"He wanted to kill me. Unspeakable murderer," Tanith's voice trembled. "Just as he killed my little gift brother's family at Iliac."

"What is this tale of Iliac?" Kestrel asked. "Both you and Giles have spoken of it."

"I will tell you," said Tanith, "and then you will see what cause I have to hate Giles de Sorell and all his kind."

Tanith settled herself and began her story.

"The Island of Iliac, in Lake Iliac, is not in the Guadja – the Valley of the Sun and Moon Lakes – it is far off, over the Guadja Mountains. My aunt, Belladonna Cressida, found it. She and my uncle, Griolin Helianthus, and my cousins, are always flying off on adventures and finding strange and wonderful places. They saw this beautiful lake and its island below them as they flew, but did not visit it, immediately. However, they told us of it and many of us set off to see it.

"It was the most wonderful place. The lake was bright blue and the island was as green as...as..." she sought for a comparison, "as the Lady of the Mountain. We went across to the island. It was magnificent. The grass was soft and sun-warmed; but as soon as we reached it, we knew that there was something wrong. The birds had stopped singing. There was a terrible silence and a feeling of death in the air.

"We wanted to leave at once, but something kept us there. We walked as if drawn by some horrid magic. Then we came upon it. The reason for our feeling of horror. Outside a cave lay a beautiful mother dragon. She had been murdered. Her shining green scales were covered with blood and one of her lovely wings was torn and bleeding. And her little ones…"

Here Tanith's voice caught as her tears began to fall. "They, too, lay slaughtered around her. The terror was still frozen in their eyes. A little further ahead, we found the father dragon, who had died, defending his family."

She could not go on. The memory was still too terrible.

Kestrel and Droco put their arms round her and stroked her hair until she was calm enough to continue.

"We knew it was the work of armoured ones by the dreadful sword wounds on those poor, sweet creatures, and we swore that, when we found the murderers we would be avenged. We were about to leave, for the Isle of Iliac no longer held joy for us, when we heard the sound of terrified weeping. We followed the sound. It led to a cave. At first we could see no one, but we kept following the sound of that pitiful sobbing, until we came to a tiny dragon. Perhaps his mother had hidden him when the armoured scum came, or maybe he had hidden himself in terror. In any case, he had escaped the slaughter.

"We found him, trembling and weeping at the back of the cave. He was so young, so tiny, he could not even tell us what had happened. He was trembling from head to foot. We took him home with us and cared for him. Now he is part of our family and is happy again, though, sometimes, he still takes a false turning in the labyrinth of sleep and wakes screaming. And if you had seen how the poor little quodling cried for his mother in the first few moonturns he lived with us, you would understand why we have sworn vengeance on the murderer of Iliac. The Lady Hochma Sofia, Dragon of Wisdom saw in her meditations that the murderer's name was Giles de Sorell. Now he is here, amongst us, and has tried to kill me."

There was silence. Tanith's eyes were full of tears at the terrible recollection of her story.

Kestrel drew Tanith to her and held her in her arms. "It must have been an evil day for you to witness such horror. But your little foster brother is safe and happy now, is he not?"

Tanith nodded.

"Then you must try to put aside your enmity with the Knights of the Falcon, at least while we follow our quest."

"Yes," Tanith agreed, "and I would have done so, had he not attacked me. But once our quest is over, we shall fulfil our pledge and destroy the evil murderer of Iliac."

Kestrel answered, "Don't think about that now. Come, lie down and try to sleep."

So peace returned, if a trifle uneasily.

In her dark tower, Zephrena saw all in her scrying glass, and smiled to herself.

"I have sown the seed," she murmured. "Let the harvest be fruitful."

Chapter Nineteen

Crossing the Lake

At the edge of the Forest of Svorg-Skenda, was a vast lake, so huge that its further shore could not be seen. Kestrel unrolled her scroll.

"This," she said, "must be the Lake of Khond. We must cross it to reach the Port of Kyrd and from there we cross the Zarish Sea of Xegos to Xegeron."

Torvic looked about him.

"But there's no way of crossing."

That was true enough. There was neither bridge, nor a ferry boat, nor even stepping stones.

Kestrel stared at the endless water, thinking deeply. Giles stood beside her, looking troubled.

"This is an evil place," he said. "I can sense it."

Kestrel was surprised at his words. Concerned as she was about how they would cross the lake, she felt, nonetheless, a sense of peace and security.

Tanith, who was grooming herself and bathing in the lake, turned on Giles, at once.

"Ignorant grutsk! There is nothing evil here. It is a good place, a place of safety and blessing."

"So you say!" Giles returned with scorn. "Which probably means the opposite is true."

"I confess," said Kestrel, gently, "I feel only peace and tranquillity here."

As if to belie her words, there came a cry of terror, and Droco appeared, drained of colour and shaking. He had been exploring, to see if there might be a bridge or a boat.

"What is it? Islarians?" asked Kestrel, who could think of nothing else that could terrify him so greatly.

Droco shook his head and tried to compose himself enough to speak. Tanith stroked his hair and crooned to him in the dragon tongue, as if he had been one of her own younger brothers. At last he became more collected.

"Dragons, Lady Kestrel. Two enormous dragons on the lake!"

Tanith broke into a smile, "Droco, you have nothing to fear from the dragon people"

Then, she turned to the others and added, a little complacently, "I told you this place held no danger. Were they she-dragons or he-dragons?"

"I didn't stop to look!" said Droco.

Giles had already drawn his sword. "My lady, let me go and dispatch them."

Torvic swung Valdur, his great double-axe. "Too much for you, spratling. I'll go."

Tanith gave a hiss, like an angry snake. "Murderers, both! Leave my kindred in peace, or I'll turn you to stone. Creatures of bloodlust and cruelty!"

Kestrel pacified her. "No one will harm your kindred," she assured her. "Sheath your sword, Giles, and Torvic put away your axe. I fear we shall have need of weapons more than I could wish; but not now."

Torvic grunted disapprovingly, but lowered his axe. He had great faith in Kestrel.

Giles protested, "But, my lady..."

"Oh, stop your prattling, whelp, and do as Lady Kestrel says. She knows what she's doing," growled Torvic.

"And who asked you for your opinion, you stunted crag?" asked Giles.

"This is no time for squabbles," put in Zakarius, in his mild way. "We have to think of a way to cross the lake."

"I will ask my people," said Tanith, her face alight with joy. "They will help us."

Impatiently she led the way, taking the path along which Droco had come, and turning every few steps to ask, "Is this the way?"

Kestrel followed, cautiously. She had no fear of the dragon-folk, but knew they had to be treated with care. Lindor was almost as anxious to see the dragons as Tanith.

"To meet dragons! What a wonderful adventure!" she kept saying. Already she was trying out songs about it all.

Zakarius, like Kestrel, was careful, but unperturbed, while Torvic and Giles, grim-faced, prepared to do battle. Droco, most reluctantly, brought up the rear. He would scale a tower, and take jewels from a safe before the eyes of the most ferocious of guards, without a shred of fear, but dragons were a different matter.

At last they rounded a bend of the lake path and there, close to the shore, dipping graceful necks beneath the water, to crop the lush lake plants, were two immense, shimmering blue dragons.

Tanith, transfigured with joy, ran towards them, her arms opened wide.

"*Ushai! Ushai!*" she cried. "*Esqai Tanith-Medea Shirakalinzarin. Thelada vri Morgana-Semiramis Shirakalinzarin, Kjan maierenda Shirak-Shagreet Talahindra. Nirandis levan ekri vinalis khan.*"

The beautiful shining blue dragons turned large, gentle, lustrous eyes upon her.

"*Ushai, Tanith-Medea!*" they replied in unison. Then one spoke alone.

"*Esquai Freja Higdrasil Sa'arourat, thelada vri Melisande Velalinda Sa'ariurat, kjan maierenda Zouron Ozandiles Sa'arourat.*"

Then spoke the other, "*Schai esquai Solveig Nehelenia, ozhu thelada vri Melisande Velalinda Sa'arourat, kjan maierenda Zouron Ozandiles Sa'arourat. Edai elandi.*"

And they bent down their long, slender, shining blue necks and Tanith put an arm round each. And they embraced and chattered in the dragon tongue, oblivious of all but each other.

Giles was tense. His hand never left his sword hilt. "What are they plotting in their evil tongue that no one understands? Lady Kestrel, let me put an end to these monsters."

"No, Giles," said Kestrel. "They mean no harm to any of us. They are simply happy to see each other. You do not need to understand their speech to know that."

It was true. The joy was in their voices and in their eyes and in every movement. The dragons, majestic though they were, frolicked with Tanith, splashing and frisking their tails in the lake.

Kestrel spoke gently. "Tanith, would you introduce us to your friends?"

Tanith hastily remembered her manners. "Forgive me, Lady Kestrel. How rude you must think me."

Then, with a simple dignity and solemnity, that was oddly touching, she announced.

"This is Lady Freya Higdrasil Sa'arourat and this is her twin sister, Lady Solveig Nehelenia Sa'arourat, daughters of Lady Melisande Velalinda Sa'arourat and her consort Lord Zouron Ozandiles Sa'arourat. They have a large family across Lake Zjara, but, by a stroke of luck, have come exploring and found that the Lake of Khond opens out from their own lake. Just think, if they had not done this, we would never have met them."

She introduced each of the travellers in turn, but when she came to Giles, she spoke in the dragon tongue and once more the word "Iliac" was spoken. The two dragons looked at him and the friendliness of their eyes turned to deep hostility, which Giles returned in full measure.

Kestrel thought that, kindly as these dragons appeared, she would not care to get on the wrong side of them.

Then, their expression of sweetness returned and one of the lovely, shining creatures spoke to Kestrel.

"Our little cousin, Tanith tells us that you wish to cross the lake. As you are friends of Tanith's, we will take you across; all except that murderer," she pointed a long claw at Giles.

Giles's face grew pale with anger, and his expression hardened even more.

"I certainly travel with none of the dragon demons," he said.

"Indeed you will not!" replied the other dragon. "We carry no armoured scum. Least of all the vile slaughterer of Iliac."

"But how will he cross the lake?" cried Kestrel. "He is needed on our quest."

"There is a boat further along the shore," replied the other dragon, waving her tail in the opposite direction from which Droco had taken. "If you need him with you, he can take that. But none of the armoured blood spillers come with us. Least of all the slaughterer of Iliac."

Giles gave the dragons a look of disgust, and without deigning to speak, set off in the direction of the boat.

Torvic looked as if he might join him. He had no desire to be carried over the lake on a dragon's back.

"Fear nothing, honoured dwarf, may the glory of your valour be renowned," Lady Freya Higdrasil assured him, as if she read his thoughts. "You will be quite safe."

Torvic scowled, and grasped his axe. "I *do* fear nothing," he snapped.

"You are courageous indeed, may the glory of your valour be renowned," said Lady Solveig Nehelennia, Tanith was already seated on Lady Freya's shining, scaled back, one arm lovingly round the dragon's neck. The other around Lady Solveig's and her head leaning against Lady Freya.

Kestrel thanked the dragons and seated herself on Lady Solveig. Droco drew, cautiously closer. Tanith was chattering happily in the dragon tongue and he heard his name mentioned. The next moment, Lady Freya turned to him.

"Tanith says you have been very kind to her. We are grateful. No dragon ever forgets a kindness or a wrong. Please honour us with your presence."

"Thank you, madam," Droco replied, with all the charm he could muster, and he sat with Tanith, feeling he would be safest under her protection.

Lindor then climbed onto Lady Freya and began playing the qu'enga and making up a ballad about the kindness and help of the two beautiful dragons, who were both charmed, and gratified.

Father Zakarius seated himself by Lady Kestrel on Lady Solveig, and Torvic, muttering and cursing to himself finished the party.

"If everyone is ready," said Lady Solveig Nehelennia, "we shall commence our voyage."

With that they moved off, smoothly, gliding, like two enormous swans, across the Lake of Khond.

Tanith was transfigured with delight. The others had never seen her so full of joy before. She laughed and chattered to the two dragons, in the dragon tongue, and then translated for everyone else. The dragons, too, were full of delight to meet their little cousin and her friends.

Luna fish and water creatures plunged and dived out of the great dragons' way. The water rippled and made calm musical sounds as the dragons swam serenely onwards, their heads held proudly, their glorious wings raised, sheltering the travellers on their backs. Lindor's sweet voice and the gentle strains of the qu'enga echoed the river sounds.

Kestrel felt at peace here on the lake. The water was soothing, Lindor's music was enchanting and the dragons were remarkably reassuring. They passed strange water flowers. Squin and Llhira birds watched them from holes in the trees growing by the lake's edge. They passed the twisted roots of trees that had reached into the lake, for moisture, and now grew there, snaking and looping their roots into the lake bed and out again into the air, groping for the lush banks.

Finally, they were out in open water and could see no land at all. The ripples twinkled in the sunlight and the Llhira birds and twen flew, warbling, overhead, their iridescent colours flashing like jewels.

Sometimes a water creature plopped its head up to look at them, or a fish leapt and then plunged back into the water.

On they travelled. Kestrel wondered how Giles was managing. She hoped he was safe. She also wondered where he would come to land. Would they meet each other safely?

"We have reached our journey's end now," announced Lady Solveig. "See, here is the shore."

The two dragons swam close to the lakeside and their passengers dismounted.

"Farewell, kind friends," said Kestrel. "On behalf of us all, I thank you for the kindness you have shown us and the honour you have done us."

The two dragons inclined their graceful heads in acknowledgement. Tanith, however, dissolved into tears. Now that the time had come to part from her people, she was desolate. Her arms encircled the dragons' necks. Her weeping was piteous and the tears flooded down her cheeks.

The two lake dragons enfolded her in their glittering wings, caressing her and speaking to her persuasively, encouragingly as one would speak to a child, and drying her tears with their claws. The name Neis-Durga was mentioned many times.

Finally, Tanith nodded and seemed to rally. There was a last, long and loving farewell. Then Tanith shook back her hair and stretched out her arms for one last caress and kiss. Then she rejoined the others, a little solemnly, but determinedly, and they moved away. Many times, Tanith turned back to wave and blow kisses. And as long as the travellers remained in sight, Lady Freya and Lady Solveig remained at the lakeside, raising their magnificent wings in salutation.

"That was quite an experience!" exclaimed Zakarius, as they moved along the lake shore.

Lindor was dancing and singing about their glorious ride across the lake, her face translucent with joy, and Torvic muttered and groused about the music and the ride.

Kestrel had enjoyed travelling across the lake and was very grateful for the dragons' help, but now she was worried.

"How shall we ever meet with Giles? Who knows where he will come ashore on this huge lake?" Maybe, she thought, he did not even get across, but she did not like to speak such thoughts aloud.

"Let us go on without him," said Tanith. "He is a vile creature, cruel and evil. We are better off without him."

"No, Tanith. Our party must be whole," remonstrated Kestrel. Though once again, she wondered if this were true. The Crone of the Moondark had said nothing about any of her companions being with her for the whole journey.

"Give him an hour, Lady Kestrel," suggested Torvic. "It'll take longer to cross the lake by boat than on those huge dragons."

"And he might have drifted, or lost his bearings," put in Zakarius.

"Should we split up and walk along the shore in different directions," asked Lindor, "in case he *has* drifted?"

"No," replied Kestrel, at once. "We don't want any more of us getting lost. Let us wait two hours and then we must think afresh. I do not want to proceed without him."

"Such a loss of time for such a worthless creature," said Tanith. She hoped Giles had drowned.

They camped by the lakeside while they waited and Kestrel started a fire. But even with magic, this proved difficult, for she was tired now.

"What about your fire spell, Zak?" asked Droco. "It was pretty good at burning my fingers, I remember. How about using it now?"

"Father Zakarius, if you don't mind, my good fellow," replied Zakarius amiably. "Zak indeed! Yes, I shall use my fire spell. That will work, I'm sure."

Torvic looked doubtful. Magic was not something of which he approved, but Father Zakarius was already raising his staff and chanting, "*Quai en shan hadra a saira*!"

There was a dazzling flash. When it cleared, Lindor appeared to have vanished and in her place was a beautiful wood nymph, who looked at her reflection in the lake, in amazement.

"What have you done to me?" cried Lindor's voice.

"Oh, strangest magic!" cried Tanith in awe.

"Oh dear! I seem to have turned you into a dryad, instead of making a fire," said Zakarius apologetically.

"All this messing about with magic!" grumbled Torvic.

"Well, kindly change me back again!" insisted Lindor.

"I'm afraid I've forgotten how to," said Zakarius. "But don't worry. You look very beautiful and accidental magic always wears off by itself."

Once Lindor found she could still play the qu'enga, she cheered up.

"I suppose I must be thankful he didn't turn me into a kraul," she said, resignedly.

Kestrel finally got a fire going with her own, more reliable brand of magic, aided by Lindor's charmed music. As they sat and enjoyed their meal, Kestrel was relieved to see Giles walking towards them. He was soaked to the skin and looked tired and dishevelled, and was furiously declaring that the lake dragons had deliberately sent him out on the water in an unstable boat, which had capsized three times.

Tanith broke into a peal of laughter, which did not help matters, and Droco provoked Giles still further, by saying, "It's not their fault if you don't know how to row."

"Not all of us have experience as a galley slave," returned Giles.

Kestrel calmed Giles down and told him to sit by the fire and get dry. She produced a wonderful liquid from her pack, which apparently had restorative properties, for Giles appeared to recover greatly. He was very taken with Lindor.

"Good evening, madam. May I have the honour of asking the name of so beautiful a maiden?"

"It's the elf, you twag!" snapped Torvic. "One of the old sorcerer's spells gone wrong."

"It will soon wear off," Zakarius repeated, mildly.

They sat and finished their meal. All was now contentment. The fire blazed brightly and everyone felt at peace.

They might not have felt quite so contented had they known that Zephrena was observing them all in her scrying glass.

Chapter Twenty

The Darkness Gathers

Zephrena sat by her scrying glass, watching the band of travellers at the lakeside. She gave a cold smile. The hatred between Tanith and Giles pleased her greatly.

"At last, they are divided," she thought. "But not as much as I could wish. Kestrel Moonblade holds them together. She is the one at whom I must strike. If I could catch her soul, it would be a great possession. But now I have something a little more entertaining to attend to."

She clapped her hands and Thirghiz Gorblitz appeared, cringing and sycophantic.

"You called, Your Greatness?"

"Bring in Zanto Elaris, the priest of the Mystic Unicorn."

Sensing something exciting, Thirghiz ducked and cackled in delight.

"I'll bring him, Your Greatness. Right away."

"Tell them they may all watch," Zephrena said magnanimously.

"Oh, Your Greatness, I thank you," and she left, grovelling in delight.

Zephrena sat alone in the torch-lit throne room. Then she rose and moved to a black bell-pull. Her slender, jewelled hand reached up and pulled the velvet cord.

At the summons, the kraul servants filtered in, slinking to the sides of the room, ready for orders. Ready to watch this long-awaited sight, with muted murmurs and chucklings.

Zephrena rose and said, "Reveal the kridrogh!"

There was a ripple of terror amongst the krauls, as one of them pulled an iron lever in the wall. Instantly there was a grinding sound and the floor of the throne room opened to reveal a huge, water-filled pit. In the pit lay the kridrogh, vast and bloated, a sickly yellow-green colour, its tentacles gently winnowing the water in which it lay, searching for its next meal.

The kraul guards entered now. Between them, in chains, was the old priest of the Mystic Unicorn, Zanto Elaris. He need not have been chained, for he seemed to come quite willingly. He was calm and serene.

"Bring the priest here," ordered Zephrena, "and let him see his fate."

The kraul guards pushed him forward, till he stood at the edge of the pit. He looked down at the hideous creature, but his expression did not change, except perhaps for a look of pity that the monster was captive, when he should have had the freedom of the open sea.

Zephrena watched him closely.

"Well, Priest of the Mystic Unicorn," she spoke the words with scorn. "Now you see my power and the fate that awaits you if you do not agree to use your powers to help me. Come," her voice took on the coaxing tones of reason. "I offer to make you a ruler by my side, if you will but lend your great powers to my scheme. You and I will share Zar-Yashtoreth between us. On the other hand, if you refuse to assist me... Well...the kridrogh must be fed...and what other use shall I have for you?"

"Sorceress of Xegeron," the old man's voice was gentle, but had great strength and showed how powerful he was. "My powers were given to me by Shara Sorian to use in the service of the light. You ask me to betray these powers, but I will not do so. Even if I wished to, it would be of no use to you, for, as soon as I tried to serve you, my powers would vanish. But I would never put my strength at your disposal, under any circumstances. You have tricked Lord Aragal's soul from his body. Now you have me in your clutches. Nevertheless, you shall not succeed. Zar-Yashtoreth will never fall to you."

Zephrena's face darkened with anger. "Insolent old man! You dare to say this to me! You think, no doubt, that that wretched band of travellers that follow Kestrel Moonblade can defeat me?" She laughed and the krauls chuckled in echo. "They will perish long before they reach Xegeron. Already they are beginning to destroy each other. You shall die knowing this truth, Zanto Elaris!"

"Truth can never come from your lips, Zephrena of Xegeron," replied Zanto Elaris. "It may be that Kestrel Moonblade fails in her mission, and I should be sad beyond all measure if she did, but others will follow her and you will be defeated at the last."

"Enough!" Zephrena cried "Let the kridrogh be fed!"

The kraul guards pushed the old man, who staggered and fell. "Shara Sorian, receive me into your light!" he cried, as the monster's tentacles reached out and crushed him, instantly.

Zephrena's face took on a look of triumph. The krauls, who had witnessed the scene in silence and fascinated horror, now broke into a cacophony of malicious glee. Then Zephrena spoke the words that opened the Globe of Souls so that she could imprison yet another soul of light. No need to fear saying the words of power before the krauls. They would never remember the spell, or even understand what she was doing.

"*Lour ab volenzur*!" she said, and the great black globe opened and sucked its new victim into its never satisfied darkness.

Zephrena pointed a long finger at the kridrogh. "Cover the beast!" she commanded. The kraul keeper of the kridrogh pulled the iron lever in the wall and the water filled pit was covered over. With a wave of her hand, the sorceress dismissed the krauls.

Alone, amongst the shadows and the sickly pale candlelight, Zephrena stood, victorious. "And now," she murmured to herself, "I shall turn my attention to Kestrel Moonblade and her friends."

Chapter Twenty-one

The Mists of the Faldras

Giles de Sorell had taken the last watch, and, as the dawn broke, he watched Kestrel awake. She bathed in the stream that ran through the field in which they had camped for the night. Purified, she now began her meditation and prayers.

Giles watched her with unbounded admiration. She was everything that chivalry could strive for. Courageous, gentle, good, kind and beautiful. It was too bad that he was the only one she could rely on in her quest. For on whom else could she depend? A scatterbrained old wizard. A frivolous elf minstrel. A common thief from the gutters of Kironin. A monster from the most evil race ever to darken Zar-Yashtoreth. And that conceited old has-been of a dwarf who couldn't even swing an axe straight.

But it didn't matter. He, Giles de Sorell, would be there to defend Lady Kestrel in danger, cheer her in sadness and support her every step of the way. He would shed his last drop of blood for her. To die for her would be an honour and a privilege. And she needed his help. She was so good that she could see no evil in others. That was why she allowed that vile dragon-spawn Tanith-Medea to accompany them. Giles was sure she was a spy of Zephrena's. Kestrel had forbidden him to harm her, but he would watch Tanith's every move and protect Kestrel from her.

Kestrel finished her devotions and turned. She saw Giles and smiled at him. Her smile was, for Giles, the rising of the sun.

"Good morning, Giles. I hope you had a quiet watch."

"Yes, I thank you, Lady Kestrel, and I hope your dreams were peaceful."

"Ah, what a glorious day!" came Zakarius's voice. "And where are we going this morning?" He made the journey sound like a pleasant little stroll and a picnic.

Kestrel consulted the scroll. "Today we must cross the Faldras Pass. From there we make for the Port of Kyrd and from there we cross to the island of Xegeron."

"My daughter," said Zakarius, "if we are to cross the Faldras Pass, we should start while the sun is rising. It is beset by mist and many other dangers."

"You are right, Father Zakarius," Kestrel agreed.

At once, everyone gathered up their packs and they left the sunlit fields and made their way towards the Faldras Mountains.

These were not as high nor as barren as the Nagli Mountains, but they were pitted with great holes and caves, reputed to be the homes of monsters. Thick mists descended upon these mountains and the Faldras Pass was the only safe way to cross, but even this was a perilous path.

As they saw the Faldras Mountains looming nearer, all the travellers fell silent, under the shadow of their menace. As they began to climb the foothills, they could hear the eerie singing of the wind and feel the damp mists clinging round them, like clammy hands.

Tanith began to shiver and her steps slowed. Used to the steamy heat of a tropical land, she felt the cold more than any of them. Her very blood seemed to freeze within her.

"Here," said Kestrel, "put your blanket round you." She took Tanith's blanket from her pack and was concerned because Tanith did not seem to notice. She wrapped the blanket round her like a shawl and then added her own, but it had little effect.

Lindor played and sang as they went and her music seemed to ease their journey, and even disperse the mist a little. Even in this desolate and cold place her steps were light and she walked with ease.

Torvic muttered about the Elvish racket as he marched stoically on, ignoring the cold and the clutching mist, but, for the others, Lindor's music and singing lightened their hearts and gave them courage as they walked.

As they continued, the mist grew damper, colder and thicker. It became more clammy and more clinging. There is evil magic in this mist, thought Kestrel, though she said nothing, for fear of disheartening the others. In a little while, however, Zakarius said to her.

"My daughter, do you not feel that the mist has something strange about it? It does not feel like natural mist to me."

"That is just what I have been thinking, myself," Kestrel replied. "I believe it has been sent by Zephrena. I often get the feeling she is watching us."

At that moment, Tanith, overcome by the cold, collapsed and lay unconscious upon the rocky path.

Lindor and Droco knelt down beside her, put their blankets over her and gently rubbed her hands to get them warm. "She's frozen," Lindor said "Feel her face, Lady Kestrel, it's like ice."

"Her hands too," said Droco. "And she's gone so pale."

Tanith's skin, usually a glowing emerald green, had a sickly yellowish tinge.

Kestrel searched her pouches and found a bottle of golden liquid, which she put between Tanith's lips. Tanith's eyelids fluttered. She moaned and then lay still again.

"Will she be all right, Lady Kestrel?" asked Droco.

"She might if only we could get her warm," Kestrel said, "But there is no way to kindle a fire, unless I use magic, and even if I did, I fear it would have little effect in this dampness, and may even make our presence known to evil things."

The mist was beginning to grow thicker and darker, blotting out everything. Tanith lay quite still. Torvic muttered inaudibly at the delay. Giles was less reticent.

"Are we to be hindered on our quest by this creature? Why not leave her here and go on without her?"

Kestrel was too busy trying to restore Tanith to consciousness to hear this remark. Zakarius, however, remonstrated gently.

"My son, that was not well spoken. Surely the Knights of the Falcon are pledged to help those in distress."

"And so we are, Father," Giles replied. "But we are also pledged to destroy the dragon race and cleanse Zar-Yashtoreth of their evil."

"I have found no evil in Tanith," Zakarius told him. "If anything, she is naïve and innocent."

Another one, Giles thought, bewitched by her spell, and not seeing what she truly is. Aloud he said, "But she is all but dead and we must go on. There is no more we can do for her."

"Oh, very noble and high minded, I'm sure," said Droco. "Very honourable."

"What would a common thief from the gutter know of honour," replied Giles, scornfully.

This was too much even for Droco's good nature. His professional pride was injured, and he replied, indignantly, "I am no common thief from the gutter! Zirax Busko's band is the elite. I may not wear a sword, but at least I wouldn't leave one of my companions to freeze to death."

Torvic has been sitting on a boulder of rock all this time, morose and still as if he were stone himself. Now he rose, his face dark with annoyance.

"By Thorgrist, are we to sit here all day arguing over that little green-skinned squin? Lady Kestrel, what do you say?"

"We can't leave her!" Lindor cried, in anguish. "That would be a heartless thing to do!"

"We shall not proceed without Tanith," Kestrel said, and her voice, for all its gentleness, held such a note of determination, that no more was said, though Giles's eyes were troubled.

"I once knew a spell that could warm the air," Zakarius said, mournfully, "but I've forgotten it."

Kestrel laid a hand upon his arm, "Father Zakarius, can you not try to remember it?"

Zakarius shook his head sadly. "I have been trying ever since this mist arose, but it's gone. Quite gone. Ah, my poor memory!"

For a while they sat helplessly on the rocks around Tanith's unconscious form. Lindor strummed softly and sang in Elvish, her voice, and the qu'enga's sweet melody sounded strange and eerie, coming from the white mist.

"Skad it, minstrel!" Torvic grumbled. "Here we are, stuck in this blagging mist and all you can do is twang that thing and squawk!"

"Of all the ungracious, miserable, soulless—" Lindor began, but Zakarius cut in, suddenly.

"No! No! Keep playing, and singing too, Lindor. You are awakening my memory! Your music has true magic in it. Don't stop."

"With pleasure," Lindor replied, "Nice to know someone appreciates my music." And, with a mischievous smile at Torvic, she played on. The silver notes sounding clear and pure as they cut though the clammy grey mist.

The old wizard sat, concentrating deeply, while the mist curled and wisped and danced around them, blotting out all the landscape before them and behind them and beneath them. He sat with his eyes closed, unmoving, as if he were trying to drag the missing spell back into his memory by very stillness. And all the time, the elfin melody laughed and sang and called, as if it, too, were pulling at the old man's memory.

Suddenly Zakarius rose to his feet. "I have it! The music recalled it to me!"

He raised his staff and chanted:

Asanari tol gerion,
Asamari tol erion
Aia chan aia
Ouela shar lerion!"

At once the chill died out of the air. Then there was a pleasant warmth, which increased until the heat became quite intense. Tanith's eyelids fluttered and at last she stirred, stretched, luxuriously, and then sat up.

Apparently, she believed she had just woken up in the morning, for she began greeting them all by name and wishing them a happy day, as was the dragon custom, except for Giles, whom she ignored. Then she became puzzled at her surroundings.

"Where are we? What has happened?" she asked.

"You were overcome with the cold and the mist," Kestrel explained. "But Father Zakarius, with Lindor's help, has cast a spell to warm the air."

"I thank you," Tanith replied. "You have saved my life. I am quite well now."

"So we can go on," Kestrel was relieved.

"But which way do we go?" asked Droco. "The air is warm, but the mist is still here."

"I'll walk ahead and guide you," Giles volunteered.

"And how will you do that, you stupid twag?" snapped Torvic. "Do you have eyes that can pierce the mist?"

"I shall find a way, dwarfling," replied Giles. "I fear no mist, even if you do."

Torvic's face grew dark. "Never tell me that I fear," he said in a voice so threatening, that all stared at him. "I am no coward!"

"Neither of you will go through the mist alone," commanded Kestrel. "You will be no use to us if you fall over a precipice. I will try to disperse the mist by magic, for I believe it is caused by magic. By Zephrena's evil sorcery."

"Oho! So the dark sorceress is up to her tricks again," an enormous voice came through the mist, startling them all. "I thought as much."

An enormous red dragon appeared before them. Tanith ran to him.

"*Ushai!*" she cried in delight. "*Esquai Tanith-Medea Shirkalinzarin, thelada vri Morgana-Semiramis Shirakalinzarin, kjar maierenda Shirak-Shagreet Talahindra. Nirandis levan ekri vinalis kahn.*"

The red dragon folded his wings round her.

"*Ushai! Elin Tanith-Medea. Esqai Glautur-Meriog Talahindra, Thelis Favarona-Fuji Talahindra kjan maierenda Uzalaon-Palassai.*"

For a while they conversed in the dragon tongue and Giles grew uneasy.

"Lady Kestrel, this evil creature certainly serves the dark sorceress."

"What do you say, you vile armoured murderer? That I serve the sorceress Zephrena?"

He sprang forward and with a blow of his powerful tail, sent Giles sprawling down the mountainside. Tanith clapped her hands in delight and laughed. She spoke again in the dragon tongue and again they heard the name Iliac and Giles's own name spoken. The dragon's bright scales darkened in anger. Kestrel was relieved to see Giles return, shaken and furious, but, apparently, unhurt. He drew his sword.

"Please let there be no bloodshed," Kestrel said. "We seek to destroy the dark sorceress and we must cross these mountains. But the mist is hindering us."

"I am Glautur-Meriog Talahindra" replied the dragon. "I am the guardian of the pass, here to help all who follow the paths of light. I do not know why you have with you one of the most vicious of all the vicious armoured ones. One who has caused so much misery to our people. But you, Kestrel Moonblade, are known to us as a dragon friend and you have Tanith with you, who is one of our own people. So I will help you. We can wait for vengeance on you, Giles de Sorell. We are a patient race. But now to disperse the mist. Zephrena must fear you greatly to send her powers so far."

The dragon took a deep breath and then shot forth flames of bright fire. Again and again he breathed fire. Tanith exclaimed in delight and encouragement. The other travellers took cover behind a rock.

"He means to destroy us, my lady," said Giles

"I mean to destroy this mist, you ignorant troll," cried Glautur-Meriog. And, sure enough, the mist seemed to shrivel before the flames. For some time, a battle raged between the mist, trying to return, and the dragon's fire. But, at last, the mist could no longer withstand the brightness and heat. It disappeared, leaving only a few puny wisps, and then these, too, faded and died.

"Uncle Glautur-Meriog, that was truly wonderful," cried Tanith. "I have heard tales of your powers, but to witness them is a privilege I shall always treasure!"

"Tush! Tush!" A mere bagatelle," smiled the dragon. "You are too generous in your praise, my little quodling."

"I must agree with Tanith," cried Kestrel. "We can never thank you enough."

"I am happy to serve you in your quest," replied the great dragon. "Zephrena has captured one of our people and keeps her prisoner. We will not rest until she is free and Zephrena is destroyed. No dragon ever forgets a kindness or a wrong, as your murdering companion will discover." He shot a glance at Giles. "But now, my friends, your way is clear and there is enough power and strength of magic to keep it clear till you have passed."

"Frazz me!" cried Droco. "Look at that sunshine, and look at that view!"

The mist had gone. The sky was clear and blue, and in the sunshine, the Faldras Mountains were dazzling in their beauty. Their slopes were green, nourished by the constant dampness and they were covered in flowers of the most brilliant hues. From the rocks, huge white waterfalls dropped their foaming strength.

Kestrel thanked the red dragon once more and Tanith flung her arms round his neck and clung to him, weeping, and Glautur-Meriog enfolded her in his scarlet wings.

"Oh dear," said Zakarius, "we will have this sadness at parting again."

But Glautur-Meriog spoke to her, crooningly, in the dragon tongue, and, with a huge claw, gently stroked Tanith's hair, and then they parted and Tanith joined the others, though not without several rather tearful looks back.

"It is very difficult to leave any of my dear people," Tanith confided to Kestrel, "but I am getting very brave, am I not?"

"Indeed you are," replied Kestrel. "And I cannot thank you enough for coming with us. I doubt if your illustrious uncle would have been so willing to help us, if you had not been one of our party."

Tanith glowed. Then suddenly flung her arms round Kestrel and kissed her.

"You have been so kind to me," she said, "and no dragon ever forgets a kindness or a wrong."

For a while they walked along the mountain path in the brilliant sunshine. Lindor was transported with joy, and even Torvic seemed contented, but their contentment was short-lived.

There was a sudden screeching and the air was filled with clapping wings. A flock of grazzard swooped on the travellers, their toothed beaks snapping and clattering, their claws slashing as they dived and rose.

Kestrel drew her sword and slashed at the monsters. Giles was beside her in a moment, hacking and slicing at the grey wings and undersides. Torvic uttered a blood-curdling war-cry and charged at the grazzard with his great double-axe.

Zakarius chanted magic spells, which turned one grazzard into a beautiful iridescent kula bird, one into a cloud and one into a tiny winged insect.

Tanith used her stone spell on any grazzard that was clear of the travellers and soon the ground was littered with ugly statues. However, those that swooped over them could not be turned to stone, for a stone grazzard falling on top of them would be as dangerous as the live things. However, she used her claws to good effect, whenever they swooped low.

Kestrel used her staff to shrivel the monsters and when her magic drained her, resorted to her sword, while Droco used his wonderful knife, and watched it dispatch grazzard after grazzard.

But in the end, it was Lindor's music that did the trick. She plucked the strings of the qu'enga and sang her magic. The grazzard screamed as if in pain and became paler and paler and more and more transparent, until they were no more than wisps of cloud, floating and dissolving in the sky.

As the travellers stood, gazing upwards in amazement and congratulating Lindor, a huge shadow spread over them. An enormous grutsk with a vast wingspan passed overhead, and riding it was a dark figure, whose hair streamed in the wind of its flight. The figure pointed a finger at them, and began to chant words in a strange tongue. Kestrel held her staff aloft and cried, "*Azal lai cha'ran!*" The figure stopped chanting and vanished from sight, screaming curses as it went.

"Was that Zephrena?" asked Lindor.

Kestrel nodded. "I'm afraid so, and she chanted an evil and ancient curse to hinder our travels. She must be growing afraid of us if she has left her tower and tried to confront us."

"Well, that's good, isn't it, my lady?" said Droco. "Shows she treats us seriously."

"At this stage of our journey, I would prefer her to fear us less," Kestrel replied. "It is now no longer safe to travel across these mountains."

"I've been thinking," said Torvic, at length.

"Frazz me! Thinking!" cried Droco in mock amazement.

Torvic glared at him and Kestrel shot him an appealing look. Torvic continued. "We could travel beneath the mountains. There are many caves and there are many strong tunnels through the mountains, carved by dwarfish hands." His voice took on a note of pride.

"Why, Torvic!" cried Kestrel. "What a wonderful idea. "Tell us about these tunnels. If the dwarfs made them, they are sure to be excellent."

"Don't encourage him, my lady," murmured Droco.

"My people made many underground roads for escape and ambush, during the Purging Wars," Torvic explained. "They served us well during those dark times, and shall again. We often used the Faldras Mountains. Follow me."

He climbed through a crevice in one of the rocks. No one else would have noticed it. They all followed, though Lindor flinched at the darkness.

Kestrel drew several torches and a tinder box from her pouch, and, once within the mountain, she gave torches out among the travellers, lighting them from the tinder spark. The light leapt up, showing a wide pathway and smooth walls. The travellers stared in amazement and Torvic said, somewhat smugly, "Now that's building for you. Not like your flimsy flamsy elven cities."

"Ah, but elven cities are far more beautiful," replied Lindor.

"Beautiful! Beautiful!" exploded Torvic "There's nothing more beautiful than the work of Dwarfen hands. And our work lasts!"

"And so does ours," Lindor returned.

The passages widened and the ceilings grew higher. They were indeed marvels of architecture. They twisted and turned, but seemed to lead deeper into the mountains without promising any way out. Lindor began to grow restless and uneasy away from the light and Torvic kept muttering about passages being blocked.

"How the frazz do we get out of this place?" After an hour's travelling, Droco voiced all their thoughts. "We've been walking these tunnels for ages."

"We do appear to be somewhat lost," agreed Zakarius.

"Your dwarf tunnels don't seem to be leading anywhere," said Droco. "They seem to be as frazzing useless as some dwarfs I know."

Torvic began to raise his axe, his beard bristling, when Kestrel, to her utmost relief saw some runes carved in the walls.

"Look!" she cried, thankful to find a way of diverting the quarrel, or worse, that would surely have broken out. "There are some runes here. I know many runes, but I cannot decipher these. I'm sure they will tell us which path to follow, to find the way out. What do they say, Torvic?"

Torvic, proud to be able to help Kestrel, but trying not to show it, peered at the tunnel wall by the light of Kestrel's torch. For a moment he stared, frowning, at the symbols carved into the rock, then he turned away in disgust. "These aren't dwarf runes," he said, indignantly. "No dwarf ever scrawled like that."

"I always knew you couldn't read," quipped Droco, moving nimbly out of the way, as Torvic turned on him like a thunderbolt.

A cry of delighted astonishment came from Tanith, as she looked at the runes.

"That is not a scrawl, Torvic-Shinetop-may-the-glory-of-your-valour-be-renowned," (she spoke this as if it were all part of his name.) "those are dragon runes. It says 'Keep to the left-hand path for seven turnings. These will be marked for you, traveller. Caves of danger are closed with magic'."

"Don't listen to her," warned Giles. "This path will lead to the den of some foul monster and we will be devoured."

"Scum of Kasperus!" replied Tanith. "My people have left these writings for lost travellers, in the generosity of their hearts, even while, no doubt, they were following Neis-Durga's trail. You should give thanks for their goodness. Look here they have written it again in the common tongue so all may understand."

"Monster. I know the treachery of your people," Giles retorted. "You think to trap us and murder us!"

"Don't be such a twag!" said Droco. "If the dragon people meant to kill us, they could have done it a thousand times over by now."

"They mean to deliver us to the dark sorceress," said Giles.

"Really!" cried Kestrel, "I'm beginning to feel like a nursemaid to a bunch of unruly brats! What with Droco's provocation of Torvic and Tanith's and Giles's age-long feud."

"What is unrulybrats, Lady Kestrel?" asked Tanith, with interest. Kestrel could not refrain from laughing at her innocent question, and the mood was lightened.

"All of you when you brabble, and quarrel and argue."

"I am not brabbling and arguing," said Tanith placidly. "Lady Kestrel," cried Giles. "I would not cause you pain for all of Zar-Yashtoreth, I seek only to protect you."

"I know you do, Giles. But you must see that we owe a debt of gratitude to the dragon-folk for their help."

Tanith shot Giles a venomous glance, and then spoke to Kestrel.

"There are the runes signifying the word 'path' and here it is repeated in the common tongue. We must follow these and they will lead us through the mountains."

"Then blessings on the dragon-folk, who made these signs," cried Kestrel, "or we should have been lost in these mountains for ever."

Torvic growled, "We'd have got through, if the dragon-folk hadn't blocked half the skadding tunnels. I know the way well."

"Of course you do," Kestrel placated him. "And you have saved us from great danger by bringing us this way."

"The tunnels are only blocked to save travellers from wandering off down a wrong track, Torvic-Shinetop-may-the-glory-of-your-valour-be-renowned," explained Tanith, politely.

But Torvic only snorted, "It wasn't a wrong track!"

"But it had grown dangerous over the years, no doubt"

"I am sure you are both right," smiled Zakarius.

They followed the path marked by the dragon signs. It twisted and looped, ever losing itself amongst other paths. Giles grew more and more convinced that Tanith was leading them into a trap and Torvic muttered into his beard about the dragon people ruining perfectly good dwarf tunnels with their interference. But, sure enough, many tunnels that had once been strong and safe had now fallen in, due to evil magic, or were filled with dangerous waters, or rushing rivers that could sweep you away, and which affected even dwarf building.

By keeping to the marked paths, they, eventually, reached the end of the Faldras Mountains and emerged into the gentle evening light.

Chapter Twenty-two

Grob the Troll

In the Dark Tower, Zephrena watched the travellers' progress in her scrying glass.

"These adventurers travel too swiftly for my liking," she said. "Each time I place an impediment in their way, they overcome it. They are stronger than I thought. They have almost reached the Port of Kyrd. I must increase my efforts to repel them."

She summoned Bragazh Gourbag. The kraul captain bowed before her.

"You sent for me, Your Greatness."

"The adventurers who seek to destroy me are making for the Port of Kyrd," Zephrena said. "Make sure they never reach it."

"It will be a pleasure, Oh Great One. Shall I take the gorkraks, or just ordinary troops?"

"Neither will be necessary," replied Zephrena. "The troll, Grob, lives on the road to Kyrd. Go and visit him and tell him what choice morsels await him, and to be ready when they arrive. He is stupid, as are all his kind, but he will understand that."

Bragazh Gourbag's face broke into a vicious grin. "I'll wager he will, Your Greatness. He'll make short work of Kestrel Moonblade and her companions. He'll appreciate such delicacies. Oh yes!"

"Quite so," said Zephrena, acidly. "Now be off with you and acquaint him with his good luck."

"Very good, Oh Great One." Bowing, Bragazh Gourbag left the room. Zephrena watched him retreat, and, when the door closed behind him, she turned, once more, to the scrying glass.

The unsuspecting travellers were full of hope as they moved towards Kyrd.

"Hope and dream, you foolish creatures!" cried Zephrena. "Everything is going well for you. You have no inkling how soon your end will be upon you!"

Bragazh Gourbag was as good as his word. He painted for Grob a picture of the succulent gastronomic delights approaching him that day, and now the troll sat watching, perched high on a rock overlooking the road that wound its way down to Kyrd. At last his patience was rewarded. The troupe of travellers appeared on the chalky road. Grob grunted with appreciation.

"Ah! Grob's breakfast has come. Very good."

With amazing speed and agility for one so huge and unwieldy, the troll bounded down the rocky hillside to the road and stood waiting for the travellers.

As they approached the bend round which he waited, Kestrel stopped.

"I sense danger," she said, "and it is very close."

"I sense it too," Zakarius agreed.

Lindor and Tanith nodded. They, too, felt a sense of darkness.

Giles drew his sword. "My lady, whatever it is, I shall protect you from it."

Torvic raised a sour eyebrow. He said nothing. Actions spoke louder than flowery words, but his great double-axe, Valdur, was ready.

"You are both brave warriors," Kestrel told them, "and I cannot afford to lose you, so let's proceed with caution."

"Perhaps we could go another way," suggested Droco. He looked at Torvic's and Giles's scornful expressions and shrugged. "We're not all raving lunatics who live for battle."

"No," Torvic returned, "Some of us are wretched little gutter shrikes, more at home with their fingers in other folks' purses."

Droco grinned, not at all put out. "That takes courage too."

"I'm afraid this is the only road to Kyrd," said Kestrel.

"It would be!" Droco's fingers closed round the magic knife in his pocket. Thank Zabris he had that.

They moved, slowly, round the bend of the road and stopped in horror.

"Just what we need," Droco muttered. "A frazzing troll. Look at the size of the ugly monster."

Grob peered down at them, a hideous grin on his face, his tow-coloured hair and beard bristling like a thorn bush.

"What's here?" he grunted. "Grob's breakfast. Yes! Good! Good!"

Kestrel stepped forward, holding out her staff. "In the name of Shara Sorian, depart, and let us pass."

Giles would not see Kestrel place herself in danger. In a moment he was beside her, sword drawn. "Let us pass, monster, or I'll destroy you."

Grob gave a coarse, raucous laugh.

"Little things destroy Grob? Very funny! Grob likes a joke!"

Tanith gave a serpent-like hiss and tried her stone spell. "*Zan esk maranaza!*"

To everyone's amazement, especially Tanith's, it didn't work. Grob remained flesh and blood.

"Hmm! Now that is very interesting," remarked Zakarius.

Grob gave an evil leering grin. "Grob's breakfast very lively. Talks a lot."

Droco decided that his knife could no longer be kept a secret and prepared to throw it, but before he could do so, Torvic, who had only been waiting for the best moment to strike, rushed in like a whirlwind, his axe raised above his head. Giles moved in too, his sword drawn, but Torvic pushed him aside.

"Out of the way, tin-pot!"

A bloodthirsty battle then ensued. Grob, though slow-witted and slow moving, was quicker than he looked, when he needed to be. He was also craftier than he appeared.

Little by little, he led the others on towards his cave, which had a portcullis built into it. At present the portcullis was raised and not visible.

Torvic made a rush at Grob, who stepped aside at the last minute. Torvic overshot, and found himself in the cave. Grob gave a bellow of laughter, and, in a flash, had swept all of them into the cave, and brought down the portcullis, so that they were trapped.

"Grob's breakfast safe!" he growled, with satisfaction. "I get the pan."

He set off chuckling. Torvic was in a towering rage. He hacked, vainly, at the portcullis, with his double-axe.

"You quibbing skag of a troll!" he shouted. "I'll have you. Just see if I don't."

"Oh dear, oh dear," sighed Zakarius. "Here's a fine brace of trill, and no mistake. Kestrel, my daughter, do you know any spell to release us?"

Kestrel considered. "I would need my staff, but I dropped it as he swept us into the cave."

"And I my qu'enga," said Lindor. "Or I could soon open the portcullis."

They could see the staff and the qu'enga lying, tantalisingly just out of each on the rocks.

Tanith, having explored the cave, carefully, and realised there was no way out, curled up in a corner of the cave, with a heart-rending whimper.

Droco smiled to himself. "What's all the fuss about? I'll have us out of here in a twizz."

He went to the grim iron gates, drew from his pouch a metal instrument and inserted it into the lock. For a moment a look of intense concentration crossed his face. Kestrel thought she had never seen him look so solemn. The next minute, his usual cheery grin broke through.

"Got you, my little beauty. What a nice obliging one you are."

And, with a flourish, he pushed the portcullis and it flew upward, as if on wings.

Tanith's eyes were wide with wonder. She rose to her feet. "You have magic in your fingers, Droco!"

"That's right," Droco agreed. "It *is* a sort of magic."

Zakarius laughed "I never thought I'd live to be thankful for your thief's tricks. Truly, there is a place for everyone as the Cloud Father tells us."

They emerged in delight and Kestrel retrieved her staff, and Lindor her qu'enga. The next instant, their joy was halted abruptly. Grob had returned with the pan.

When he saw the travellers free, he let out a horrifying cry of rage. Giles and Kestrel drew their swords, but Torvic rushed forward.

"Stand back, everyone. This one's mine!"

Once more he assailed Grob with his double-axe and the battle between them continued, as if it had never broken off, but now with redoubled vigour.

Torvic hacked and swung and slashed with his double-axe. While at the same time, he dodged the swinging, battering club, wielded by Grob. His skill and ferocity were truly amazing.

He snarled like a wild beast, and his single eye flashed venomous hatred, as he brought down his axe with deadly force.

Grob, though three times Torvic's height, was slower moving, and slower thinking. But he was cunning, and his great strength prevented him from being an easy conquest. He gave Torvic some ugly blows with his club, before Torvic moved, with lightning speed, and struck off the troll's head with a single stroke. It lay on the roadside, the glaring eyes round with surprise, blood staining the dust.

Torvic held his axe aloft with one hand and Grob's head with the other, as a token of victory. On his face was the nearest thing to a smile that anyone had ever seen. Then he lowered his axe and tossed the head aside.

Kestrel took his hands in hers, bloodstained though they were.

"Torvic Shinetop, that was an act of great heroism."

Torvic masked the pride he felt at this praise, in his usual ungracious manner.

"Name of the abyss! Lot of fuss about nothing. For the love of Askolan, let's find the skadding road to Kyrd."

Kestrel saw through his rudeness and hid a smile.

"Very well," she said. "I know you are not one for many words, but we all feel gratitude to you, Torvic, and to you too, Droco. Without your help we should have ended up on Grob's breakfast plate.

Giles felt a pang of jealousy. "I could have finished him quicker."

Torvic did not deign to reply, but merely uttered one of his snorts.

He's a dreadful crosspatch, thought Zakarius. But very brave. Aloud he said, "Without you and Droco we should have had no hope of survival, unless the sun had brightened. That would have finished off our friend Grob. No troll can look into the sunlight and live."

Something occurred to Lindor, and she spoke without thinking.

"But the sunlight doesn't affect you adversely, does it, Tanith. In fact you thrive on it. It must be your elven blood that protects you."

There was a deathly silence. Lindor stopped abruptly as she realised what she had just said. That Tanith had troll blood. Most would have been mortally offended, but it meant nothing at all to Tanith. She had not mentioned that her blood mother was the Troll Queen, not because she wished to hide it, but because she never gave it a thought. She was a dragon and that was all. Now she simply turned a surprised look at Lindor, and cried, "How did you know that?"

"I only realised just now when your spell didn't work on that troll."

And Zakarius added, "The only time magic doesn't work on a troll is when it is cast by one with troll blood."

"A troll by birth and a dragon by rearing! Delightful!" murmured Giles.

Kestrel, however, put her arm round Tanith and said, gently, "If you wish to tell us your story, Tanith, we will hear it. If not, it is your secret."

"Of course I will tell you," Tanith cried in surprise. "It is a story discovered by Lady Hochma-Sofia, the Dragon of Wisdom. All my people know it. Why should my friends not hear it too?"

She settled down upon a rock, and they all gathered round to listen with interest.

Tanith told her tale with charm and simplicity. Unlike Torvic, she felt no shame at her lineage, only wonder and delight at her good fortune, that had led her to her adoptive family.

"My blood mother was Mugdrug, the Troll Queen of Oglaf; a vile and fearful creature, cruel and hideous. After the terrible Purging Wars in that land, she took prisoner a young elf minstrel, like you, Lindor. He had accidentally strayed into Oglaf. She would have tortured him to death, but he sang words that charmed her, and she took him, secretly, as her consort.

"One night, she found that, somehow, he had fled, leaving her with child. That child was me. I looked more elven than troll, Mother Tiamat be praised, and Mugdrug, in disgust, threw me into the River Kvar. But praise to Mother Tiamat, who preserved me, at that moment, a grutsk swooped down, and took me up in its claws, meaning to devour me. Again the Great Mother protected me. The grutsk was shot by a hunter's bow, and, as it died, it dropped me back into the river. I was washed into the nest of my beloved mother, Morgana-Semiramis, and my dearest Father, Shirak-Shagreet. I lay amongst their eggs and they took me as their daughter – their gift child – and have loved and cared for me ever since."

They all listened intently to this tale, especially Lindor, whose amazement grew as Tanith's story unfolded. When Tanith had finished, Lindor spoke.

"Then we are kin, you and I. We are half sisters. The elf minstrel you spoke of was my father. He told us, many times, of his escape from the Troll Queen of Oglaf, though he did not know she was with child. But we always took it for one of his tall stories."

"So," Tanith said slowly, "your blood father and my blood father are the same?"

"The same," replied Lindor, taking Tanith's hands. And with that they fell into each other's arms and embraced long, while the rest of the party stared in utter disbelief.

"Frazz me!" cried Droco, as Lindor and Tanith drew apart, to talk and to revel in their new joy. "Would you ever think that?"

Giles looked scornful. "My sympathy goes to the elf minstrel, for she is a pleasant companion and brings happiness with her music and song. She deserves better than to be related to that monster."

"Who asked for your opinion, you stuck up quib?" retorted Droco.

"Lindor is happy to claim Tanith as a half-sister," put in Zakarius, gently.

Giles turned to Torvic. "Well, Shinetop, you're supposed to be a trollslayer..."

He got no further, for Torvic at once interrupted. "You think I'd waste my time on that?" He jerked his thumb in Tanith's direction. "I leave that to you. What honour would there be in slaying a silly little quppet like her, unskilled as she is in the arts of war."

"She is not so unskilled as you think," retorted Giles, who still bore the marks of Tanith's teeth and claws from their battle.

"Besides," Zakarius said, "she is only half-troll, and has no allegiance to the troll race. Why, I've heard her use the word 'troll' as an insult. She is of the dragon people despite her outward shape, as she always says."

"Giles does not mean it, I'm sure," said Kestrel. "It was just a fleeting thought, no doubt sent by Zephrena herself."

"Yes, indeed, Lady Kestrel," said Giles, though he was not at all sure that it was not his own thought. "I know we must all reach Xegeron alive, if we are to defeat the Dark Sorceress."

After that, he thought, maybe he could kill Tanith. After that, however, every dragon of Zar-Yashtoreth would want to spill his blood in revenge for Iliac. He would ask Sir Jules de Mauriac, the Golden Falcon, what to do when he returned to Eloskan. If he returned.

Lindor and Tanith, meanwhile, were blissfully unaware of this conversation or Giles's dark thoughts. They sat apart from the others, and shared one another's pasts.

Chapter Twenty-three

The Port of Kyrd

The Port of Kyrd was small and picturesque. Narrow cobbled streets twisted steeply. The harbour was crowded with fishing boats and larger vessels, riding peacefully at anchor in the moonlight. When Kestrel and the others arrived, the streets and harbour were almost deserted. The street lamps were already lit, but no lights shone in the bow windows of the little cottages. The town slept under lamplight and moonlight.

The travellers walked down the silent streets, trying to be as silent as the streets themselves. They were thankful that there were no town gates or guards. Kestrel supposed this was because guarding a small coastal town was a useless endeavour. Anyone really determined could slip in by sea. She had no wish to let anyone know their mission. They were too close to Xegeron, now, to speak of it. Zephrena could have spies anywhere and everywhere. In fact, Kestrel felt sure that Zephrena possessed a scrying glass. She felt more and more that they were being watched. Zakarius, Lindor and Tanith had also mentioned this feeling, and though neither Droco, Giles nor Torvic were magic users, their own skills made them sensitive to such things, and they, too, had spoken of the sensation that eyes were upon them.

The harbour was lit by many lamps and Droco suddenly stopped dead and pointed to some elegant ships, whose purple and gold sails showed clearly in the lamplight.

"I don't like the look of that. Those are Islarian merchant vessels. I'd rather not be anywhere near any quagging Islarians. Spawn of krauls. I'll cut my throat before I go back to the galleys."

"Proper place for you," snapped Torvic, but Tanith laid her hand, protectively, on Droco's arm.

"If they try to harm you, I'll turn them to stone. You have shown me great kindness, and no dragon ever forgets a kindness or a wrong."

Droco felt his heartbeats slowing down and the blood returning to his cheeks at the thought that he had Tanith's friendship. And with it, of course, the friendship of all the dragon people.

"Bless you, Tanith. You're a jewel," he said.

"Let us hope things won't come to that," said Zakarius.

As they reached the foot of a steep, winding, cobbled hill, they came to The Blue Mermaid Inn, a tall, narrow, timbered building. Its windows were darkened, and its huge wooden door was firmly shut. When Kestrel tried it, it was, clearly, bolted.

"I can get that open," offered Droco.

"I am sure you can," replied Kestrel, "but perhaps we had better use the bell rope, though I hardly like to disturb them at this hour."

She pulled the bell rope and they all waited. After a long time, a serving girl answered the door, in rag curlers and nightdress. She held a candle in one hand, and was rubbing her eyes with the other.

"Yes?" she asked sleepily.

"We are sorry to have disturbed your rest," said Kestrel, sympathetically, but we have travelled far and need food and shelter."

"I'll call Madam Zhal," replied the girl, and then in a shrill, powerful voice, bawled up the stairs

"Customers, Madam Zhal!"

There was a pause, during which the serving girl disappeared, leaving the travellers on the doorstep. After a while, Madam Zhal appeared. She was a tall, handsome, imposing woman, even in her night attire, and with a large lace mob cap covering her rag curlers. She glared suspiciously at the travellers.

"What do you want at this time of night?"

Kestrel repeated her request for food and shelter. Madam Zhal sniffed and looked more suspicious than ever. At last she spoke, doubtfully.

"Well...I have two rooms, but it'll cost ten silver draskas."

Kestrel hesitated. "So much? I don't believe I have..." She began, but Droco interrupted her, with a flourish.

"Ten silver draskas, madam? No trouble at all. A very reasonable price. Take twelve for your beauty."

Madam Zhal bridled and turned quite pink. "Ooh, you are a cheeky little squin, aren't you? Thank you very much, sir. Come inside all of you. You must be weary."

She bustled inside, beckoning to them to follow. Kestrel dreaded to think from where Droco's silver had come.

When it was Tanith's turn to enter the inn, she stopped, trembling and suspicious.

"What is this place?" she demanded.

"It is an inn," Lindor explained.

"Inn?" Tanith repeated, puzzled.

"It's like..." Lindor racked her brains for a comparison to something Tanith might understand. "It's...like a cave," she said, at last.

Tanith could not accept this. "I have never seen a cave like this. I think it is a trap. I shall stay outside. She settled herself on the doorstep, looking with deep suspicion at the doorway.

So Lindor took up the qu'enga and began to play and sing.

"The Blue Mermaid Inn
Is warm within,
It sings a welcome
'Come in, come in'
It sings a mermaid tune,
Under the light of the moon."

Tanith, mesmerised by the sweet singing and the music, followed Lindor into the inn, half in a trance.

The Blue Mermaid was, indeed, warm and welcoming. A huge fire was covered, and burning itself out, but still bright and warm, and Madam Zhal led them to a long table beside it. Droco's silver and flattery had put her in a very happy frame of mind and she couldn't do enough for them.

"Please be seated. Your food will be brought in a moment, and your rooms are being prepared.

"Thank you. Most kind," said Kestrel.

Madam Zhal rushed off and the inn was left silent and empty, except for the travellers.

Tanith gazed at the chairs with curiosity and sat on the floor by the fire. Lindor looked concerned. Since she had discovered that she and Tanith were half-sisters, she felt it was important to impart a few social graces to the dragon-maid.

"Tanith," she called, softly, "Would you not prefer to sit on a chair?"

Tanith looked at the chairs again, with interest. She even touched one, cautiously.

"Carven tree stumps," she said, her voice full of wonder.

"Those are chairs, Tanith," Lindor explained, as Tanith seated herself on one.

"I am sitting on a carven tree stump!" she cried in delight. She was fascinated by the chairs. She kept getting up and looking at them, and sitting down again.

"How they will laugh at home," she cried, "when I tell them that I have sat on a carven tree stump, called a chair." She went into peals of laughter and clapped her hands in delight.

Madam Zhal and Livia, the serving maid, bustled in with a dish of hot quill and a tureen of soup, crisp velta bread and two flagons of wine.

The travellers were greatly cheered by this. Kestrel requested water for Tanith instead of wine. She did not want to risk a repetition of the "water of laughter" incident here in public, and draw attention to them all.

Everyone ate and drank in silence, though Tanith had great trouble handling a spoon for the soup. She had never used such a thing in her life. Though no one ate more daintily than she did, she always used her fingers.

They finished their meal and Livia showed them to their rooms. By now everyone was feeling very sleepy. Nonetheless Torvic planted his double axe firmly across his chosen bed, and glared at Droco.

"If you try any of your thieves' tricks this night, I'll cleave your skull."

"And I'll split your heart on my sword, like a juala bird's," Giles echoed.

"By Zabris!" Droco replied, in mock terror. "I shall be afraid to sleep tonight!"

"Come," said Zakarius, who, having finished his devotions to the Cloud Father, was splashing merrily at the washstand, and wringing out his long beard, "let us spend the night peacefully and not talk of cleaving skulls and splitting hearts, or of thieving either."

"Quite right, old man," agreed Droco. "I'm for a peaceful night tonight."

Torvic grunted and laid himself, fully clothed on the bed.

"Don't you even remove your clothes and wash?" Giles was disgusted. "You dwarfs must be a dirty race."

Torvic was up like an arrow.

"Take care how you talk of my people, you tinpot whelp. Just because I don't rush to the washstand first and mince around it like a maiden princess on her bridal night, doesn't mean I don't intend to wash at all."

"By Zabris!" cried Droco. "That's a long speech for you, Shinetop. I didn't know you knew so many words."

"One of these days, thief, I'll skaberate you," Torvic replied, "and leave your carcass for the quarks."

"But not tonight, I hope," said Zakarius. "Let us treat each other with courtesy. For we all follow a path of light, though those paths may differ."

"Certainly," said Giles, without much sincerity, and washed with extreme care.

Droco grinned, "Come on, don't take all night about it. There are others who want to wash, even if our little ray of sunshine here doesn't."

In deference to Zakarius, Giles did not reply, but, with a raised eyebrow, managed to convey extreme surprise that someone like Droco even knew what washing was.

"You take your turn, thief," snarled Torvic, going to the washstand the moment it was free.

"Manners!" said Droco, with mock primness, and then, quoting one of Tanith's axioms, he added, "No more manners than a troll," which always amused him, since Tanith was, herself, half troll by birth.

Torvic ignored this and began to wash off the grime of the journey, taking as little time as possible to demonstrate that he, unlike Giles, washed purely for cleanliness and not for vanity.

Zakarius lay snugly in bed and watched them, amused. Nothing but squibble and squabble, he thought. Why can't folk get along together? And yet, when the time came to meet the Dark Sorceress, they'd fight as one. Close ranks against evil, like the best of friends.

Zakarius felt his eyelids grow heavy. Can't imagine why they can't get along better, he thought sleepily. They're the best of fellows, after all. Droco's a scamp, but he has the kindest of hearts, and Torvic Shinetop's a surly blazzard, but he's a good and brave soul, when all's said and done. And kind and generous too, though he'd die before admitting it. And that silly young gallian, Giles, is a good lad too, for all his airs and graces. Courageous and idealistic. And he and the dwarf have a liking and respect for each other under all that growling. Oh yes, indeed. I can see it clearly...silly young twags. When they've grown to my age...was the old wizard's last thought, as he drifted off to sleep.

In the room shared by Kestrel, Tanith and Lindor, the atmosphere was far more peaceful. In fact, Kestrel and Lindor, having finished their devotions, would probably have slept at once, had they not been distracted by Tanith's amazement at the wonders of the room.

It was the mirror that first caught her attention. A large, oval, bronze-framed mirror on the dressing table. Tanith examined her reflection from all angles, put out her hand to pat her reflection, and then withdrew her hand, in surprise, as she met the hard surface of the glass.

Kestrel and Lindor watched her, amused. Tanith turned to them.

"Look!" she cried, in wonder, "a pool of solid waster, standing up on end. What marvels there are here in the Port of Kyrd."

Lindor smiled. "That is called a looking glass, Tanith. It isn't water at all, but glass."

"Strange magic!" Tanith cried and continued to play with the mirror, patting it and laughing with delight.

Lindor turned to Kestrel. "What am I going to do with her, Lady Kestrel? She will cause chaos when I take her home with me to Tilioth. How can I ever teach her all she needs to know?"

"Is that what you intend to do, take her home with you?" Kestrel asked her.

"Of course," Lindor replied. "I couldn't leave my own half-sister living in a dragon's cave. I must take her home. I'll turn her into an elf somehow. It can't be impossible. She is, after all, half-elven."

Kestrel shook her head. "But Lindor, she may not wish to go with you. She is happy where she is. The dragon-folk are her family."

Lindor was undeterred. "That's only because she knows nothing else."

A startled cry from Tanith made them break off their conversation. The dragon-maid stood frozen in the furthest corner of the room, as if she were trying to press through the wall. Her eyes were wide with terror, as she stared at the large four poster bed.

"What is that?" she cried in terror. "Is it a trap?"

Kestrel sighed, wearily. "No Tanith. It is called a bed and it is quite harmless."

Tanith looked disbelieving. "It is like no bed I have ever seen. I shall not sleep there."

"As you please, Tanith," said Kestrel. "But Lindor and I shall be very happy to sleep on it, after all those nights in the open."

Kestrel and Lindor washed and then showed Tanith how to pour water from the jug into the wash bowl. This bowl delighted her.

"What a dear little pool," she cried and spent a long time splashing and playing with the water, as well as washing with great care and thoroughness. Kestrel and Lindor watched, amused as she laughed and frolicked with the water.

"Oh, look at the silver eye of Mother Tiamat in the water!" she cried, seeing the moon's reflection in the bowl, through the window. Mother Tiamat, thank you for this dear little pool and for all the wonders of this very strange place. For chairs," she still rippled with laughter at the word, "for solid water that stands on end…no, for glass," as she remembered the correct word, to Lindor's gratification, "and for dear little pools of water. Keep us safe, dearest Mother from traps and danger. Protect us on our quest and keep me safe from the evil slaughterer of Iliac."

The sweetness and simplicity of her prayers were strangely moving. Lindor found tears in her eyes and Kestrel's heart melted. But it was growing late and it was time for sleep. Kestrel and Lindor climbed into the huge bed and released the bed curtains.

Tanith, seeing the heavy drapes apparently engulfing her friend and her sister, gave a heart-rending scream.

"No, Lindor! Lady Kestrel! I knew it was a trap." She ran to the curtains, and, with a few slashes of her powerful claws, tore the curtains to shreds. They hung, in tatters, and parts of them lay in little heaps on the floor.

"Oh no! Tanith! No!" Kestrel moaned. "How am I going to explain this to Madam Zhal?"

"This is a terrible place!" cried Tanith. "It is full of wicked enchantment. I shall never feel safe near that thing with its suffocating wings. We must escape."

She walked to the wall and began to scan it for an exit. Having no idea how doors worked, she began, once more to panic like a trapped bird, rushing wildly from one side of the room to the other, beating her hands against the walls and giving blood-curdling screeches of terror.

"Hush, Tanith!" said Kestrel, alarmed, lest Tanith should rouse the whole inn. "What is the matter?"

"Look! Look! The walls have closed around us," moaned Tanith. "We are trapped! We cannot get out! We will die here!"

She sank down on the floor in a heap of desolation.

Lindor rose from the bed and opened the door.

"Look, Tanith. Here is the way out. We are not trapped at all.

Tanith's eyes widened at this marvel.

"Wonderful magic!" she cried. "You are a very powerful magician, my sister!"

"It's only a door. Look," she demonstrated the way it opened and shut, and, at last, persuaded Tanith to try it for herself. Tanith was delighted to find that she, too, could work this wonderful magic and spent a long time opening and shutting the door and crying, "Look, Lady Kestrel! Look, my dearest sister! I grow in magic skill. Now I can turn things to stone and back again and I can open and close walls! My family will be so pleased."

"Yes, Tanith. Very good," said Kestrel, gently, as she sank to sleep.

Lindor echoed, "Very skilful, Tanith," and slept too.

Tanith continued to open and shut the door, until she too felt tired. She would not trust the creature with the wings, although the wings now seemed to be useless, after her attack on them, but stretched out on the floor. She left a little gap in the door, just in case her magic was not yet strong enough to open the wall again once it was completely closed.

At last the travellers in both the rooms slept peacefully, and woke refreshed next morning. Kestrel ordered a dish of pezdas and a cup of khal for them all for breakfast.

There were several customers in the inn seated at various tables, eating and drinking. The travellers sat at a long table. Livia brought a steaming dish of crisp pezdas, warning the travellers to take care, as they were very hot.

Each of the travellers used the long serving spoon to take the crisp, light pastries, dripping with honey, but Tanith, who had all but given up on using cutlery, took one, daintily, in her fingers and dropped it with a shriek as it burnt her,

"Oh FRAZZ it!" she cried in distress "Frazz it! FRAZZ IT!"

Livia looked horrified. "Well really! There's no need for that sort of talk! I told you they was 'ot. Why did you take 'em with you fingers?"

There were one or two shocked looks from the other guests and the mother of a young child put her hands over her little girl's ears, and gathering up her own sister, who was eating with them, walked out muttering, "We can't listen to *that* kind of language!"

Tanith looked bewildered, not understanding what the fuss was about. Why, Droco said "Frazz it" all the time. What could be wrong?

Droco grinned at her, vastly amused, and said, with mock horror, "Tut! Tut! Where did you learn such *dreadful* language?"

Which bewildered Tanith even more.

Things settled down again and Kestrel said, in as soft a voice as possible, for anyone could be listening, "Today we must find a boat."

"That'll be tricky," Torvic replied.

"Indeed," agreed Zakarius. "Not many will wish to go where we are going."

"Leave it to me," said Lindor. "The qu'enga has great powers of persuasion."

"We're near, aren't we, my lady?" said Giles.

"Yes, Giles. Very near."

"Worried?" sneered Torvic.

"I fear nothing, mushrump!"

"Please," begged Kestrel. "Save your strength for the struggle ahead. We will need every kedlin of it. If you are not worried, you should be, for we will be in grave danger."

At that moment a troop of Islarian mariners and their wenches came into The Blue Mermaid. They must already have been drinking at a tavern and now they wanted a meal, and more drink, for they were very noisy. With their handsome crimped, black hair, colourful clothes and vivid jewellery, they made everyone look up, as they sat down, noisily.

Droco took one look at them and, with great speed and agility, and a cry of "Frazz it! Quirking Islarians!" he shot under the table.

"Bring us some pezdas and firkin, and a jug of prad!" cried one of them, who appeared to be the leader, a slim, good-looking man with long crimped blue-black hair and a drooping moustache and curled beard.

Livia patted her own red, curly hair and fluttered her eyelashes. "Certainly, sir. Right away," she said, and bustled off.

The crowd continued to laugh and chatter and to bill and coo with their girls, who giggled and fluttered and cuddled up to them.

As time went on, and the Islarians seemed more and more engrossed in their food and in enjoying themselves. Lindor called softly to Droco, "They seem to be more interested in eating and drinking than in anything else," and Droco emerged, cautiously from under the table.

They were nearly at the end of the meal, when Torvic took an enormous swig of the delicate khad wine in his goblet, screwed up his face, in disgust, and spat it out.

"What's this quirking rubbish?" he cried. "Bring me something I can drink. A flask of klavin!"

"No more manners than a troll!" cried Tanith, in disgust.

"That'll be another seven draskas, sir," said Livia.

"Hmph!" Torvic delved into his pouch, and finding he had only three pieces of silver, turned on Droco.

"You quirking little squag! Where's my silver gone."

Droco, who had, in fact not touched the dwarf's pouch since that first night when he had joined the party cried, "I've not been near your frazzing silver. I don't steal from those I work with. It's against our code, so lay off with your blagging accusations!"

"I'll believe that when krauls grow brains!" Torvic muttered. He raised his axe and pandemonium broke out. Everyone shrieked in horror, except the Islarian crowd, to whom the prospect of a fight was an added entertainment, and who laughed loudly and called out encouragement.

Tanith, seeing Droco about to be attacked and wishing to return his kindness to her, stretched out her clawed hand and cried "*Zan esk Maraneza!*"

To Kestrel's horror, Torvic froze into a statue. Droco laughed and the Islarians stopped their jollity and stared in fascination.

"Thanks, Tanith. You're a treasure. Doesn't he make a fine statue? He could go outside the inn and frighten off the krauls and trolls."

After much pleading from Kestrel, and assurances that Droco would not be harmed, Tanith, reluctantly said, "*Zan esk U-maraneza!*" and a somewhat confused Torvic blinked into life and sat down, wondering what had happened.

Gradually the Islarian din rose again as they discussed the strange happening and the wine restored their laughter, but all the shrieking and noise had brought Madam Zhal into the dining hall. She stood, with her arms akimbo, glaring at the travellers. They were a funny looking lot. She'd been suspicious of them all along, arriving like that in the dead of night. She was convinced they were the source of all the trouble. Not least of her fury was caused by the fact that her beautiful bed hangings, imported from Syrenia, were in tatters.

She paid no heed to the noisy crowd of Islarians, who had now been joined by a jolly, round-faced man, with a pretty, laughing girl on his arm, and who was the cause of an even greater amount of noise. Shouts of welcome and laughter.

Instead, she turned her wrath on the travellers and raised her voice, even above the Islarian din.

"That's it!" she screamed "Out! Out, the lot of you! Coming in here and upsetting my customers!"

"That's right, madam! You tell them!" cried one of the Islarians and they all shrieked with laughter.

Some customers, however, were really upset and were trying to settle their bill and leave.

"Coming in here, in the middle of the night!" went on the irate Madam Zhal, "causing trouble! This is a respectable inn, this is. You clear out and don't come back again! Magic! Fighting! Arguing! And what's happened to my bed hangings, I'd like to know?"

Kestrel was in despair. She apologised for all the fuss, tried to explain that they were respectable travellers and offered to pay for the torn bed curtains, though how she would do this, she had no idea. She was amazed to find a quantity of gold coins in her pouch. She was sure they had not been there before and Droco was looking suspiciously innocent, but she was so relieved to find she had the means to pay, that she handed them over without question. Truly, Shara Sorian moved in mysterious ways!

Madam Zhal bit each coin, and, on finding they were genuine, sniffed, put them in a pouch and put the pouch into her capacious bosom. Then ordered them out without more ado. It transpired that the gold had, in fact, come from Madam Zhal's waist pouch and that Kestrel had given her own coins back to her.

How Droco had moved them from the tightly tied bag at Madam Zhal's waist, into Kestrel's pouch, was a mystery. He was, indeed, a master thief!

Kestrel felt her heart miss a beat when she heard what had been done. Suppose she had found out?

"She wouldn't have," shrugged Droco. "When she realises she's no better off, she'll probably think the Islarians have taken her gold."

"Oh, Droco!" cried Kestrel. "What am I to do with you? I can't say I'm not thankful, though." She began to laugh, in spite of herself.

"I aim to please," replied Droco, nonchalantly.

"Well, it was time to leave, anyway," went on Kestrel. "Now we have to find a boat that will take us to Xegeron."

"That will not be easy," murmured Zakarius. "No one will want to go near that dark place."

"And," put in Lindor, "everyone will wonder why *we* want to go there."

"Yes," said Kestrel, "I know, but let us watch and wait. Maybe there is a boat sailing to Xegeron for trading purposes. Zephrena will need some things that she would not waste her magic on. Food, perhaps even armour for her krauls, for instance."

So they wandered down to the quayside. All their hearts were now very grave, for their quest was drawing to a close and the encounter with the forces of darkness was close at hand,

"Something vile and evil is watching us," whispered Tanith. "I can feel it."

"I know," said Kestrel. "I can feel it too. It is most likely the Dark Sorceress herself."

Tanith said nothing, but a shiver shook her body from head to foot.

They watched the little fishing boats and the larger trading boats. These were being cleaned and checked, tarred and mended, and loaded with cheerful shouts and much loud banter. No one would believe, Kestrel thought, how close they were to the dark island of Xegeron, which stood, just out of sight, in the Sea of Xegos. The Zarish Sea.

If Droco had realised what was happening at that moment at The Blue Mermaid Inn, he might have shivered, like Tanith. The latest addition to the Islarian crowd, whose wits were not yet quite as befuddled by drink as the others, couldn't stop wondering where he'd seen Droco before. Finally, it came to him. On those "wanted" posters. "Escaped galley slave. Reward", came into his mind. The portrait painter had done a good job. The posters had long ago become tattered and fallen down, and the Islarian guard had given up trying to find Droco, having more important things to worry about. But the mariner was sure there would still be a reward for his capture.

He called Madam Zhal over, and asked, "Who were those people you chucked out just now?"

Madam Zhal was non-committal. She didn't want any more trouble. The Islarians were merry drunk at the moment, but that could change. They were a volatile lot, Islarians.

"I don't know," she replied. "Troublemakers they were. Wizards and warriors, and such like."

The mariner held out a gold piece to her. "Anything else?"

Madam Zhal hesitated. He added another gold piece. They glittered in the lamplight as they lay in the palm of his hand.

"Well," said Madam Zhal, tempted, "I think, from their conversation, that they came from the Nagli Mountains direction."

Her fingers made a dive, snatched the coins from his hard, tanned palm, and placed them, lovingly in her bosom. She was doing quite well today.

The mariner felt he was doing well too. He turned to his companions.

"That crowd that got thrown out just now, d'you know who one of them is? That little kligg that escaped from the galleys. If we go now, we could catch him. There's a reward out for him."

The others were not so enthusiastic, especially not his girl. She had better things to do than chase runaways.

"That reward's gone cold," said one of them. "It's not been offered for ages now."

"Too right," said another. "Let's forget about him. We're having a good time, aren't we?"

So that by the time the mariner had persuaded them to try, and by the time they had paid Madam Zhal for their food and drink, and by the time they'd left the inn, there was, of course, no sign of the travellers at all.

The travellers themselves, unaware that anyone had been trying to track them, were on the quay, watching the boats. There were large boats, small boats, fishing boats and trading boats. One especially interested Kestrel. It was a small boat called "The Shadow". The boatman and his mate were loading it with boxes, but this was soon done, and it looked as though she were not going on a long voyage but perhaps taking provisions to a nearby island – Xegeron possibly?

Torvic approached her. "Are you thinking what I am, my lady? That "The Shadow" might be our boat?"

"That's exactly what I am thinking," Kestrel replied. "But how are we to get the boatman to take us?"

"We need a disguise," said Droco. "Something with hoods that hide our faces, so we could be anyone."

"And where do we get those, pray?" asked Giles, disdainfully.

"Oh, I think I might be able to provide those," smiled Zakarius.

He drew his staff in a circle on the ground, and then held it over the centre.

"*Alai rem reantra, quai potivis eloran,*" he said.

Everybody prepared to step back as something went wrong, but to everyone's amazement, there, on the ground, lay a pile of black material, and when Kestrel picked one piece up, they could see it was a black cloak with a hood.

"Ah! The Cloud Father is with me," beamed the old man. "Gentle Father, I thank you!"

"Wonderful magic!" cried Tanith.

They all thanked Father Zakarius for his help and donned the cloaks, though Torvic chuntered about "messing about with magic" and that "no good ever came from it".

"Frightened again?" taunted Giles.

"Please, no more arguments or insults," pleaded Kestrel, as Torvic's face darkened. "We do not wish to draw attention to ourselves!"

They all looked at each other. They looked strange, unrecognisable, like dark wizards. It was uncanny.

"Now let's see if we can succeed in crossing the Sea of Xegos and reaching Xegeron," Kestrel said.

Everyone fell silent. The Sea of Xegos suddenly looked very black and cold. This was the final stage of their journey. On the way they had been able to forget, to laugh and joke, to tease and squabble. Now they must put everything aside and act as one. Even Lindor and Droco looked solemn.

Kestrel spoke at last. "I think that little boat "The Shadow" is our best hope. I'll speak to the boatman."

"I'll go with you, my lady," said Giles, at once.

"And I, Lady Kestrel," echoed Torvic. Both hid their weapons under their cloaks.

Droco held out a pouch. "Here, Lady Kestrel. You may need to bribe him."

Droco had clearly had a good evening, night and morning at The Blue Mermaid. He laughed at Kestrel's expression.

"It's only from the Islarians. I thought you might need it to get to Xegeron."

Kestrel shuddered at the risk he had taken.

"When you disappeared under the table?" she asked.

"I didn't stay there all the time," replied Droco.

Kestrel couldn't even pretend to disapprove. "Thank you," she whispered, taking his hands.

"All in a day's work," he replied lightly.

"Shara Sorian forgive me," thought Kestrel. "I have taken tainted money to slay the greater evil," and she set off towards "The Shadow", Torvic and Giles following her like shadows, themselves.

The boatman, a certain Skofflaw Snollygoster by name, had just finished loading and checking his craft and was lounging against her side, waiting for the tide and smoking a long-stemmed pipe.

"Good day," said Kestrel. "I would ask you a favour. Do you sail to Xegeron today?"

Snollygoster regarded her and her companions with deep suspicion.

"I may be," he replied, evasively.

"My companions and I would be grateful if we could go with you."

"What's yer business?" asked Snollygoster, even more suspiciously.

"Secret business," said Kestrel. "But important and we will pay well."

She tipped the contents of the pouch out onto her hand. At the same time, Lindor began to strum her qu'enga. Soft, persuasive, seductive music. Snollygoster's heavy eyebrows lifted at the sight of so much gold and his eyes glazed over at the sound of the music.

"Just you three?" he asked, as if in a hypnotic trance.

"Seven of us, master," replied Kestrel.

"Seven! She's but a small vessel."

Kestrel tipped the rest of the contents of the pouch onto her hand.

"Half now. The rest when we reach Xegeron." Lindor played even more sweetly in the background.

Snollygoster whistled. "Very well. Get aboard then. The tide be ready for us. Have ye luggage?"

"No," Kestrel replied.

"Well, that's a mercy, anyway," said Snollygoster.

Seven black-cloaked and hooded figures walked up the gangplank, and onto "The Shadow".

Snollygoster eyed them suspiciously.

"I don't like it," he murmured, "but gold is gold, I suppose."

The hypnotic music continued and Snollygoster said no more.

Chapter Twenty-four

The Mists of Despair

In the Dark Tower, Zephrena sat before her scrying glass. Her face was impassive, but her eyes blazed with fury, as she watched the travellers embark. Did these creatures have charmed lives? She was the most powerful sorceress Zar-Yashtoreth had ever known and yet she was unable to stop this small, foolish band of travellers. It was ridiculous. They had come through everything, more or less unscathed. They had almost reached Xegeron.

"No matter, for now they come beneath my power," she said aloud. "Here the powers of light weaken and die. Now they are on my sea and sailing ever nearer to my strength. And now I shall destroy them."

She thought for a moment. What should she send? A great storm that would scuttle that tiny boat? No, they would probably manage to swim ashore. But what about the Mists of Despair? An evil smile crossed the sorceress's face. Yes. The Mists of Despair. Her trump card. No one ever escaped the Mists of Despair!

The seven travellers, cloaked and hooded, sat in the small boat, as Snollygoster and his mate trimmed the sails and did other tasks on the small craft. They were aware of the suspicious looks darted in their direction, as the everyday work of the boat went on. Each of them sat, unmoving, their eyes fixed on the horizon, hoping for, and yet dreading the appearance of Xegeron's coast.

"Mist comin' up, Cap'n," said the mate, as from the blue and cloudless sky, a greyness appeared far off.

"Just a heat haze," returned Snollygoster. "We'll sail through her."

The haze thickened into a dark mist, which blotted out the sky and the sun. Snollygoster and the mate, Encarno, looked up and blanched. "The Mists of Despair!" they cried, as the clamminess and dankness of the mist descended and clung to them.

Both turned their eyes to the seven travellers. Had they brought this evil on their little craft?

"What are the Mists of Despair?" asked Kestrel, dread filling her heart along with a feeling of hopelessness that they would never reach Xegeron, never destroy Zephrena, never restore Lord Aragal's soul.

"*She* sends them," replied Snollygoster. "To her enemies. You lose all hope. They drain you. You can't fight them. You lose the will to live, the spirit of life. We'll all perish now."

To Kestrel's horror, both Snollygoster and Encarno sank to the deck, leaving the little boat untended and lay there, quite lifelessly. Kestrel started to go towards them, to help them, but, the next moment, a clammy coldness entered her heart. What was the use? She could do nothing to help anyone. The quest had failed. The powers of evil had won. Zephrena was victorious. The forces of light were defeated for ever. Kestrel collapsed on the deck, her tears flowing for the end of all that was good, all that was beautiful.

Giles made a vague movement towards her, but he too felt it was useless. He could not help Lady Kestrel. He had failed her utterly, failed in his quest. The dragon people would kill him in revenge for Iliac and would go on to slaughter all the Knights of the Falcon.

Zakarius struggled to cast a spell to dispel the mist, which now clung to the boat like some dismal coverlet, heavy, grey, and draining the life force from them, but his efforts were in vain. What could he do? He was a poor, powerless old fool, whose memory had deserted him. He must sleep. He was so tired...so tired. He would go to the Cloud Father. If there *was* a Cloud Father. Probably not... He drifted into uneasy dreams.

Droco's lightness of heart left him, completely. He crouched on the deck, and thought, this is the end. All our marvellous adventures were a waste of time. I'll be taken by the Islarians and end my days in the galleys. I'll never see Pa or Zirax, or any of my friends, or The Red Cat or Kironin again. He put his arms over his head and gave a soft moan.

Torvic chafed that his skreely manling blood had weakened him and made him unable to fight this evil. Now he would die with dishonour and never reach the halls of his ancestors, for they would disown him.

Lindor plucked listlessly at her qu'enga, but the sound was dull and muted by the grey fog. If she could not make music, she had no way of combating evil. She was trapped in its coils. She felt a creeping coldness in her heart and mind. All was finished. They were all destroyed.

Tanith lay curled in a crumpled heap on the deck. The physical cold of the fog had overcome her first of all the travellers and now despair entered her mind. Evil was victorious and she would die here, away from her loved ones. Her tears poured down her face. She tried to speak the dragon call to aid, but had no strength left to do so. Automatically, her lips formed the words of farewell in the dragon tongue.

And miracle of miracles, those soft despairing words were heard. At the sound of the dragon tongue being spoken, apparently by one in trouble, Lady Thetis Ariadne, Queen of the Sea rose, towering from the waters, her two heads glistening from the waves.

"Brrr! These mists are a curse!" cried one head.

"Evil things, out of Xegeron!" said the other and both heads drew a deep breath and sent forth, not fire, but a glowing substance like subterranean sunshine. The mist wavered. Again the two beautiful heads breathed out gold and the mists began to shake and move. Again and again came those huge shining breaths, until at last the cold clammy greyness was pushed further and further away, growing smaller and smaller, until they shrivelled up.

Twice the mists tried to return, but each time the glowing sunshine, breathed out by the two-headed dragon, pushed and shrivelled them, until there was the warm sun and the blue sky and the calm sea, sparkling.

"Frazz me!" cried Droco's cheerful voice.

"Aunt Thetis Ariadne!" cried Tanith, in delight.

"Tanith-Medea!" cried Lady Thetis, and she approached the boat and bent her shining heads to kiss Tanith. And Tanith put her arms round first one of Lady Thetis's necks, and then the other, as far as they would reach and kissed and hugged her, while they chattered long and brightly in the dragon tongue.

"Swig me! A ligging sea monster! It'll sink the boat!" cried Snollygoster. "Nought but trouble since I took this blagging crowd on board!"

"Fear not, little man" laughed Lady Thetis. "My niece tells me you are bound for Xegeron. I will guide you there, though I could wish, for your sakes, you did not have to travel to that evil place."

And she swam behind the boat and began to push it, gently.

"Lady Shai protect us!" cried Encarno, making the star sign over his heart and forehead.

"Blagging Kasperus!" cried Snollygoster, less reverently. "Who's its niece, in the name of the Kallybargo?"

Tanith and Lady Thetis were now deep in conversation, forgetful of all around them. Kestrel could have cried with happiness. Zakarius chuckled gaily, "All is well. The Cloud Father provides. I thank you, Holy One."

Lindor played and sang. Even Torvic allowed himself something approaching a brief smile. Only Giles was suspicious.

"That monster is pushing us towards Xegeron!"

"Of course she is, you twag," returned Droco. "That's where we're going, isn't it?"

"We are sacrifices to the Dark Sorceress, you ignorant little squin," said Giles. "That must be what they are talking about in their evil language."

"All is well. Everyone is arguing again," said Kestrel. "Tanith will you please translate and stop Giles thinking the worst."

Tanith, her eyes alight with joy, cried, "Lady Kestrel, Aunt Thetis has a brood of 12 little ones – and every one two headed."

"So she says," muttered Giles. "Who knows what they are really plotting."

"Oh, Giles!" cried Kestrel. "When will you realise that the dragon people are with us and against Zephrena. Why she has captured one of their own. Would they help her after that?"

"That could be a trap, my lady," said Giles.

"Frazzing Kasperus!" Droco turned his eyes heavenwards. "You'll never talk any sense into that curly golden head of his, Lady Kestrel," and he ruffled Giles's curls. Giles was incensed. Such disrespect to a Knight of the Falcon was unthinkable. Automatically, he laid his hand on his sword hilt, but Kestrel stopped him.

"No, Giles, I beg you. We will need Droco if we are to enter the Dark Tower, I am sure."

"If you ever come to Eloskan, I'll have you flogged and set in the stocks for a week."

"Alas!" said Droco, in mock despair. "Another place closed to me. Zar-Yashtoreth is shrinking.

"You can come to the Guadja," said Tanith, with such innocent sincerity, that it was all Kestrel could do not to laugh.

Laughter, she thought, I never thought I'd feel it again.

Droco laughed too. "Thanks, Tanith. Good to know I'm welcome somewhere."

They were travelling, at a steady pace, towards the dark island. Lady Thetis saw Kestrel's solemn look and spoke to her gently. "You are a noble and courageous lady. I wish the dragon people could go with you. We have tried and tried to reach Neis-Durga Talahindra, but the place is surrounded by such powerful spells against us, it is like a thick wall. You must have very strong magic to have come so far."

"I also have very good companions," replied Kestrel.

"Yes, indeed," agreed Lady Thetis. "Every dragon of Zar-Yashtoreth wishes you well. That is, except for the slaughterer of Iliac."

"He is very young, and has been led to believe things that are not so," Kestrel said, hesitantly.

"All armoured ones are evil, Lady Kestrel," replied Lady Thetis. "You think us cruel and vengeful, no doubt, but you cannot conceive of the misery they have inflicted upon our innocent race."

Kestrel said no more. She knew that, for now, there must be only one aim. Zephrena's destruction and the return of Lord Aragal's soul. She spoke to Zakarius. "Zephrena is watching us all the time. We will lose the element of surprise if she sees us arrive. I propose that we use our magic to confuse her."

"That is a good plan," replied Zakarius. "I think she must be using a scrying glass, for I feel her eyes on us too. If we can send a false image into the glass and make her think this craft is wrecked and we are destroyed, that may lull her into a sense of false security."

"I think we will need all our magic users to do this," said Kestrel.

Lindor said she could play storm music, that would create the illusion of a storm, while protecting them from a real one.

Tanith said she would try, though she had not yet learnt this magic.

"Come to me, little quodling," called Lady Thetis Ariadne, "I will show you how to do this. And don't forget my own magic, Lady Kestrel. Dragon magic is very powerful."

"Why, thank you, Lady Thetis Ariadne," cried Kestrel.

"Snollygoster and Encarno are very quiet," said Droco. "I've not seen or heard them for ages."

"I have put them into a deep sleep," smiled Lady Thetis. "They will remember nothing. Now, little Tanith, all you have to do is to see a great storm in your mind and our little boat being wrecked and everyone drowned, and think of nothing else."

"I think I can do that," said Tanith.

"First," said Kestrel, "Father Zakarius and I will put spells of protection around our boat and upon these seas. Then, we will send a spell into Zephrena's mind, so that she thinks she, herself has caused the storm. Then, when I give the word, let all of us who have magic, confuse the scrying glass.

"Now, Droco, can you keep a look out for quarks, sea-grutsk or other monsters, or sea-raiders, and can you, Torvic and Giles, deal with them. Once we start the spell of confusion, it would be dangerous to leave it."

"Lady Kestrel, we can do that without any difficulty," Giles promised. "I could do it on my own."

Torvic gave one of his snorts. "Less boasting and more action," he snapped. Droco had already climbed the rigging. "And you, thief," called Torvic. "Keep your mind on what you're doing and tell us the moment you see trouble."

"Don't worry about me, Oh Grumpy One," Droco called back. "I won't let a sea monster gobble you up. It would give him indigestion to swallow one so knobbly!"

He checked that the magic knife was still with him, in his body pouch. There it lay, safe and sound. What a laugh if he made the first kill of a sea-raider or sea monster.

"All ready?" cried Kestrel

"Ready, Lady Kestrel," they replied.

"Our people beneath the sea will help too," added Lady Thetis.

"My thanks to them all," replied Kestrel. "Now we will start."

And now the magic users concentrated on seeing a great storm. In their minds arose huge billows, dashing the boat to and fro, up and down. The wind howled and ripped the sails and dashed the little craft on the rocks, pitching them all into the deadly foam. Lindor played storm music on the qu'enga, forming vivid images. Zephrena, in her dark tower, received Kestrel's powerful magic into her own mind and believed she had sent this storm. It was not as difficult to do this as Kestrel had believed it would be, for the thought was, already, half in the sorceress's mind. But Kestrel's and Zakarius's own spells protected "The Shadow" and she sailed peacefully on, pushed by Lady Thetis Ariadne.

"Grutsk! A huge flock of them!" shouted Droco from the rigging and Giles and Torvic got ready with their weapons.

The sea grutsk clapped their toothed beaks as they dived at the little boat. Droco felt his knife twitch in his pouch. He withdrew it and it flew, felling the leader of the flock. The great beast dropped into the waves. Leaderless, the flock became confused. Torvic and Giles hacked and slashed at them as they came near the boat. Ugly heads fell to the deck, drenched in blood. Droco, perched in the rigging, threw the magic knife again and again – or rather, it threw itself – killing one grutsk after another, and each time returning to his hand. It was marvellous.

Then, one of the creatures gashed his arm with its enormous claws. Droco felt his head spin and darkness flickered before his eyes. But the knife went on doing its work, even though he could no longer aim or throw. The pain of the wound made the dizziness return.

Torvic and Giles were also badly wounded by the poisonous beaks and claws, but continued hacking and slashing at the grutsk, until finally the survivors took flight and flapped off, clattering their beaks. Away, over the horizon.

Torvic and Giles wiped the sweat from their foreheads. A strange bond seemed to join them all. Torvic even called up to Droco.

"You all right, thief?"

"More or less," said Droco. He took a flask of flange wine from his body pouch and took a draught from it. Then climbed half-way down the rigging and handed it to Torvic and Giles. Both took a grateful gulp.

"Where'd you steal this?" asked Giles, but not ill-naturedly. "No matter. It's come in more than useful."

And indeed, the strong wine did much to alleviate the pain of their wounds.

"You're not a bad hand with that catapult," Torvic admitted.

"Well, thank you!" grinned Droco, who had not used his catapult once, but only the wonderful magical knife. "Maybe I'll become a warrior!"

Suddenly all their petty squabbles had vanished. They were now brothers in arms.

The magic users were still concentrating deeply. Droco climbed the rigging again, and watched the sea.

All of them cleaned their wounds as best they could. Lady Kestrel would heal the damage later, if there were only time.

Torvic and Giles had thoroughly enjoyed the combat. This was what they had waited for. They were coming into their own at last. The tensions and discontent they had been feeling, vanished. They were wounded, but they were alert and ready for the battle ahead, which they knew would surely come.

Droco had quite enjoyed it all too. Normally he believed fully in the thieves' motto "Better flight than fight", but it had certainly relieved the boredom of the voyage.

Zephrena, seeing, as she imagined, the little boat dashed upon the rocks and the seven travellers disappear, struggling, beneath the heaving sea, laughed.

"Farewell, my friends. I win once more. Now I have Lord Aragal's soul for ever, and soon, all the souls of light will be trapped and darkness will prevail!" She laughed and retired to her chamber.

Kestrel felt her retreat and saw the coast of Xegeron appear.

"We can stop now," she said. The magic users relaxed, exhausted. Lady Thetis stretched her two long necks. And kissed Tanith

"Well done, little one. You now have another magic skill, but do not practise that one without help."

"Thank you for showing me how to do that, Aunt Thetis," cried Tanith, half dead with weariness. "How pleased my family will be when I return." *If* I return, came the afterthought.

Kestrel examined the wounds of Torvic, Giles and Droco. Lindor played and the poison was drawn from their wounds.

"Don't tell me there's a use for that Elvish racket!" grumbled Torvic, but Kestrel noticed that his voice was less harsh than usual. The little group was beginning to unite.

Snollygoster and Encarno were up and about, bringing "The Shadow" to land as if nothing had happened, unaware that they had slept through the voyage, though they were puzzled to see so many grutsk heads on deck.

Kestrel dressed the wounds of the three who had kept the sea grutsk off. There was joy and congratulations all round. Kestrel called her thanks to Lady Thetis and to all the sea dragons for their magical help.

Tanith was a little tearful at leaving Lady Thetis, but, Kestrel noticed, nowhere near as bad as she had been at the lake. Partly because she was so weary, but also, because she had matured, Kestrel thought. They both embraced and murmured cooing endearments, and then separated.

Snollygoster and Encarno moored the little boat and everyone thanked them as they left.

"We have reached Xegeron. May Shara Sorian be with us all," said Kestrel, and each of them offered up a silent prayer to his or her own particular deity.

This was the purpose of their journey, but they had all pushed it to the backs of their minds. No one had even dared to think that they would get this far.

The island was dark with clouds overhead. It was full of shadows, and very silent.

"There are no birds singing," observed Lindor.

"Not even kritch-kratches," said Tanith.

"The very air is steeped in evil," put in Zakarius.

"But, with Shara Sorian's help, not for long," said Kestrel.

She consulted her scroll again and pointed the way they must take to reach the Dark Tower.

Chapter Twenty-five

The Dark Tower

Kestrel gathered her little troupe around her.

"We must never lose sight of the fact that Zephrena may still know we are approaching," Kestrel told them. "So we must be prepared for her to send her minions against us. We must move towards the Dark Tower with caution and be ready for an attack. We must also make ourselves as invisible as possible."

"How do we do that?" asked Droco.

"I have magic for that," said Kestrel.

"And so do I," added Zakarius.

If it works, thought Droco.

"I can do that too," said Tanith, unexpectedly. "I know a camouflage spell. I'd forgotten I knew that."

"I can wrap us in invisibility with a silent music," said Lindor.

"A silent music. Now that's more like it," put in Torvic.

Lindor began to strum but no sound came forth, only a kind of shimmer seemed to surround the qu'enga.

"Torvic and Giles, have your weapons ready in case of ambush," said Kestrel. "And Droco, take care, stay protected, and don't try any heroics with your, er, catapult. We can't enter the Dark Tower at all if anything happens to you."

"Whatever you say, Lady Kestrel. Better flight than fight. The thieves' maxim."

And wonder of wonders, neither Giles nor Torvic sneered. They knew how vital Droco's skill was. The little group was uniting, as she had feared it never would.

"We'll look after him, never fear," said Torvic.

What next? Wondered Kestrel, astonished, Giles a dragon friend?

Droco gave a sidelong glance at Kestrel. He did not care for the way she had said, "With your, er, catapult". How much did she know about the magical knife? Could *anything* be hidden from Lady Kestrel?

Kestrel, Zakarius, Tanith and Lindor began their invisibility spells and, to the amazement of Droco, Giles and Torvic, they all seemed to fade and then vanish.

"Here!" said Droco, "How will we know which way to go, if we can't see Lady Kestrel?"

This was a problem, indeed. Then Lindor spoke. "Lady Kestrel, my qu'enga sings silently, but I can also play so that only we can hear it. Everyone can follow the sound."

"Then that's our solution," cried Kestrel. "How skilful you are. But Lindor, how will you yourself find the way?"

"The music will lead me," Lindor replied. "The qu'enga never fails. And I can feel your footsteps, Lady Kestrel."

So they set off, following the sweet strains of the qu'enga. It was the strangest feeling, having nothing else to guide them, for of course there could be no word spoken, and it required perfect trust in Lindor's music. But, by now, Kestrel knew that trust was there. There would be no more squabbling or arguing. Now the little band would act in perfect unity.

It seemed a long way that they travelled, but at last there stood the Dark Tower before them, black and threatening against the sky.

They stopped. Lindor's playing dropped to a mere sweet humming. Outside the tower stood two enormous krauls.

"Shall we attack, Lady Kestrel?" whispered Giles.

"No, Zephrena must have no warning that we are here," Kestrel whispered back. "Tanith, how far can your stone spell carry?"

"I think it could reach them." She gathered her energy and focused it on the two krauls. She felt her magic ready to throw, like a weapon.

"*Zan esk Maranaza!*" she whispered.

The krauls froze into monstrous statues. Tanith felt elated, for truly, she had never sent her magic as far as that before.

"That was well done," cried Kestrel. "We can approach now. But take care."

Inside the Dark Tower, Zephrena felt the magic. She looked into her scrying glass and though she saw nothing, she felt the approach of the travellers.

"So, they still live, and they are here," she murmured, "but they shall never enter."

She raised her staff and set up solid barriers, invisible, but strong, to surround the seven travellers. Now they were trapped, in a kind of deadly courtyard. Kestrel and Zakarius felt the magic surrounding them.

"Zephrena has trapped us," Kestrel cried. "There are invisible walls around us."

And now, Zephrena's krauls, led by Bragazh Gourbag, the kraul captain, appeared. Torvic swung Valdur, his great double axe. Giles and Kestrel drew their swords, and the battle began.

The seven travellers were hopelessly outnumbered, but Giles and Torvic were like 20 warriors, slashing and hacking. Kestrel, Zakarius and Lindor used their magic powers, Tanith turned krauls to stone by the dozen, and when her magic drained her, simply disembowelled them with her claws. Droco's magic knife flew like a shining zanta bird, killing where it struck.

And then Tanith, casting her stone spell on a huge kraul, found it didn't work. She realised he must have troll blood, but, in that instant of hesitation, he was upon her, with his scimitar. Tanith gave a screech of terror and the next instant, the kraul's head lay, beside his body, on the ground, sliced by Giles's sword. Both of them stood, transfixed for a second. Tanith, amazed that Giles should save her life. Giles, horrified that he should have done so. There was no time to wonder about it, however, for the battle raged on.

The krauls seemed infinite in number and as strong as stone. To make things worse, Zephrena had now joined the battle, casting spell after spell, poisonous and powerful from the battlements of the tower.

Again and again, Tanith sent out the dragon distress call. Now, if ever was the time to call her people. But the dark sorceress had surrounded her tower with such powerful spells to protect herself from the dragon people, that no call for help could reach them.

And then Kestrel left the battle, drew aside and gathered her energies. She was badly wounded, but she raised herself above her pain and began to summon her magic. Zakarius, knowing what she was doing, lent her magical strength. The others did not know what she was doing, but they could see she was seeking magical help. It came. Her spell was successful. The spell of multiplication. Suddenly there were a hundred Kestrels with bright swords and powerful magic staffs. A hundred Zakariuses, lending their strength to the old man's magic and their cover to the "Kestrels" when their magic drained them. A hundred Taniths, clawing and turning krauls to stone. A hundred Lindors, filling the courtyard with magical music, which sent the krauls, screeching for cover, hands over their ears. A hundred Drocos, each with a magical knife that never missed its mark. A hundred Gileses, with gleaming swords, that slashed and stabbed with the speed of lightning, and a hundred Torvics with huge double axes, charging, like living rocks into the ranks of krauls.

It was an energy draining spell and it could not last for long, but while it lasted, it had the most wonderful results. Zephrena, crumpled by the spells of the many Kestrels and the music of light from the many Lindors, retreated, in a fury, from the battlements. She attempted to retaliate with her own spell of multiplication, but the qu'enga music and the light from the staffs of all the Kestrels and Zakariuses, burned her as a fire, in her very veins, and weakened her.

Bragazh Gourbag, the kraul captain, lay dead, surrounded by his troops. The few survivors had collapsed on the ground, horribly wounded. Kestrel had to put several out of their misery and the others were too badly wounded to do anything but retreat, nursing their wounds, as the multiplying spell ended, leaving only the seven travellers in the courtyard.

Zephrena, seeing the krauls slaughtered, charmed the locks of the Dark Tower's doors.

"You'll never reach me. Never recover Lord Aragal's soul," she whispered venomously.

The travellers, wounded and exhausted, sat down on the ground to rest, before their final and most deadly struggle. All seemed quiet. The invisible barriers that trapped them were still there, but Kestrel believed she could remove them, once they she had rested. Zakarius and Lindor, and maybe Tanith, could help. Now she could only manage to cast her invisibility spell, while Zakarius created a circle of protection around them.

"That was some spell you cast, Lady Kestrel," said Droco, as Kestrel bathed their wounds with her salves. "A whole army of us. Frazzing Kasperus!"

"It is a useful spell," replied Kestrel, "but it does not last long."

"Long enough," said Torvic.

"''Yes, Shara Sorian be praised," said Kestrel. "Long enough."

She looked round at the others. Tanith had curled up into a little ball and fallen asleep. Droco had also stretched out, quite unconscious. Zakarius was gently snoring and Giles was also out of the arms of Zar-Yashtoreth. Lindor was strumming sleepily; slower and slower came the notes.

"No stamina!" growled Torvic.

"Never mind. Let them have the luxury of sleep," replied Kestrel. "It will be for too short a time and no one can say they don't deserve to rest."

"Hmm!" Torvic was doubtful. "If the Dark Sorceress sees us in this state..."

"She won't. We are invisible and within Father Zakarius's protective circle. But soon we will have to take the final step of our journey. How far we have come. Sometimes I thought we would never come this far. But this last part of our journey is the most important, and the most dangerous."

"We'll make it," said Torvic, and for the first time, ever, Kestrel heard something in his voice approaching warmth. Torvic must have heard it too, for he hastily cleared his throat and repeated, "Yes, we'll make it," much more gruffly.

Kestrel smiled. "You have been a great strength to me, Torvic Shinetop, to us all. Thank you."

Torvic gave one of his snorts. "No more than my trade, Lady Kestrel. I'm a warrior and a trollslayer. I fight evil where it rises."

"Yes," said Kestrel, softly. "You certainly do. Now, on to our final battle. Do you not want to rest a little, Torvic?"

"Not me!" replied Torvic. So Kestrel woke them all as gently as she could and raised her staff and put forth spells to make the barriers around them disappear. This was a battle in itself, for each time they vanished, Zephrena replaced them, until finally, Lindor began to play her magical music, which strengthened the seven travellers and weakened Zephrena, blocking her energies, and so the barriers melted away.

Kestrel's heart almost failed when she thought that it took seven of them to defeat Zephrena at every stage of their journey. Her powers must be enormous. Then she recalled Shara Sorian's writings, "The light will always win, however slow she may be." It gave her courage to continue.

They were now before the great black doorway of the Dark Tower. It was, of course, locked, and Kestrel could feel that the lock was heavily charmed.

"I can't do anything with a charmed lock," said Droco in dismay. "No one can."

"I can draw the magic away, though," said Lindor, and she began to play again, though the strains were weaker than before, through her wounds and her weariness.

Zephrena, hearing the music grow fainter, smiled. "She grows weak, that wretched little musician. Soon she will be able to do nothing."

But the music kept playing, till Zephrena could bear it no longer and sank upon her throne in a half faint.

Thirghiz Gorblitz fanned her, vaguely.

Kestrel, feeling Zephrena's weakness, rallied her own strength.

"The magic has left the lock. It is now no longer charmed," said Lindor.

Torvic grew impatient.

"Stand back. I'll cut it through."

He raised Valdur, but Droco stopped him.

"Do you mind? You need a little finesse with locks. He produced his lock pick and held it delicately. "Finesse. Never one of your strong points, was it, Shinetop?"

Droco inserted the pick. Once again there appeared that look of deep concentration. Almost reverence, thought Kestrel. In a short time, his face relaxed and the door swung open.

"Call that a lock! I call it an invitation!"

"You have true magic in your fingers, Droco," cried Tanith in awe.

Droco waggled his fingers and put the lock pick back in his pouch

"Magic? Well, yes, I suppose it is a kind of magic," he said, nonchalantly.

"We must be very silent as we enter," warned Kestrel.

They entered the Dark Tower. At once five enormous nvarwolks bounded towards them, growling, manes bristling and teeth bared. But Kestrel and Zakarius held their staffs towards them and they leapt back. Tanith turned two of them to stone and Lindor's music lulled the other three to sleep.

They mounted the spiral stairs slowly and silently.

Torvic and Giles dispatched the troll guards who challenged them and Droco's magical knife slew Zephrena's personal bodyguard, who guarded her chamber. Thirgiz Gorblitz, seeing the travellers enter the chamber and feeling the powers of light, even in her dull body, gave a squeak of terror and scuttled from the chamber, never to be seen again.

Zephrena watched them approach and rose from her throne with deadly calm. She knew they could never kill her while her life force was not in her body. She smiled a deadly smile, so soulless that it chilled the travellers' hearts.

"Welcome my intrepid adventurers. Your quest ends here!"

Kestrel summoned all her powers, while Zakarius drew a circle of protection around them. Kestrel marvelled to see how his bumbling manner and magical mishaps had vanished. He knew exactly what to do now the time had come.

"Zephrena of Xegeron," Kestrel spoke with a confidence she was far from feeling, "We have come to demand the return of Lord Aragal's soul, taken, by trickery, before its time, and imprisoned by you!"

Zephrena's smile was even colder. She raised her black, carved staff.

"That shall never be, Kestrel Moonblade. Lord Aragal's soul is mine forevermore!"

Then, with icy deliberation, she raised her staff even higher and cried, "*Bragazh n'agour!*"

A flash of lightning flew from the staff. Kestrel had, inadvertently, stepped forward, out of the circle of protection and the lightning caught her and almost crushed her with its powerful energy.

Torvic and Giles drew her back into the healing circle of magic. Their weapons were powerless in this final battle between Kestrel Moonblade and Zephrena of Xegeron.

Chapter Twenty-six

The Final Battle

Zakarius whispered to Kestrel, "The circle of protection is complete again."

But Zephrena heard him. "Your circle is powerless against my magic!" she cried. "*Ergah Zhavour!*"

Again Kestrel was shaken with the pain of the evil of this magic. But now, she recovered enough strength to hold up her own staff and retaliate.

"*Ailan shara ni!*"

This time Zephrena recoiled and crumpled with pain.

And now light and dark magic were flung back and forth like some terrible tennis match, with neither gaining the ascendancy and everyone at a loss as to what to do to help Kestrel. It was as if their magic strength and their skill were frozen within them.

And then Tanith heard a voice calling her name and speaking in the dragon tongue. Clearly no one else could hear it and she wondered if it was a trick of some kind, but the sweet voice continued.

"My quodling, do not show in any way that you are hearing this. Reply to me with your thoughts only. I am Neis-Durga Talahindra."

Tanith said, in her thoughts, "Where are you?"

"You will find me later. But first, can you see a black jewelled casket on the table to your left?"

Tanith tried to look, without appearing to. "Yes," she thought, "I see it."

"This is where the Dark Sorceress keeps her life force. You will need the elfin minstrel to draw the charm from the lock, and the thief to open it. Then you will be able to freeze the life force to stone."

"I will try," Tanith said, in her thoughts.

Back and forth flew the magic between Zephrena and Kestrel. Zephrena now conjured up legions of demons, of krauls, of trolls.

Giles and Torvic began to use their weapons and Droco reached for his magical knife, but Tanith stopped him.

"No, we have something else to do. Come with me. You, too, Lindor, my sister."

Surprised, they followed her and Zakarius followed to redraw the circle of protection around them and then returned to give his magical protection to Kestrel, Torvic and Giles. Droco decided he must make the sacrifice. He handed the knife to Torvic.

"Here, you old grouch, one of you two can use this, and make sure you give it back to me afterwards."

Torvic took the knife and immediately saw what it could do. He understood, at once, how Droco had killed so many grutsk on board "The Shadow". He grunted his thanks and returned, with new strength to the battle around Kestrel and Zephrena. He didn't like messing around with magic, but needs must in this case.

Tanith led Lindor and Droco to the casket on the table.

"Can you open this, Droco?" she asked.

Droco examined it. "It's triple locked, but that's no trouble, but each lock is charmed."

"And *that's* no trouble" put in Lindor and began to play, while Tanith held her long-clawed hands over the casket.

After a long time, Tanith whispered, "The magic has left the lock. I can feel it."

"Then the rest is easy," said Droco, drawing forth his lock pick. Again the look of reverence crossed his face, as he worked, deliberately on the complicated triple lock. At last, he smiled with satisfaction. "Got you, my little beauty," he said, and opened the casket.

Inside shone a dull green light, which throbbed and pulsated. Zephrena's life force. And through the battle, the Dark Sorceress felt that it was vulnerable.

"NO!" she uttered a hideous scream, as Tanith held out her hands, and, gathering all her strength, cried, "*Zan esk maraneza!*" she felt Neis-Durga throwing her own powers towards the life force and helping her.

The green light grew dark, flickered out, and shrivelled to dust. Zephrena collapsed, gasping, onto her throne.

"You think you have won, Kestrel Moonblade, but you will never return Lord Aragal's soul to him, before the Sands of Doom have run. As for me, I shall gather my powers in the abyss and I shall return for vengeance!"

Her magic staff fell to the ground and Zephrena lay dead on her throne. Kestrel took up the staff and snapped it into several bits. Now that Zephrena's soul was dead, the staff broke like a dry twig.

"She's right, though, Lady Kestrel," said Torvic. "We'll never reach U-Llashkar, before the Sands of Doom run out."

"We must try," Kestrel replied.

"We must find the Globe of Souls"

"I think I can do that," said Tanith. In her mind she spoke to Neis-Durga.

"Lady Neis-Durga, can you guide us to the Globe of Souls, please?"

"Yes, I will do so," replied Neis-Durga, in Tanith's mind. And she proceeded to do so.

"Just follow me," said Tanith, and to everyone's amazement, she led the way, without a false step, to the Dark Chamber, in which stood a great iron globe. Beside it was a beautiful young woman, chained to the globe.

"My speech has returned, now that the Dark Sorceress is dead," she said. "Now I can ask for your help to release me."

Giles, of course, unable to see a lady in distress, stepped forward and cut the chain with a blow of his sword. "Allow me, madam."

There was a gasp from Tanith, and from the lady.

"So, Giles de Sorell, you redeem yourself a little, and I must thank you for that," said the lady.

Giles looked puzzled and Kestrel explained. "This is Lady Neis-Durga, the fire dragon. She changed her shape to thwart Zephrena's evil work."

And to Giles's horror, the beautiful lady became a scarlet dragon. She and Tanith nestled together, chattering nineteen to the dozen in the dragon tongue.

Torvic snorted, "You stupid twag. You've rescued a dragon!"

And Droco said, laughingly, "What's it worth not to tell your fellow knights in Eloskan?"

"How was I supposed to know?" said Giles, in great distress, but Kestrel, hoping this inadvertent good deed might mitigate the dragon people's vengeance for Iliac, said, "Giles, sometimes it is better to say nothing."

She held the chalice out, towards the iron globe, and it opened at once. A great stream of light poured from it.

"See, the souls of light are free and can return to their home," cried Kestrel. But one globe of brightness flew into the chalice. The soul of Lord Aragal.

"I have freed his soul, but I will not be able to restore it," sighed Kestrel, "for the Sands of Doom will have run before I can bring it to him."

"Not so," said Neis-Durga, "for I will call my family. We can take you to U-Llashkar long before the Sands of Doom run out."

Tears of joy ran down Kestrel's face. "How can I ever thank you?"

"But it is for us to thank *you,*" replied Neis-Durga. "You have defeated Zephrena, set me free and taken care of little Tanith and brought her safely home."

The next moment, two extraordinary things happened. First Lindor's elven shape returned. They had all grown so used to her as a dryad, that it startled them. Lindor felt the magic and drew a small mirror from her pouch.

"I have my own form back again!" she cried in delight.

"Ah! I knew the magic would wear off, eventually," said Zakarius.

The next extraordinary occurrence was at the Pool of Azolak.

Ishta'aren rose up, shining and beautiful, her face alight with joy. "You have set me free from my vile servitude to the evil sorceress!" she cried. "I can now return to my home and dance in the rivers and fountains again. Thank you with all my heart. Please can you free the poor kridrogh too? He is a fearful monster, but not so fearful in the great seas, where he belongs."

She led them to the kridrogh's pool and they all gasped in horror at the terrible creature. But Kestrel held out her staff, and cried, "*Oushana lai keranni!*" and the Kridrogh vanished before their eyes.

"He has gone home. My thanks to you all," said Ishta'aren. "And now I must go too. Farewell!" And she vanished as well.

"And what about my knife?" Droco asked Torvic.

Torvic handed it back, "That's quite a weapon," he said, unable to hide his admiration. "Where in Kasperus did you swig that?"

"Present from the great god Zabris, God of all thieves," replied Droco. "Well, I suppose you could have refused to return it, or told me you'd lost it in the battle, and, as Tanith always says, "a gift demands a gift" so if you still want the Lady of the Mountain. She's yours for the asking."

"You've got her?" cried Torvic.

"Oh yes. Quite safe. Waiting for the right price. But there you are…I must be frazzing mad, but you can have her back."

"Well I never!" cried Zakarius in amazement.

There was a beating of wings and a flock of shining red dragons came flying through the air and landed wherever they could in the tower.

"My family have come to take you back to U-Llashkar," announced Neis-Durga. "You will be back long before the Sands of Doom have run. Come."

"The birds have started singing," cried Lindor. "And look at the light!"

It was true. The whole of the dark land of Xegeron shimmered in a new light, brilliant and shining.

The scarlet dragons greeted Neis-Durga and Tanith joyfully, and prepared to take the travellers home, but refused to carry Giles. And he refused to go with them.

"They may have helped us against Zephrena," he admitted, but they have dark plans of their own."

Then Lord Ashanti Coriolis stepped forward. The Talahindra hero, destroyer of many armoured ones.

"We must take the armoured murderer," he announced. "If we do not, he will escape our vengeance. But he travels as our prisoner, not our guest."

Kestrel stepped forward to plead for him, but the scarlet dragon shook his head. "There is nothing anyone can say for him, not even you, Lady Kestrel, whom we all love and revere."

Before anyone could say anything, Lord Ashanti Coriolis had struck Giles's sword from his hands, as he drew it, and, snatching him in his claws, flew off with him.

The other dragons invited the travellers to climb upon their backs and they all rose into the air. Kestrel clutched the precious chalice, as they swooped and dived through the clouds.

Tanith chattered joyfully in the dragon tongue to all around her and the dragons chattered back. They laughed and called to one another. But Kestrel's heart was troubled for Giles. They would kill him without mercy, she knew. They had waited for this a long time.

The flight through the air was magnificent. The dragons soared and dipped and finally alighted before the Temple of the Golden Unicorn in U-Llashkar.

Giles, guarded by Lord Ashanti Coriolis, was already there. He looked pale and shaken, but not broken.

"We must all enter the temple," Kestrel told the dragon.

He nodded, "That is permissible. We will surround the temple. There will be no escape. The secret underground tunnels will be guarded also."

Kestrel's eyes widened in surprise. How could they know about the secret tunnels of the temple?

"Are you hurt, Giles?" she asked.

"Not yet, Lady Kestrel, but they will kill me."

"I don't think so," Kestrel replied. "You saved Tanith's life in battle and set Neis-Durga free."

"Not intentionally"

"Still, by the dragon code, that means they cannot kill you."

Giles's lips curled in disgust. "Dragons have no code, Lady Kestrel."

Kestrel put a hand on his arm. "You will find they do. Their code is very strong."

By this time, they had entered the temple courtyard and all of them gasped at its beauty and splendour.

Selana Oreole, who was on watch that day, gave a cry of joy and rushed into the temple. "Lady Maia Palladine! Lady Kestrel Moonblade has returned!"

Such a commotion! Such an eruption of happiness was never before heard in the hallowed halls of the Temple of the Golden Unicorn. Everyone gathered to watch as Kestrel and her companions walked into the golden sanctum. How long ago it seemed to Kestrel, since she had last seen it. Nearly a half-year's turn ago. Yet here it still stood, as if she had never left and still Lord Aragal lay, white as death upon a couch.

Lady Maia Palladine led Kestrel to him and all stood and watched her, fearfully, but hopefully. A little uncertain as to how to achieve the transfer of his soul into his body, yet obeying the inner voice that told her what to do, Kestrel held the silver chalice to his pale lips and prayed aloud.

"Oh, Shara Sorian, giver of all blessings. Grant Lord Aragal his life. So mote it be."

"So mote it be," echoed the followers of the temple, and also Zakarius, who knew the prayer in a slightly different form.

There was a moment in which nothing happened, and all hearts quailed. But then Lord Aragal's eyelids flickered, his eyes opened and he sat up on the couch, slightly bewildered, but then smiling in remembrance.

"Kestrel Moonblade," he cried, rising and taking her hands. "You have restored my life and my soul, and saved Zar-Yashtoreth from a great evil. For to save me, you must surely have destroyed the Dark Sorceress, Zephrena. And who are these?" He looked around at Kestrel's companions and all stared at them, taking them in for the first time, for a stranger group of beings had never been seen at the Temple of the Golden Unicorn.

"These are the companions of my journey," Kestrel replied, "without whom I could have achieved nothing."

"They are welcome," replied Lord Aragal, "and I thank you all from the depths of my heart. You must all rest and refresh yourselves. Then we shall hold a great feast of celebration, where we shall give thanks to Shara Sorian for your, and for my own deliverance, and for the overthrow of evil. Then, Kestrel Moonblade, if you are refreshed enough, perhaps you will tell us some of your adventures?"

"Gladly," said Kestrel. "But Lindor Estoriel here can tell our adventures far better than I can."

For, indeed, Lindor had been playing and singing, all the way home, to the delight of all the dragons.

But now Tanith approached Kestrel, shyly, but determinedly and whispered that her family's voices were speaking to her in thought, demanding that Giles be brought out to them.

Kestrel's heart grew sad at this. May he not be permitted one more night, to share the celebrations, and to rest, before facing the vengeance of the dragon people? Reluctantly they agreed to this.

"For your sake only, Lady Kestrel, but do not think you shall turn our purpose, and let there be no thought of escape."

Kestrel spoke nothing of this to Giles. Let him enjoy his last happiness, without this shadow over it. Giles, however, seemed aware of what was to happen to him.

"I am happy to die, knowing I have served you, Lady Kestrel, and that I have fulfilled my quest and helped to destroy the Dark Sorceress."

"We shall see, Giles," replied Kestrel, gently. "It may not be as bad as you think."

She was touched by the way he regarded his death, with such apparent unconcern. He must be terrified, beneath it all, but not a tremor shook his demeanour.

"May I ask a great favour of you, Lady Kestrel? Will you send news to the Castle of the Falcon at Eloskan, and to my parents?

Let them know that I have succeeded in my quest, and have been slain by the dragon people. They will avenge my death."

"Of course," Kestrel assured him, but she hoped there would not be more bloodshed.

They were given food and bathed and shown to rooms in which to sleep.

Tanith was terrified of sleeping in what she called "One of those traps," so Lindor asked if they could share a chamber.

Before she entered her chamber with Lindor, Kestrel attempted, one last time, to speak for Giles.

"Tanith, you will tell your people, won't you, that Giles saved your life in battle. And surely the Lady Neis-Durga will say that he severed her chains?"

Tanith looked at her in surprise. "Of course we must tell this. We are bound by our code and our laws. Any kindness must be returned, any wrong avenged. But, Lady Kestrel, neither of Giles's 'kindnesses' were meant. They were accidental."

"But still kindnesses," persisted Kestrel.

"And, as such, will be spoken of," Tanith replied. She put a hand on Kestrel's arm.

"Do not fear, Lady Kestrel. Those two accidental kindnesses will probably save him from death. He will be treated with more generosity than he has treated us. But do not expect him to be dealt with lightly. He has caused great harm and distress to the dragon-folk."

She saw the relief that flooded Kestrel's face, but that her eyes were still troubled, and suddenly put her arms round Kestrel and kissed her lightly on the cheek.

"How good you are, Lady Kestrel. You would protect even the most vile amongst us. I believe you would even try to help a kraul."

Kestrel returned her embrace. "Shara Sorian tells us that there is a spark of light in us all and we must strive to free that spark."

"Even Zephrena?"

"The Dark Sorceress had turned away from all light and smothered every vestige that might have redeemed her."

"You are composed of light," said Tanith. "You are all light. I will miss you, sweet Lady Kestrel."

She embraced Kestrel again and followed Lindor into the sleeping chamber.

***

On the following day, the great celebrations were held. There was feasting and jubilation. Lindor sang a long and beautiful ballad, recounting their journey, and all listened, enthralled. Even Torvic sat without grumbling and Kestrel suspected that he was secretly rather flattered to hear his exploits told in song, though he pretended to snort into his beard, as if it were all a lot of nonsense.

Cleander Larkrise had drawn close to Kestrel and listened nestled in her arms. Her face a picture of peace. She had carried on bravely while Kestrel was away, never wavering, but now that Kestrel was returned, she felt complete again.

The dragon people spoke in Tanith's thoughts and Tanith reminded Kestrel, gently, of what must be done.

Kestrel rose, "My Lord Aragal, there is something unfinished, that must be done. It will not take long, I think. I will return very soon. Before nightfall."

Giles rose too. He knew that this was the moment. The colour drained from his face, but he said, "I'm ready, Lady Kestrel. You do not need to go with me."

"We will all go with you," said Kestrel. "You will not go through this alone."

"I do not know if this will be permitted," said Tanith, doubtfully. "No one has ever been to the dragon gathering place, who is not of our people. But you have all a special place in our hearts."

She went out into the courtyard and all from the Temple of the Golden Unicorn followed and cried out in amazement, for the courtyard was filled with dragons. They sat on the mosaic floor, perched on the roofs, on railings, stairways and towers. A cry of delight and welcome greeted Tanith and the dragons surrounded her, all trying to kiss and hug her at once, and Tanith trying to embrace them all in return. Kestrel feared she would be crushed with love, but she emerged, laughing and crying with joy. Then she began to speak in the dragon tongue.

There was a lot of discussion and then the clan matriarch of the Shirakalinzarin spoke. Kestrel recognised her from that day at the Sun and Moon Lakes – so long ago at the outset of their journey. When she had finished, Tanith embraced her and there was more general embracing. Kestrel recognised Tanith's foster parents and her two eldest foster sisters.

"You may travel to the gathering place," Tanith translated, but you must be sent into a sleep so that you do not know the secret way. This is a special favour to you Kestrel Moonblade and to all who have set Neis-Durga free and taken care of me when I was far from home."

Kestrel sent thanks to the dragon people for their generosity.

What happened next, no one could have said, except Tanith, for all succumbed to the dragon magic and knew nothing, until they arrived at a plateau set amongst great mountains. The heat was intense and humid, and glorious flowers grew everywhere in profusion. Birds, the colours of brilliant jewels, darted amongst these flowers, with liquid calls, and waterfalls foamed down the cliffs.

This then was the gathering place and Giles was guarded by two enormous green dragons. He looked pale and drawn, but his face was disdainful and he regarded his captors with the utmost contempt.

Tanith had her arms round the necks of her foster parents, and then tound her two eldest sisters, and they spread their wings over her to shelter her. She greeted the two dragons who guarded Giles, her uncles Phineus Coprineus and Apollonius Mercury. They embraced her and murmured to her in the dragon tongue, while not taking their eyes off Giles.

Then Lady Tiamat Ananta spoke in the dragon tongue. The tone of her voice chilled Kestrel.

"What is she saying?" she asked Tanith.

"She says they have waited long years to avenge the crimes of the slaughterer of Iliac and they will now kill him. Wait, she will speak in the common tongue, so he knows what she is saying."

Sure enough, Lady Tiamat Ananta's words came now in the common tongue, informing Giles of his fate. He stood as if a victim of Tanith's stone spell, but showed not a trace of fear, though he must have been terrified. Kestrel marvelled at his courage, and even Torvic muttered approvingly into his whiskers.

"Giles de Sorell," said Lady Tiamat, "you have brought distress and misery to our happy and innocent people. You have passed into legend as the evil slaughterer who darkened the sweet Isle of Iliac. You will now be destroyed. The first of your vile race to perish."

Torvic grasped his double-axe. "Lady Kestrel…" he began, but she shook her head and laid a restraining hand on his arm.

"Wait. This cannot be solved by more bloodshed. I think he may escape death. The dragon-folk are generous, especially at this time of joy."

"Do any of our people speak for the slaughter of Iliac?" asked Lady Tiamat.

There was silence. Then Lady Neis-Durga, shimmering scarlet in the sunset, stepped forward.

"By the law of our people," she said reluctantly, "I am bound to say that he severed my chains when the Dark Sorceress had me chained to the Globe of Souls. Though I think he set me free by chance, rather than intention."

There was a murmur of surprise from the gathering of dragons. Then Tanith stepped out from the shelter of her family's embracing wings. She, too, spoke with reluctance.

"By the law of our people, I, too, am bound to say that he saved my life in battle, when one of Zephrena's troll guards would have slain me. But that, too, was by chance, I think, and not by intention."

"It was by chance," cried Giles. "I would never help one of your vile race by intention."

"You stupid twag!" murmured Droco, who could have talked himself out of Giles's predicament with ease.

"So, by your own admission, any kindness that you ever showed our people was not meant," said Lady Tiamat Ananta. "However, by dragon law every kindness, even an accidental one, must be returned. A gift demands a gift. We may not destroy you. However, you will remain a captive of the dragon people for the rest of your days. You will never be set free as long as you live."

For the first time, Giles's terror showed.

"No!" he cried. "Rather kill me than let me live as your prisoner in slime and filth and darkness."

"The word is spoken, murderer of Iliac. There is no more to be said," said Lady Tiamat.

"Come," said Lady Neis-Durga. "It is time to return Lady Kestrel to the Temple of the Golden Unicorn. Tanith, my little quodling, do you go with them?"

"Yes, Aunt Neis-Durga. To say farewell."

"Give the call when you are ready, and your mama will fetch you. She is overjoyed to have you back."

"And I to have returned," said Tanith. "Just think, tonight I will sleep amongst my family, again, at last!"

And, as it seemed to Kestrel, the next moment they had returned to the Temple of the Golden Unicorn, but Giles was no longer with them. The one shadow of their joyous return.

Tanith, seeing her sadness, put her arms round her

They'll treat him badly, won't they?" asked Kestrel.

"As well as he deserves," replied Tanith. Then seeing how this distressed Kestrel, she went on. "Lady Kestrel, we are not as they are. He will have food and water. He will not be kept in chains, or tortured. Visit the Guadja and see for yourself. You will always be welcome."

"I may do that?" asked Kestrel.

"Of course," replied Tanith. "And this time you will receive a better welcome from us than that first time – so long ago."

This cheered Kestrel greatly. If she could visit the dragon-folk, she could continue to plead for Giles's freedom.

"You'll get him out, Lady Kestrel," said Droco. "I always said you were very persuasive."

"Why, Droco," laughed Kestrel, "have you learnt to thought read?"

"Not thoughts. Just faces," Droco replied.

Now the moment of leave taking had come. Lord Aragal thanked them, once again for their help and courage and then left Kestrel to say her own farewell. Suddenly everyone felt a tug of sadness in their hearts.

One by one they embraced Kestrel.

"'Bye, Lady Kestrel," said Droco. "I've enjoyed every minute of our adventure. If you ever want a little discreet burgling done, you can usually find me at the Red Cat in Kironin."

"Goodbye, Droco. May Shara Sorian protect you. Thank you for everything." She gasped as Droco held out her purse and her ring.

"Droco! You haven't..."

"Just to prove to myself, I can still do it, my lady! Bye everyone. I'm sure our paths will cross again. And you, you old twadge," he said to Torvic. "The Lady of the Mountain's yours, if you care to turn up at the Red Cat. I'll treat you to a glass of klad wine. Bye, little Tanith. I told you you'd go home, remember? That first night."

"Please come to the Guadja," said Tanith. "My family would like to give you thanks for your kindness to me on our journey."

"Thanks. I will," said Droco. "'Bye, Father Zakarius. Take care of your fire spells. So long, Lindor, I'll miss your music."

He turned and walked away with his graceful, easy gait.

Tanith turned to Kestrel.

"Farewell, Lady Kestrel. Farewell everyone. Please visit the Guadja. I shall miss you. I have grown to love you all so much."

She embraced them all in turn. Even Torvic was treated to a kiss, to his disgust, as he muttered about "slushy nonsense".

Lindor stepped forward. "Tanith, my sister, will you not come home with me to Tilioth? Consider, once more. It is Zar-Yashtoreth's most beautiful city. And you father lives there."

Kestrel had heard this discussion a few times, since Lindor and Tanith had discovered their relationship. Now Tanith replied, as she always did.

"No, Lindor. He is my blood father, but my true father is Shirak-Shagreet-Talahindra, who has loved me and protected me from my babyhood. But will you not come back with me and live in the beautiful Guadja? Mama and Papa will embrace you as a gift child and my brothers and sisters as a sister."

"Why no, Tanith. I cannot live in a dragon's cave."

They paused, looking at each other. "But we will not lose each other again, will we?" asked Lindor.

"Never!" cried Tanith. "We have not found each other to lose each other again. Dearest sister."

They embraced, tearfully, clinging to each other. The delicate golden elf-maiden, and the little green creature with her mass of long black hair.

Never, Kestrel thought, were there two stranger sisters in all Zar-Yashtoreth, and truly, perhaps, it was fortunate that Tanith did not wish to live in Tilioth, for Shara Sorian alone knew what the elves would make of her, or she of them.

Tanith closed her eyes and was, clearly, making the dragon call. The next moment, a shining green dragon appeared.

"Mama!" cried Tanith, opening her arms.

"Tanith-Medea, my little quodling!" cried the dragon, and they embraced.

"I thank you once more for your kindness to my little one," went on Lady Morgana Semiramis. We will never forget. No dragon ever forgets a kindness, or a wrong." (Everyone mentally joined in this sentence, having heard it, so often, from Tanith.)

"This is my sister by blood," said Tanith. "But alas she will not return with me."

"Her own home calls her," Morgana-Semiramis understood this so well. "But you are always welcome at our home, little quodling."

More embracing all round. Torvic snorting more and more in disgust and grasping his double axe as if for moral support against this sentimentality. Then Tanith climbed upon her mother's back and they were gone. Everyone waved till they could no longer be seen.

Now Zakarius came to say farewell. He looked tired, but his eyes were bright and Kestrel thought he held himself more erect, and his step was firmer.

"The Sacred Cats of Kushli. That's where I was supposed to be going," he cried. "The Dark Sorceress took away my memory, but the Cloud Father guided me to you instead, my dear daughter. I'm glad. I've made some good friends."

"Dear Father Zakarius. What should I have done without your wisdom?" Kestrel replied, embracing him. "Would you like a carriage to take you home?"

"No, no, I thank you, I shall go on foot. I like to travel on foot. It keeps me young and helps me to think. Farewell to you all, my good and dear companions." He started to leave, and then turned back to Kestrel.

"Don't worry about Giles. The dragon-folk will keep their word. They won't kill or torture him."

Kestrel smiled and nodded. She watched the old wizard walk away, with great sadness in her heart. A wise, true friend indeed.

Now Lindor stepped forward, light of foot, sweet and graceful. She kissed Kestrel, lightly. "Goodbye, dear Lady Kestrel. Light has prevailed, thanks to you. I will miss you, and I will sing of your courage and goodness when I return to my family at Tilioth."

"Do not forget your own part in our victory," Kestrel reminded her, embracing her in return.

"I won't," Lindor said. "Nor you, you valiant old crosspatch," she said to Torvic.

Torvic muttered something indistinguishable and shuffled his feet in embarrassment. Then he managed to say, "You've been a good companion, Lindor Estoriel, despite that elvish racket."

Lindor laughed and then she, too, was gone, the strains of the qu'enga lingering in the air behind her.

Now it was Torvic's time to say farewell. He struggled with the words. So swift in battle, so slow of speech, thought Kestrel. She caught the glint of tears in his single eye, and pretended not to notice.

Awkwardly, the dwarf trollslayer held out his leathery hand and cleared his throat. Kestrel could not stop herself. She took his hand, but then embraced him, her tears flowing freely now.

"Farewell, Torvic Shinetop, my dear friend. You are the best, the noblest, most honourable of dwarfs. Thank you for all you have done. I do not have words enough to say what I wish to say."

"No need, Lady Kestrel. No need," he replied. "It has been an honour and a pleasure to serve you."

"What will you do now?" she asked

"Go to Kironin and make sure that little squin keeps his word and returns the Lady of the Mountain."

"He will," Kestrel assured him. "And after that, why not visit your father. He will be proud to hear of his son's adventures."

Torvic looked at her. "You know my secret, don't you, Lady Kestrel? Did that little twag of a thief tell you? I swear I'll kill him one day!"

"By Shara Sorian's grace, I can look into others' hearts sometimes," Kestrel replied, avoiding a direct reply. Do not let this sour your days on Zar-Yashtoreth. Your blood father was a good and honourable man. You need not be ashamed of him. And your adoptive father loves you like a son."

Torvic sighed. "You are right as always, Lady Kestrel... but..." he could not find the words, and merely said, "We shall see. We'll see."

He kissed Kestrel's hands, turned and marched away.

All had gone, and Kestrel stood alone in the courtyard. Her tears flowing freely.

She felt a gentle hand on her arm and turned to see Lord Aragal standing beside her, and young Cleander Larkrise hovering anxiously near. It was time to take up her old life again, to return to her old friends and fellow followers of Shara Sorian. Time to give thanks to Shara Sorian for their safe return. And, when all was told, it was good to be back again, with all that was familiar. She smiled at them and followed Lord Aragal into the temple, her arm round Cleander's shoulders.

"I did everything you told me, Lady Kestrel," the young acolyte said proudly. "But it was very lonely without you."

"I am very proud of you, Cleander. I missed you very much too," said Kestrel, and Cleander glowed with pride and happiness.

In the temple, everyone surrounded Kestrel, embracing her, questioning her, gazing at her. Kestrel suddenly felt very tired, and strangely lonely. She felt an inexplicable faintness. The room swam. Lord Aragal and Lady Maia Palladine caught her and guided her to a quiet chamber, where Cleander bathed her temples and wrists, and Lady Maia gave her a draught of ashka. Kestrel felt her strength return.

"Lie down, Lady Kestrel," said Lady Maia Palladine softly. "You have been through a time of great danger and darkness, May Shara Sorian be praised, you have returned safely."

"Shara Sorian be praised!" murmured Lord Aragal, Cleander Larkrise and Kestrel.

Then Kestrel felt herself enveloped in a sweet sleep.

***

The candles had burned low and the temple was silent, save for the soft chanting of the night guardians. Kestrel's fingers ached. It had taken her three seven nights to complete the story of her quest. Now she was nearly at an end.

"Xegeron," she wrote, "will become a place of light again, and the birds will sing once more. But it will take a long time for the island to recover. Lord Mischa of the Reeds has visited Eloskan and informed Giles's family and the Knights of the Falcon of Giles's fate. They are distraught. Jules de Mauriac wished to lead a party to the Valley of the Sun and Moon Lakes, to rescue him, but were, fortunately, dissuaded. They would be hopelessly outnumbered by the dragon-folk, and besides, I am told, the cave where he is held, though open to all others, is sealed by magic against Giles, and all Knights of the Falcon. I will visit the Valley of the Sun and Moon Lakes myself and try to persuade them to release him. If they slaughter the dragon people, Giles will never be released for they alone know the magic of the cave."

Kestrel yawned and stretched.

"Light has prevailed," she wrote, "and the powers of good have triumphed, Shara Sorian be praised."

She paused and added some last words.

"But as I close the story of the Quest to Xegeron, I am reminded of the last words of Zephrena, the Dark Sorceress, and a tremor of fear enters my heart. Were those words merely spoken in anger and vengeance? Or does she truly have the power to gather her strength in the abyss and return to Zar-Yashtoreth? Shara Sorian tells us that the powers of light will always triumph in the end, but that we must never cease our vigilance against the powers of evil and darkness.

THE END